PENGUIN BOOKS
BBC BOOKS

JIMMY McGOVERN'S
THE LAKES

D1150725

K. M. Lock

JIMMY McGOVERN'S THE LAKES

PENGUIN BOOKS
BBC BOOKS

PENGUIN BOOKS
BBC BOOKS

Published by the Penguin Group
Penguin Books Ltd, 27 Wrights Lane, London w8 5tz, England
Penguin Books USA Inc., 375 Hudson Street, New York, New York 10014, USA
Penguin Books Australia Ltd, Ringwood, Victoria, Australia
Penguin Books Canada Ltd, 10 Alcorn Avenue, Toronto, Ontario, Canada m4v 3b2
Penguin Books (NZ) Ltd, 182–190 Wairau Road, Auckland 10, New Zealand

Penguin Books Ltd, Registered Offices: Harmondsworth, Middlesex, England

First published 1997
1 3 5 7 9 10 8 6 4 2

The publishers and authors gratefully acknowledge permission
to quote from the following copyright material:

'When I Leave the World Behind' Words and Music by
Irving Berlin © 1915, Irving Berlin Inc, USA.
Reproduced by permission of B. Feldman and Co Ltd,
London wc2h 0ea

'The Shield of Achilles' from Collected Shorter Poems 1927–1957 by
W. H. Auden, published by Faber and Faber Ltd

'Party Night in Bedlam' by Kevin McCann © Kevin McCann, 1993

Set in 10/12pt Monotype Sabon
Typeset by Rowland Phototypesetting Ltd, Bury St Edmunds, Suffolk
Printed in Great Britain by Clays Ltd, St Ives plc

PROLOGUE

The lake swallowed them casually, like a great whale sucking in a school of tiny fishes in a yawn. The only sign that they had been gulped into its 200-feet-deep belly was the capsized wooden rowing-boat which, even as Danny watched, disappeared beneath the calm surface too. He scanned the water with a growing sense of horror as none of them reappeared. Without thinking twice, he plunged off the jetty, striking out towards the spot in a frantic crawl. Cold, a glacial coldness many millions of years old, engulfed him as he dived downwards. At first it was clear enough to see and it flashed through his mind that this was what it was really like to go through the looking-glass, to observe the world above as shimmery and fragile as its reflection normally was. Then, as he descended, the light grew more and more faint, making it difficult to identify the fleeting shapes in the murk. Were they bodies? He swam towards one, reached out and touched human hair streaming in the opaque water like a mass of dark weed. Wrapping an arm around the unresisting form, he kicked upwards. They didn't seem to make any progress. Blood roared in his ears. Danny tried again but suddenly their bodies had an impetus he couldn't control, the weight of their saturated clothing dragging him even deeper. His lungs were bursting. He had almost no breath left; molecules of oxygen were leaking from him in a stream of bubbles and he thought then this was how it was for them, that they were all going down together, and there was a peculiar comfort in it.

ONE

'This is a dangerous corner,' Emma announced, sitting forward, animated. 'There's always crashes here. People get killed. They don't notice how sharp it is because they're distracted by the lake. Look, there it is.'

A vast body of water slid into view, gleaming silvery blue in the late afternoon sun. A flotilla of small crafts flashed bright sails on the far shore, while a bigger boat ploughed a wide wake closer to them. 'Steamer,' she explained. 'They drop off at a landing stage the other end – it's one of the longest lakes in Cumbria. Lovely, isn't it?'

Danny leaned over her shoulder, purportedly to get a better view out of the coach window, and drank in the scent of her warm skin. One of her springy curls brushed his cheek as she turned her head back towards him. For a second their faces were close, then she said abruptly, 'Mine's the next stop.'

He stood up to let her out and as she put on her jacket and reached for her bag, he suggested, casually, 'I could phone.' What he really wanted to do was beg, 'What's your number, where do you live, will I ever see you again?' Emma knew it, too; she wouldn't look at him now. 'See you,' she said, and left.

As the coach pulled away, Danny realized why. He half-raised his hand to wave and lowered it again as he saw Emma being greeted by a dark-haired youth. They kissed and strolled off up the street, hand-in-hand. This was obviously not to be his date with destiny. And yet, her candid eyes, her smile, her relaxed manner, the way she'd teased him earlier, all seemed to invite a different interpretation, despite the freezing out he'd just received.

'Where's the next stop?' he asked the driver.

'Half a mile up the road, just past the hotel.'

It was a gamble and he was an outside runner, but Danny liked long odds. 'Drop me there, will you, pal?'

Danny had decided on the Lake District the night before, after his parents locked him out. He had trudged round to Spanner's house and dossed down on his sofa. Going to Cumbria was, in fact, Spanner's suggestion. Over breakfast (cold curry and flat lager) he told him that several of his mates had got seasonal work there. 'Hotels always need staff and you get your bed and board thrown in for nothin'. Scenery's great – beats Liverpool in the summer – plus there's loads of birds lookin' for a little holiday romance. I'd go with you but my Maureen would freak.'

No contest, thought Danny. Especially compared with flogging the *Big Issue* to woollybacks doing the Beatles tour, which was probably all he'd get now, having been made homeless. He staked his last £20 on a ticket and boarded a coach for Keswick.

He had just chosen a seat near the back and was, by force of habit, checking the racing results in the paper, when he saw a girl coming down the aisle towards him. Danny, behind shades, automatically flicked an eye over her. She stopped at the seat in front and shrugged off a denim jacket, reaching up to put it on the overhead shelf. He ogled the vision unexpectedly presented: her breasts – braless; he was an expert – in the tight, white cotton top; the flash of tender midriff, the way the long blue skirt clung to her mobile hips. He leaned forward and addressed the back of her creamy neck. 'Where are you going?'

She glanced round, revealing a frank, open face. It wore a vaguely scornful expression. Apparently such an inadequate chat-up line wasn't worth answering because she settled back in her seat again. He tipped the shades

4

down his nose and tried looking rueful. 'You've recognized me, haven't you?'

'No,' she said, staring straight ahead.

'Well-known television programme.' Say someone cool, he thought. A long-lost Gallagher brother?

'*Survival?*' She was pretty cool herself.

'*Top of the Pops.*' He leant back, arms folded. No bite: she was staring out of the window again, not impressed by smart-arses, obviously. He dropped the act. 'So where are you going, then?' Silence. This was hard work. He supposed it was obvious. She must think him a right dork. 'Lakes?'

'Yeah.'

'Then you're in for four or five hours of challengin', stimulatin' conversation.'

'Really?' She sounded very doubtful.

'An example. Right? Sir Isaac Newton – y'know, the apple and gravity and all that? He only ever spoke once in about twenty years in parliament. You know what he said?'

She turned round and fixed him with her cat's eyes. '"Anybody want the core?"' Clearly she had a bratty younger brother. He suddenly felt about ten. 'D'you mind if I open the window?' he asked lamely.

The coach wended its way through the grey urban landscape, a formless sprawl of factories, shuttered shops, derelict buildings, tower blocks. Me Liverpool home, Danny thought bitterly. Doesn't feel much like home any more.

There was a vending machine at the back of the coach. It gave him an idea. 'Want a coffee?'

She gave him a sudden, quick smile. 'Thanks. Milk, no sugar. D'you need any change?'

'I'm all right.' He was. He could dance down the aisle. Not sidelined yet then, my son, he told himself. He returned gingerly holding two brimming paper cups with ridiculous flimsy cardboard handles. Scalding coffee splashed on his fingers. 'Be careful,' he warned, handing one to her. He loitered for a second by her seat, wondering if he should sit by her. Presumptuous; it was too soon. He sat back down behind her again, feigning disinterest.

'So why are you going to the Lakes?' This time it was her asking, peering back at him between the seats. Danny found himself captivated by the freckles dusting her translucent skin, her smooth forehead, her heart-shaped face.

'Had a bit of a row with me mam and dad, y'know what I mean?'

'What about?'

'They want me to go to Oxford, study law. I want to take a year or two out, see the world.' It was a blatant lie but he didn't want her to think him a loser.

'Cumbria?' She wasn't fooled.

'It's a start, isn't it? Cumbria today. Tomorrow – who knows?'

'Benidorm even.' She grinned wickedly. He took the plunge.

'I'm Danny.' She looked like she'd opened a door and then wished she hadn't. 'It's an old English custom: someone tells you his name; you tell him yours,' he persisted. Still no reply. 'I've got this gift,' he gabbled, slightly desperate now and hoping it didn't show. 'A girl tells me her name, I come up with a poem about it. Just like that.' He snapped his fingers.

She hesitated, then couldn't resist the challenge. 'Emma. Emma Quinlan.'

God. Emma, Emma, Emma. 'Some names take longer than others,' he waffled, buying time. 'Some can take up to a minute.' He paused and took a deep breath.

> 'There's a beautiful woman called Emma
> Sends Danny's heart into a tremor.
> But he's on a bus,

6

He can't make a fuss,
Oh dear, what a fuckin' dilemma.'

Emma ducked her head, trying to hide her smile. She was intrigued by Danny; he seemed so confident – OK, so full of himself – and yet, well, charming.

They were on the motorway now, hemmed in by high embankments. 'Can I sit by you? To avoid givin' you a crick in your neck,' he added hastily. She nodded. He switched seats and extended a hand. 'You're daft,' she said, but shook it anyway, won over by his smile. If she was honest with herself, she was flattered by this streetwise Scouser's attentions.

'So what were you doing in Liverpool?' he asked.

'Interview. Uni. For sociology.'

'So you live in Keswick?'

'No, a village called Hawksmere. You wouldn't know it, unless you're a walker.' She checked his physique. He was wiry but had an unhealthy pallor, as if he'd spent a lot of time indoors living on junk food. 'I don't see you in stout boots and Gortex.'

'I love mountains. Climb every one of 'em, as the Mother Superior says. They bring out the Wordsworth in me. So who do you live with?'

'There's my mam and dad; Pete, my brother; Annie, my little sister; and Granddad.'

'No Grandma?'

'She died years ago.'

It was hard to know what to follow that with. After a while she closed her eyes, shutting him out, but he couldn't tell whether she was asleep or not. Certainly she didn't snore or drool, or – very disappointing this – nod off on his shoulder. Lulled by the steady motion of the coach he let himself drift off, floating in and out of consciousness.

He wondered, hazily, if his parents were worried by his sudden disappearance, then dismissed the thought.

After all, they'd effectively kicked him out; presumably they thought they were well shot of him. He was twenty-one years old and hadn't contributed to the housekeeping since – when? he couldn't remember the last time he'd had a job – and there was never anything left out of his giro. That, in fact, was what the bust-up had been about.

He was lying in bed, waiting for it to arrive. Of late Danny had tended to hibernate in his room to avoid hassle from his mam and dad. All they seemed to do was give him grief about his giro, about not working, about not having a life. He had been awake for ages listening for the post. He needed to be quick off the mark.

The letterbox clacked and Danny leapt out of bed in one bound, naked. Wrapping a towel around his waist he slithered downstairs, trying to avoid the creaky treads. Something was wrong. There were only two white envelopes on the mat. He pulled open the door and collared the postman, who was remounting his bike. 'Is this all?' Danny waved the envelopes at him indignantly.

'What are you expectin'?'

'You know what I'm expectin'. Me giro. Brown envelope. Little window in it. Sees you through the next two weeks.' Behind Danny, Megan, the Kavanagh's elderly mongrel, started to bark, her tail wagging, wanting to play. A woman across the street twitched her curtains at the racket, clocking Danny's scrawny skeleton and mushroom-pale skin. 'Nose,' he mouthed, goosebump-defiant.

'You mean this?' The postman produced the envelope, holding it up teasingly.

'Yeah.' Danny lunged and snatched it from him, giving Megan the opportunity to score her best trick. She yanked his towel away and ran back up the hall with it, leaving Danny with his giro as his only means of protection. The woman across the way was still gawping. He backed into the house, hiding his genitals with the brown envelope, and flashed his backside at her triumphantly as he slammed the door.

Bounding up the stairs, he made it to the bathroom and bolted the door with split-second timing. His mam was on the rampage.

'I want that giro, m'lad.' She banged on the frosted glass, furious. 'The only time I see you move is once a bloody fortnight when that thing comes through the door.'

He got under the shower to drown her out. He knew the litany by heart. To appease her he shouted, 'I'll split it with you. I'll see you all right.'

'When you get your glasses, yeah.' She knew the responses as well as he did. 'I want some money off you. I want some bloody keep. I don't know what you think this is – some kind of bloody charity or something.'

He combed his wet hair, giving it a flick and mussing some gel into it. 'I've got to shoot out for half an hour. Right?'

'He's gonna have something to say. When he gets home, he's gonna have something to say to you.' Threats now, true to form.

'I can't give it to you 'cause I've got to cash it, right? Me name's on it,' he retaliated, hopping on one foot to get into the jeans he had stowed in readiness behind the laundry basket the night before.

'Your name'll be on a bloody slab if you go out of this house with that in your pocket. You need straightening out, that's what you need. Lying in bed for two weeks, thinking about your bloody giro.'

Danny brushed his teeth vigourously, with lots of whooshing and slooshing, running the taps full blast. Outside, the diatribe had stopped. He stepped cautiously on to the landing and made a dash for it. She heard him and was out of her room like a greyhound from a trap.

'You'll get it,' he cried, belting down the stairs two at a time.

'When?'

'After.'

'There'll be nothing left *after*.'

Charlie, an independent bookmaker Danny had come to rely on, had a lucrative sideline cashing giros. This one-stop service suited Danny well; he peeled a tenner off the small bundle of notes Charlie had just given him and put it on the first race, joining the group of diehards staring fixedly at the TV screens mounted on the wall.

'And as they round the bend, it's Silver Searcher in the lead. Silver Searcher from Hometown Boy and making good running on the outside it's April Fool followed by What's My Line.' A horse pecked and stumbled, causing a wizened old man in a greasy cap next to Danny to turn away, shaking his head. 'Go on. Go *on*!' Danny could hardly bear to watch, his fists bunched into tight balls, the sinews in his neck rigid. Another bloke was practically riding his horse, making sawing motions with imaginary reins, while a woman with a deeply lined face took rapid repeated drags on a cigarette, the smoke spiralling upwards like puffs of rapidly evaporating dreams.

'As they come to the last it's Hello Dolly leading the field. Oh, and there goes the favourite. And that's brought a few others down too.' Despair all round. Danny bowed his head, unclenched his fists and exhaled slowly. There was always the next race. He pulled a betting slip out of a dispenser, studied the *Racing Post* and got out his pen.

By the time he left Charlie's, Danny had lost every penny. He wandered the streets listlessly, ending up by the old docks looking out over the oily Mersey as it slapped against its concrete bulwarks. That's it for the next fortnight, he thought. Back to the nagging, back to nothing. Thanks for nothing. Nothing will come of nothing . . . Where was that from? *Lear*? I used to be good at English, he reflected; not the spelling and stuff; literature and poetry. Could have been good at the rest, if I'd wanted to. Not that it made you any friends. Swots weren't sexy. Not exactly magnets for the birds. They liked scallies like him, scallies who could duck and weave and cheek their way out of trouble. In Liverpool you survived on your wits. Until you got to your wits' end. He lobbed a stone into the water and watched it sink, the ripples pulsing outwards in concentric circles. 'I am a man more sinned against than sinning,' he murmured. 'U SUK' contradicted a graffiti-strewn wall. He trudged off past disused warehouses to blag a bus-ride home.

'I'll give y' me name and address, right? I'll give y' me name and bleedin' address.' The bus conductor could spot a fare-dodger at a hundred paces and was having none of it. The doors sighed shut and the bus moved off, spraying Danny's legs with water. Big fat raindrops hit him in the face. He pulled his sweatshirt hood up, hunched his shoulders and set off, resigned to a long wet walk.

It was another thirty minutes before he got home. A light shone from the hall. Time for a bollocking. He fumbled with chilled fingers, trying to work his key, but the door wouldn't open. 'Shite,' he swore and knocked loudly. He could hear heavy footsteps approaching but it wasn't the door that opened, it was the letterbox.

'What?' shouted his dad belligerently.

'The bolt's on.'

'I know.'

'Well, I can't get in.'

'That's the idea,' his dad said sarcastically.

'Look, I'll give you the money tomorrow,' Danny pleaded, squatting and peering back at him through the flap.

'Then you'll get in tomorrow.'

'It's pissing down out here.'

'Language.' The letterbox snapped shut.

There was nothing for it but to use the old escape route. At thirteen he could scale the drainpipe out the back no problem, usually pretending he was in one of those reruns of *Mission: Impossible*. Now he was heavier and less agile and more than a little out of practice. He stood on an upturned bucket, grabbed the collar of the pipe – at least his arms were longer now – and heaved. Raindrops trickled down the inside of his sleeves. He made painful progress, slipping frequently and breathing hard. From inside the house he could hear raised voices. The words weren't clear but he definitely recognized the theme: Danny is a Useless Get.

He made the bedroom window, arms quivering from the strain of holding his weight. Squishing his adult body through the opening proved another challenge but Danny was still slim enough, just. He dropped to the floor like a cat burglar and stole across the room, pausing on the landing to catch what was being said. His dad was ranting, 'What more do you want me to do, for Christ's sake?'

'I want you to talk to him.' His mam always was that little bit more understanding, though she pretended not to be.

'I'm sick of talking to him.'

'You don't talk to him. You just explode every now and again. You never sit down and talk. You never ask him what he thinks he's doing with his life.'

'Oh, for God's sake, woman, you've been watching too much telly. "What he thinks he's doing with his life",' he mimicked her voice squeakily.

'You never have a conversation, it's always a two-minute explosion, a two-minute row.'

'He's got no bleedin' idea what he's doing with his life 'cause he's a lazy bastard, right? He's a lazy bastard who needs a good kick up the arse. And that's down to me. Right? My job is to give him a good kick up the arse every now and again and that's what I do.'

A treat I can hardly wait for, thought Danny, making a decision. He went to his room, found a holdall and stuffed in underpants, jeans, T-shirts, a couple of sweaters, a Walkman and tapes, then decided to sacrifice a bulky jumper for his two favourite anthologies, one of poems by Dylan Thomas, the other of works by Gerard Manley Hopkins. In the living room his folks were still at it, so loudly that they didn't hear him creeping down the stairs. He saw his dad's jacket hanging up, located his wallet and extracted £20, leaving him a scribbled IOU. Cheap for a kick, he wanted to add, but decided not to – it would probably be lost on his old man. Megan waddled out of the kitchen, cocked her head inquiringly and beat her stumpy tail against the wall. 'Good girl. Shhh,' he whispered, opening the front door. His mam was still batting for him: 'He needs a bit of help, that's all I'm saying. He needs to find himself. He needs to find something he –'

'He needs to find himself my arse. This is Liverpool, woman, it's not bleedin' Tibet. I'm not the bleedin' Maharishi. He needs to find a bleedin' job, never mind himself. He'll have plenty of time to find himself once he's found a bleedin' job.'

Your mission, should you choose to accept it, Danny thought, is to prove that anything's possible – on condition that it's better than this. Else I'll be what self-destructs.

Less than twenty-four hours later he woke up with a dry mouth on a coach in a new country with a beautiful girl sitting next to him. It was definitely an improvement.

TWO

The Ullswater Hotel stood on the lakeside, an imposing L-shaped building constructed, like most of the houses, of locally quarried slate. The slates, with their irregular shapes and different colours – iron grey, seal grey, bluey-grey, silvery-green, ochre, aubergine – gave the village, encircled by peaks, an organic quality, the hotel seeming almost to have grown out of the dark crags rearing up behind it. Wood smoke from numerous chimneys flavoured the crisp air, underpinned by a clean, fresh tang from the lake that caught at the back of Danny's throat. The hotel drive's entrance and exit, he noted, both had cattlegrids across them. To stop sheep, he supposed. There were a lot of them about.

He went through a kissing-gate and scrunched up the drive, which was lined with trees festooned with lights. An acned young man with a scrawny neck and a Tin-Tin style haircut was having a sly smoke outside. Judging by his white kitchen porter's jacket, he was obviously staff. Danny buttonholed him. 'Where will I find the manager?'

He started, making wild rabbit eyes. 'In r-r-r-r-r-r-r-r-r-r-r-' Danny had never been so sorry to have opened his mouth. It seemed condescending to finish the word, rude to walk off. He waited. 'In there,' the young man said suddenly, pointing to the hotel's revolving doors.

'Ta.' He went in and found himself in reception, which was decked out like a mock gentleman's club, all stuffed leather sofas, wing chairs, mahogany furniture and potted ferns, made all the more incongruous by the tiled, low modern ceiling with integral spotlights. A portly, self-important-looking man behind the desk eyed him suspiciously, while a heavily made-up woman, whose garish ensemble clashed with an adjacent floral arrangement, was gassing on the phone.

'Yes?' the desk clerk inquired condescendingly.

'Can I see the manager?' Danny dropped the holdall and ran his hands through his sticking-up hair.

'Yes.' The man looked at him and didn't move. The woman was no help either; she was oblivious to Danny's presence and was carrying on an intense running commentary worthy of Sybil Fawlty herself. 'She phoned in the early hours. Well, about half-past one. Drunk. Well, I assume drunk, slurring her words and whatnot. I mean, short of saying, "Call me back when you're sober," what can you do?' She covered the receiver and hissed, 'Bridge tonight, darling, don't forget,' and trilled gaily on.

'Today if possible,' Danny reminded the desk clerk, annoyed at the standard of service.

'I am the manager,' he replied, indicating several framed certificates on the wall behind him that stated Mr C.H. Archer's numerous qualifications for running the establishment. Danny pondered his next move, distracted by the wittering woman, who was obviously his wife.

'I won't have the answer-machine on of a night. Well, what happens if someone phones urgently and just gets the machine?' She paused briefly to examine her nails. 'At least, if it rings and rings, you'll wake up. Have you seen anything of Jean? Oh? When was this? Wednesday? Was she still going on about Wimbledon? She was? Boris Becker, my eye. Why can't she age gracefully? She might have a chance with Martina.' There was a cackle, followed by a split second of silence. 'It wasn't Centre Court, it was court Number One. I've told her; there is a difference.'

Danny waded in: 'I was wonderin' if you had any jobs goin'.'

'Scouse?'

'Yeah.'

'I sacked a Scouser yesterday.' Archer cracked his knuckles. 'You want to hear my theory about Scousers?'

Did he have any option? 'OK,' Danny shrugged.

'Bone idle. It's not your fault, you understand, it's in your genes. You're all descended from the feckless Irish. Half-starved, you get on a boat, you get as far as Liverpool and you say, "Sod that, I'm going no further. This'll do." The ones with any gumption moved on a bit. Leeds, London, America. The feckless all stayed in Liverpool.' The pebble eyes remained fixed on him during this outburst.

Danny thought, 'Do they have segregation or somethin' up here?' but kept it to himself. 'I'll take that as a no, then,' he said pleasantly. He glanced at Mrs Archer, who was still talking nineteen-to-the-dozen, only occasionally coming up for air.

'Hilda? Oh, *Hilda*. How is she? Really? For God's sake, Hilda and her cruises. She goes in a "friendly four". Honestly! Bowels of the ship, cooped up with three total strangers. I'd sooner work my passage. Did she meet someone? Come on. You know exactly what I mean by "meet".'

Archer was a bully but he needed staff. 'Hands,' he barked.

'Sorry?'

'Show me.' Danny proffered his mitts, palms up.

'And over.'

This was like bloody Dickens. No wonder he'd done out reception like that.

'How often do you take a bath?'

How often do you have a wank? Danny thought. Shouldn't think you get near her knickers very much, mate. Not without gagging her first. 'Pretty often,' he said, controlling his urge to tell Mr C.H. Archer to stuff the job.

16

'Once a month whether you need it or not?'

'No.' Twice at least.

'Any health problems?'

'I've got an infectious laugh.'

Stalemate. Would he crack?

'Follow me,' said Archer grimly, coming round the desk. Mrs A was patting her hair, fluting, 'Oh, I hate name-dropping. Virginia Bottomley does as well.'

He took Danny to a secluded part of the lounge – more luxuriant foliage, elaborate drapes, fringed lampshades – where a couple were sitting, knees almost touching, on a chintz sofa. The man stood up as they approached; the woman – elegant legs, Danny noticed – stayed seated, her face shielded by a wing of fair hair.

'This is Chef,' Archer announced.

'All right,' said Danny, wondering whether to shake hands. He clocked Chef's bulging forearms and thick neck in his sleeveless T-shirt and realized he could probably wring his arm off if he was of a mind to do so. Chef scowled at him.

'Can you use him?' asked Archer.

'What's your name?' demanded Chef.

'Danny.'

'Scouse?'

Here we go again. 'Yeah.'

'You think you're a comedian?' Chef pushed his face at him.

'No.'

'You think you're hard?' So close now he could feel his hot breath.

'No.'

'I am. I'm very hard.' The woman glanced up at him with a half-smile. Danny and Chef were practically nose to nose. Don't stare back, it antagonizes them, Danny told himself. He had heard that once on a wildlife documentary and it sounded like good advice. Chef was definitely an animal. He had a skinhead haircut and a thuggish demeanour and looked as if he spent his spare time beating people up in dark alleys. The woman was a classy piece of work; Danny wouldn't have had him down as her type.

'Right,' he agreed.

'I've got a theory about Scousers. You're all descended from the bastard children of slave owners. So you can't help it. You can't help standing by and watching others do the work. It's in your genes.'

'Right.' Well, you pays your money and you takes your choice.

Chef stood back, folded his arms, glared at him and turned to Archer. 'OK.'

Only so he can torture me with a selection of painful kitchen utensils, thought Danny, trotting behind Archer, who was away again. Archer stopped at the doorway and jerked his thumb. 'Lounge and lobby.'

'Right.'

'You keep out of them.'

They headed through double doors and made a right into a room set with dark green tablecloths and white Lloyd loom chairs. 'Dining room. You keep out of here as well.'

'Right.' They went on through the kitchen and out into a yard stacked with crates. Archer led him to a squalid tip of a room in a single-storey slate building – 'Staff common room. Do what you like here' – and along a corridor to a tiny damp-smelling cell which was presumably where they had kept their last prisoner. 'Your room. Any questions?'

'Is there a betting shop around here?' No harm in asking.

Archer gave him a withering look and turned on his heel.

Orange flames roared from a central bank of cookers where trainee chefs were frying spitting pans of eggs.

Rashers of bacon curled and sizzled under a massive grill, sparks cracking like pistol shots as the fat caught light. A white-coated porter strained a cauldron of boiling potatoes over the sink, disappearing in an explosion of steam. Someone shouted, 'Stand back,' as a tray of grilled trout went up with a loud whoomph, belching blue smoke, causing Chef to swear horribly. It was like being in Hell's kitchen. Everybody was moving, moving, moving, yelling strange commands in a frantic shorthand over which a transistor radio blasted out pop music. Minions hunched over stainless steel preparation tables, chopping and slicing deftly with rapid knife movements. Waitresses swung in and out, carrying dishes and pinning up orders. Danny – not usually conscious until *Channel 4 Racing* came on in the afternoon – was suffering; his biorhythms were all fucked up, having been rudely woken at 5.30 a.m. and told to get his arse in gear. The fever-pitch activity in the kitchen was taking on a surreal quality, making him feel as if he was the only thing in focus in one of those blurred motion photographs you saw in colour supplements. Danny had been put on dishwasher duty and was keeping a low profile. Chef's bollockings were like being flayed alive. Fortunately, someone else was getting a roasting.

'Did you make this mess on the floor? You did? *Get rid of it. Now.* That's a hazard. Right? Any mess, any obstruction, it's a hazard. And there'll be no hazards in my kitchen. Safety and cleanliness at all times. *Is that clear?*' He grabbed a platter of Full English Breakfasts from another trainee and slammed it down on the counter. 'Would you eat food served up like that? If you wouldn't eat it, don't expect them to eat it. This is good food. Good food deserves a bit of presentation. OK?' The sausages, bacon, eggs, tomato, mushrooms, sauté potatoes and black pudding having been rearranged and garnished to Chef's satisfaction, he cuffed the beetroot-faced culprit round the head and stomped off to do battle with a complaining waitress.

Joey, a kitchen porter with a mop of auburn hair and sideburns, approached Danny, who was stacking plates and bowls. 'He looked at the stranger,' said Joey in a soft Scottish burr. Joey did indeed proceed to study Danny, before adding in his odd, third-person way, 'He smiled a knowing smile. He walked away,' and doing just that.

In a corner, two more porters, Albie and Julie, were having a heated discussion across the toaster. Albie, whose cockney accent marked him as an East End wide boy as surely as Danny's accent made him a shiftless Scouser, seemed to be undertaking a half-hearted apology. Julie, who was brandishing a bread saw, didn't appear to be having any of it.

'What did you expect?' demanded Albie, aggressively.

'I didn't expect two halves of lager then grievous bodily harm,' she retorted.

'Oh, be'ave.'

'You practically raped me, you dirty little get.'

'I tried it on, that's all.'

'You *what?*'

Joey, who was also listening in, shouted, 'He could see she was upset.'

Albie, who had a hide like a rhinoceros, insisted, 'I thought you were playin' 'ard to get.'

She shook her head in disbelief. 'Well, I wasn't. I was playin' impossible to get, 'cause you' – she waved the knife at him – 'make' – she prodded his lapel with it – 'me' – she prodded harder – 'sick.' She fixed him with a killer glare. Joey was reminded of the vicious-'raptor-in-the-kitchen scene in *Jurassic Park*.

'Don't beat around the bush, will you,' said Albie, brushing crumbs off his front.

'He wondered, should he intervene?' Joey kept up his third-person commentary, infuriating Julie.

'You keep your nose out, you bloody loon,' she snapped, before rounding on Albie again. 'Who d'you think you are? You spend £1.60 on me, two halves of bloody lager, and you think I'm yours for the night.'

'You're forgettin' the crisps,' he said, stepping smartly backwards out of range of the knife.

Just as it seemed that bloodshed was inevitable, the impossible occurred. The frenetic tableaux froze. All male eyes had swivelled round to the kitchen door, where Archer's pneumatic fifteen-year-old daughter, Lucy, had made an entrance and a half. She had a mane of thick, wavy, dirty-blonde hair and was pure jailbait, dressed in a cherry-red shirtwaister mini-dress that emphasized her well-developed figure. Despite the fact that it was early April, her slender legs, encased in knee-high kinky boots, were bare. Sauntering like a catwalk model – she's practised this, thought Julie, gritting her teeth – Lucy walked the length of the kitchen, porters parting like waves to let her pass. Even Chef was too gobsmacked to rant about this flagrant incursion into his territory, something he had been upbraiding waitress Sheila Thwaite about only ten minutes earlier. Humming blithely, Lucy went over to a tap and stooped to get a glass, flashing a pert bum. Someone dropped a fork. It clattered on the floor, making several people jump, just as Archer burst into the place and demanded to know why they weren't working. He spotted Lucy, who was pouring herself some water, and roared, 'What have I told you?'

'I'm thirsty.' Lucy pouted, looking like butter – or indeed anything else – wouldn't melt in her mouth, but Archer had hold of her arm and was already marching her back past the frothing stockpots, one of which had boiled over in a cascade of bubbles and was hissing on the burner.

'Out. And stay out.' He looked around the room, saw Chef's glazed expression and barked, 'There are people waiting to eat,' before striding off again. The kitchen started back to life.

Once breakfast had finished and the kitchen had been swabbed down, Danny got a break. He decided to explore and took a footpath up out of the village alongside a beck, breathing in the odour of sheep dung and panting with the unaccustomed exertion. Walkers toting rucksacks and clad in fluorescent jackets strode past, casting odd looks at his parka and trainers. Twenty minutes or so later, he reached a boggy bit and admitted defeat. He turned and looked down on Hawksmere, where the houses lay like a scatter of children's toys in the lap of the lake. Coughing, he lit a fag and parked himself on a boulder, winking at another disapproving bobble-hat brigade. They sloshed through the mire and tramped on, disappearing behind a bend. Silence descended, broken only by the distant cries of ewes and the hurrying beck. Danny felt his chest open up and a strange kind of peace pour into him. He shaded his eyes and squinted up at the ridge. A bird of prey was gliding effortlessly on a thermal, broad wings outstretched and unmoving. Unprompted, the words of 'The Wind-hover' began to unfold in his head:

'I caught this morning morning's minion
Kingdom of daylight's dauphin,
Dapple-dawn-drawn Falcon, in his riding
   Of the rolling level underneath him steady air, and striding
High there, how he hung upon the rein of a wimpling wing
In his ecstasy! then off, off forth on swing,
   As a skate's heel sweeps smooth on a bow-bend: the hurl
      and gliding
      Rebuffed the big wind. My heart in hiding . . .'

The bird became a dark speck, then faded from view. Danny shut his eyes, felt the breeze kiss his face and fantasized about Emma.

Amazingly – or perhaps not; this was, after all, the only nightspot around – he saw Emma that very evening. With her boyfriend. Danny had located the hotel's disco by the faint thumping and the flashing lights issuing from the Ramblers Bar, an unadorned slate-built annexe with bare walls and rustic fittings. He stumbled into the warm, beery fug in dire need of a bevvy, but having been forced by Chef to work late cleaning down the surfaces, he found they had finished serving. As he turned to go, he noticed Tharmy – the Brummie with the stammer – waving at him from the staff table and pointing at a couple of pints. 'Cheers.' Danny downed the first in a few gulps, nursing the second as he surveyed the dance floor. Julie, tarted up in a low-cut orange dress and smudged mascara, was grinding her hips and giving him the eye. Danny was about to take up the invitation when he suddenly spied Emma with a group of others. She looked like an angel. His heart did a funny double beat, giving him a fluttery sensation in his chest. He went over and shouted, 'Can I join y'?' above the hubbub. Emma smiled. Robert, the boyfriend, scowled and snarled, 'No.'

'Come on, I know Emma. We met yesterday. Swapped life stories. She wants to be a Liver bird. So how yer doin', Emma?'

She looked between them dubiously. Robert said, 'You stay away from her. Wisecracking Scouser. A quip for all occasions. Thinks we're all country bumpkins, a bit slow, a bit soft. Aye? Wanna prove it, do yer? Come on then, you show me.' He rolled up his sleeve and planted his elbow on the table. Danny did the same. They locked hands, Danny's white, scrawny forearm against Robert's brown, corded forearm. There wasn't really much of a contest. Danny gave it his all but Robert won easily, forcing Danny's arm to the table with a stab of pain and winning applause from his mates. Emma was silent. Danny said, 'Strengthens the muscles, doesn't it, a lot of that,' making a wanking gesture.

'No, that's you lot. We shag sheep.'

It doesn't sound like something I'd boast about, thought Danny, but kept it to himself. He glanced at Emma. She held his gaze for a moment, then looked away. He decided to live to fight another day and backed off. Julie was waggling her arse at him. He didn't need asking twice.

Julie proved be an absorbing diversion. Soon, she was swaying against him with her hands in his back pockets, working his bum with her fingers and pushing her pelvis into his throbbing crotch. They necked, long, slobbering, tonsil-searching kisses, making a meal of it, and continued to eat each other's faces when the music speeded up and other couples broke apart.

For Albie, this was too much, especially after his humiliatingly public scolding earlier. He headed for the kitchen, Tharmy – who had earned his nickname after he once confessed that his ambition was 'to join th' army' – dogging his heels like a terrier. Albie went to the knife drawer. Tharmy, so beside himself that he forgot to stutter, clutched his sleeve and yelled, 'He's not worth it. Just forget him, right? He's just some silly bastard. And she's a silly bitch an' all,' but Albie was still choosing his weapon, holding up blades in the harsh artificial light, then rejecting them. 'We'll go back and finish our ale, right? We'll finish our ale, go up to the staff room.' Tharmy's pitch rose as he saw Albie weighing a mighty meat cleaver in his hand. 'For Christ's sake, Albie, put the bloody thing down!' To no avail: Albie, jaw set, had a very sharp axe to grind.

Doreen Archer, who was in the lounge holding forth to her bridge party, did not see Albie materialize in the lobby behind her and continued regaling them with tales of her upwardly mobile lifestyle. 'They took me through a door and she's standing there. Princess Anne. We said hello. As you do. And she asked me for the recipe.' Doreen was pleased with the effect this produced. Her guests (who had spotted Albie, cleaver raised, haring past, screaming, 'I'm gonna chop his bloody head off') sat frozen, gin and tonics halfway to their lips, mouths agape. 'I know,' she boasted delightedly. 'I couldn't believe it either.'

Fortunately, Danny was tipped off about Albie by the barman, Arthur Thwaite, and fled the disco just in time. He belted out into the car park and, hearing Albie and Tharmy approaching, swarmed up the nearest tree, thankful for his recent drainpipe training. Julie, the little minx, blew his cover. 'He's up here.' Albie hacked at the branches furiously, but Danny was out of his reach. 'Look,' Danny said desperately, 'I didn't know. Right? I didn't know you were going with each other. The signs weren't there, y'know what I mean?'

'Get down 'ere, you Scouse bastard!'

A small crowd was gathering, among them the lissom Lucy. Julie, with two men fighting over her, was in seventh heaven. 'I couldn't live with meself. If someone was to die because of me, I just couldn't live with meself. Could you? Could you live with y'self?' This was said to rub Lucy's sassy underage nose in it, and Lucy knew it. She despised and hated Julie for getting all the attention.

'I mean, if a bird's got her hand down your kecks, you tend to think you've got a bit of a chance, you tend to think there's not much in the way of complications.' Danny peered out from the branches like a frightened cat, but his defence didn't wash with Albie.

'I've got all night. Right? I'm gonna wait all bleedin' night.'

His stake-out was interrupted by Archer, who told them all to get back inside and stop disturbing the residents, who were complaining about the noise. Danny, invisible among the dark leaves, stayed put. Time passed. At last he whispered, 'I know you're still there. I'm not soft, you know what I mean? I know you're still there,' but it remained quiet. Cautiously, he slid back down and headed for the disco. 'A man's gotta do . . .' he told himself in a John Wayne drawl, and went inside. Julie, the drama queen, was all over him like a rash. Danny glanced around for Albie and saw that the conquering hero had won himself a new bird. He walked over. The music stopped.

'Anything could happen,' commented Joey.

'Want a pint?' Danny asked.

There was a pause. The girl licked Albie's ear and snaked her hand inside his shirt. The debt was apparently Albie's. 'Towel's on,' he muttered indistinctly through a mouthful of hair.

'Tomorrow.'

'Nice one.'

'You'll get over it, Albie,' laughed Julie, putting her arm around Danny. Lucy Archer curled her lip in disgust – or possibly jealousy – before stalking manless from the room. Chef, who had been keeping out of it, sitting in the corner with the fair-haired woman, disappeared too. The party was over. But the serious stuff was just about to start.

THREE

In room 34 of the hotel – the pokiest, without a lake view and hence always the last to be let – Chef was giving his lover, Simone Parr, the headmaster's wife, a lesson in sexual techniques she had never experienced before. The way he handled her body, placed it just where he wanted it, ordered her when to move, when to take it, consumed her. When she wasn't with him, when she was out shopping, or walking, or cooking or driving, it was all she thought about. Sometimes she had to pull over into one of the little vantage points by the lakeside until the image of his powerful form and the memory of his hard fingers had subsided along with the buzzing between her legs.

The moment she loved best, though, best of all, was when he collapsed beside her afterwards, spent, and traced her cheek gently, and said, 'You're the greatest, you are. D'you know that?' He didn't do it very often. They always had to get up too soon and there was little time for soft words. Not that it's his strong suit, she thought, smiling to herself, as she drove him the short distance home in silence. Well, who cares? She got more than enough talk from her husband, John, only they had nothing left to talk about. Simone let Chef out of the car and said goodnight. They did not kiss. As usual, his wife, Ruth, was at the bedroom window, watching. He said Ruth knew, that she didn't mind. I bet she does, really, thought Simone, but she was too sated and tired to care.

Despite having been up and at it for over twenty hours, Danny was finding that, with Julie, he could stay up and at it all night, too. She was athletic and uninhibited and had straddled him facing his feet, giving him a pleasing view of her arse. The fact that she was fucking him while swigging from a bottle of lager did not detract from his enjoyment. He didn't like girls getting moony-eyed and serious. It was a little impersonal, having her come with her back to him, but then she turned round and gave him another ride facing forwards, her skunky hair swinging wildly, and he let go too and felt pulsating waves taking his body, dragging him down into oblivion.

Afterwards they rested for a while, her head snuggled on his shoulder. Next door they could hear Tharmy's bedsprings creaking rhythmically, the headboard slapping urgently against the wall, then a long shout, 'Oh, G-G-G-G-God!' On Albie's side it was strangely silent.

As soon as the first pink streaks of dawn painted the sky, Danny was out of bed, charged by some sort of febrile electricity, intoxicated by a sense of being vividly, utterly alive. Julie stirred, moaned, 'What are you doing?' and he threw her his shirt. 'Get up.' Clad only in his boxers, he led her down the corridor and outside on to the grass. She stifled a scream as they stumbled over the cold, wet lawn, leaving a trail of dark footprints. They reached the edge of the lake and he knelt, looking out across the mist-smoking surface. 'What are you doing?' she asked again, giggling, getting down on her knees, too.

'Shhh.' He put a finger to his lips. She listened.

'What? I can't hear anything.'

He held up a hand, like a conductor raising a baton. There was a sudden change of light as if a curtain had been drawn back and the sun swept over the fells in front of them. Danny sat back on his heels and whistled the first three notes of Beethoven's Fifth. Silence. He did it again. A bird replied, the same three notes floating back to them across the water. Danny whistled it once more. Again, the response, then another bird and another joined in until the dawn chorus burst full-throated into glorious music.

Laughing, Julie and Danny stood up and danced in the dew until, overcome by the cold, they were forced to run back inside. Hearing Archer banging on doors, shouting, 'Get up you lazy bastard,' Julie went to dress. She pulled on her knickers and was fumbling with her bra when Danny came round behind her, cupped her small breasts, and whispered, 'We've got five minutes yet.' She turned, put her arms around his neck and felt the heat of his blood, pumping, pumping. Outside, the band played on.

There was a final act of initiation into the group. Danny learned about it during a lull in breakfast when Joey shuffled up to him and announced, 'They were planning on robbing a car. He thought: count me out.'

'Count me in,' Danny said to Albie later in the staff common room, a graffiti-plastered den full of mismatched chairs, tatty posters, dirty mugs and overflowing ashtrays (Chef had no jurisdiction here: the place was littered with unhygienic hazards).

'Sure you're up to it?' he asked, champing on gum.

'I'm a big fan of *The Bill*.'

'OK, you're on.'

They nicked it from a car park provided for walkers. 'They'll be gone all day,' said Albie, knocking in the window and fixing the wiring like a pro (it became obvious to the others why he'd got out of London). He reversed rapidly, forcing Tharmy to cling on to the back of the seat. 'Go for it,' he squealed, thumping Albie on the shoulder. Danny donned his shades, switched on the stereo and they rocketed out of the side road in a cloud of exhaust. After passing the boat yard, the church, the school and the two-up, two-down police station without incident, they started to relax. 'Got any of them funny cigarettes?' Albie asked. Tharmy rolled a joint and they passed it round.

'How was she last night, then, that blonde?' Danny asked Albie, exhaling with a satisfied sigh.

'OK.'

'Only you were a bit quiet. Didn't sound like you were havin' much fun.'

'Short but sweet, that's me.' He looked embarrassed.

'How long?'

'Depends.'

'On average.'

'About fifteen seconds.'

Danny caught Tharmy's eye in the rear-view mirror. Albie noticed. 'That's too quick, isn't it?'

'A bit, yeah.' Tharmy, Albie's devoted shadow, was none the less pleased that he was able to do something better than him, especially since Albie was older, better looking and built like a brick shithouse.

'Get her to punch y' on the nose, soon as you feel y'self comin',' said Danny.

'What'll that do?' Albie was not convinced.

'It'll stop yer comin'. Honest. Something to do with the nerve endings there.'

Driving through the next village they saw three girls waiting at a bus stop. Albie slammed on the brakes and skidded to a halt alongside them. Danny leaned out of the passenger window and called, 'Wanna ride?' The girls – Lucy clones, all bare legs and long hair – looked at each other and shrugged their shoulders.

'Take 'em off,' said one.

'It's a bit early in our relationship, isn't it? A bit premature,' Danny clowned, the lovable Scouser.

'The shades.'

He swept off the sunglasses, giving her his big blue eyes, his puppy-dog grin.

They got in the car.

The heavily laden vehicle – it was a squash in the back; Tharmy, to his delight, got one of them on his knee – chugged through the pass, a tortuously winding road between high crags with scree-covered slopes. Albie had to take some of the one-in-nine stretches in first gear, the engine howling in protest. He got stuck behind a caravan and swore. 'Fuckin' tourists. Pull over.' The elderly Volvo with its equally elderly occupants stuck grimly to twenty-five m.p.h., blocking the middle of the road. 'Give me strength,' he shouted, hand on the horn. They reached the top of the pass. In front of them the narrow road snaked down through folds of fells like the supine backs of animals. 'Hold tight.' Albie, the gradient now to his advantage, put his foot down and they hurtled past the caravan, missing the rock face on the other side by an inch. The girls screamed. 'Roll up for the mystery tour,' Danny called over his shoulder. 'Can y' find us a betting shop, my son?'

'So what do you all do?' asked Tina, who had blue nail varnish, black hair and a pierced eyebrow.

'We're ho-ho-ho-' began Tharmy.

'S'right. We're dead funny. Travellin' comedians,' cut in Danny. 'Cabaret, like. We've got this act.'

'Yeah? You gonna give us a performance, are y'?'

'We might. Shall we, lads? If they're good girls?'

'Sneak p-p-p-p-preview,' agreed Tharmy. 'We'll show it you for free.'

They parked in Bowness. Albie, Tharmy and the girls waited in the car, drinking cans of lager and surreptitiously smoking dope, while Danny nipped into the bookie's. He was gone a long time. 'P'raps he's makin' our fortune,' said Tina, hopeful of being taken on a bender.

'Losin' one, more like,' Albie predicted, wiping the misted-up windscreen. Danny reappeared, his long face confirming just that.

'How much?' asked Tina.

He shook his head, unable to answer.

'Much,' said Albie.

They drove on alongside Windermere, doubling back up the other side and following a narrow road into Grizedale Forest. Albie pulled over into one of the numerous secluded picnic spots. 'Driver's privilege. I get the car. And Trish. You lot, find a leafy glade or summat.'

'What for?' asked Trish, a vacant-looking brunette.

'We're going to put on the show right here,' said Danny, getting out of the car and taking 'Manda, a frizzy-haired bottle blonde, with him. 'See you later.' His heart wasn't in it but he wanted to blot out the thought of losing his first week's wages. They disappeared into the undergrowth. 'If you go down to the woods today, you're sure of a big surprise,' he said, unzipping his trousers. 'Manda put her hand inside. 'I like surprises, me,' she slurred, kneeling down.

Tharmy, meanwhile, was beginning to wish he'd never started trying to get inside Tina's knickers and had taken her for a nature ramble instead. First, she complained about lying on prickly beechnuts; then, when he found her a nice mossy bank, it was too damp and finally, when he tried to take her standing up against a tree, she screamed because a caterpillar fell on her head. Added to which she wouldn't stop talking. He shut his eyes and tried to think of Kim Basinger – it usually worked – but even when he did, eventually, achieve penetration (back on the moss: he had sacrificed his anorak), she continued to spout, hardly pausing for breath between thrusts.

'He came to me room. He said, "What are you doing here?" I said, "I'm finished." He said, "You're not." I said, "I am." He said, "You haven't folded the end of the toilet paper." I said, "You what?" He said, "You fold the end of the toilet paper into a triangle." I said, "Why? Are you expectin' people with funny-shaped arses?'

'Did you come?' asked Tharmy.

Back in the car, Albie had discovered that Trish's dad was an ex-boxer and that he'd taught his daughter how to do a fair right hook. There was blood all over the back seat and he thought she might have broken his nose.

Three days and several more shags later – all with different girls; Spanner was right, particularly about Danish back-packers, one of whom had invited him into the shower without even asking his name – found Danny suffering from an inflamed penis. He went to the village medical centre – a down-at-heel prefabricated bungalow with damp creeping up the walls and a vase of dead daffs in the window – and laid it out for the inspection of Dr Sarah Kilbride. She examined it with a gloved hand and tutted. 'When did you last have sex?' He glanced at his watch: about five hours ago. She saw this and looked at him severely. 'Do you take precautions?'

'I lock the door.'

'I'm sorry, was that meant to be funny?' She was definitely not laughing.

Suddenly, he felt really worried: suppose it was something awful? Her face was grim.

'Mildly amusing rather than funny.'

'You've heard of AIDS?'

'Yeah. Can I put it away now, please?' Oh God, he thought, this is it, I'm going to snuff it. And all for what? A bit of skirt.

'Yes. There's nothing wrong with you. But take my advice: lay off it for a bit.'

Reprieved. Thank you, God, thank you.

The lads were not especially sympathetic: Danny had a higher scoring rate than any of them.

'Change yer doctor,' advised Albie, who was chopping vegetables.

'Nah. I'm sick of it all anyway.' Danny stared at the huge mountain of dirty dishes in front of him.

'Bollocks.'

'*Work!*' Chef spotted them from the other side of the kitchen, which was mad busy with dinner.

Danny ignored him. 'D'you like any of them? OK, it's nice to bang them, but d'you like any of them? Do y' give a shite about any of them?'

Chef took a menacing step or two towards them, his face like thunder. They got the message.

For the next two hours Danny moved like an automaton, loading, unloading, stacking, rinsing, in his own little steam-filled world. There wasn't time to think; his hands did the job without any instructions from his brain. The rhythm of the work took him over: man and machine, Danny and the dishwasher were as one.

'Is it rough where you come from?' He jumped, so tuned out to the activity in the rest of the kitchen that he hadn't even noticed Lucy coming up behind him.

'You get stopped going into every pub, asked if you've a weapon. If you say no, they give you one to take in.' Her mouth dropped open. Chef flapped a tea-towel at her, shooing her out. 'You leave that Scouse scumbag alone. You don't know where he's been.'

The Friday-night disco was in full swing by the time Danny and Albie got off. They drank, lounging against the wall, surveying the scene. 'Not bad tonight,' Albie shouted in Danny's ear. 'Seen anythin' you fancy?'

'Yeah.' Danny had, as he hoped, seen Emma, her distinctive mass of spiral curls backlit on the dance floor. Better still, there was no sign of lover boy. 'Over there,' he indicated. Albie whistled and winked at him. 'Stunner.'

'Yours is the other one.'

They pushed their way through the packed crowd to where Emma and Delilah, her plump friend, were getting down to harsh jungle music. Emma, in wedgies, hipsters and halterneck, looked drop-dead gorgeous. Delilah, who was three sizes larger and similarly dressed, looked ridiculous. Eventually they all collapsed exhausted and giggling at a table. Albie bought a round and squeezed in next to Emma. She was polite but unforthcoming. When she talked to Danny, he noticed, her eyes crinkled and her face lit up. He knew he'd drawn the short straw. He supped his beer gloomily.

They walked the girls home under a black sky heavy with stars, the noise of the disco still ringing in their ears. Albie and Delilah, trailing some fifty yards behind Danny and Emma, walked in silence, knowing they were the also-rans. Nevertheless, he decided to make an effort. She did, after all, have big tits. 'You like livin' up 'ere?' he asked.

'Yeah.' She knew her tits were good and he wasn't going to get his sticky fingers on them.

'You've never fancied livin' in the city?' Albie walked closer, bumping against her shoulder.

'No.'

'Not even in the winter? I mean, don't y' get bored stiff in the winter?'

'No.' Did he call that a chat-up line?

Albie gave up and went for the jugular. 'What's it like being so fat?'

Ahead of them, Danny was strolling with his face tipped up to the constellations. 'You never see them like this at home. City lights give off too much glare. I never knew there were so many. They're so bright. 'S brilliant.'

'What's it like?'

'What?'

'Liverpool.'

'It beats Bosnia.'

A car pulled up alongside them. 'Want a lift?' This was addressed to Emma.

'All right?' Danny recognized Arthur and Sheila Thwaite from the hotel. They did not respond.

'I'm fine, thanks,' said Emma. 'Honest.'

'If you're sure then. Night-night.' They drove off.

'My auntie,' Emma explained. 'She's my mother's sister. Lives in the same street.' She stopped under a street lamp, stooped, and picked a flower. 'Star of Bethlehem.'

'You live around here?'

'Yeah.' She picked another. 'Red campion. Look, it's all closed up.'

'You're minted then?'

She snorted and jerked her head at the estate in front of them. 'No. We've got a council house.'

Delilah stomped past, breathing hard, distressed. 'Pig,' she yelled back at Albie.

Danny and Emma tried not to laugh. They came to a stop. 'Night,' she said, softly.

'Night?' Danny was crushed. He thought he was really getting somewhere.

'My boyfriend's over there. See? That's my brother, Pete, with him.'

He looked and spotted the sheep-shagger Robert and another bloke about the same age sitting on a low garden wall, obviously waiting for her.

For God's sake, ask her this time, insisted the voice inside his head. 'Can I have your phone number?' he blurted out. She hesitated. 'Please.'

'Gotta go.' She made her way over to Robert and pecked him on the cheek. He put his arm round her possessively, giving Danny a filthy look, and they walked off up the hill. Pete remained where he was, glowering.

'Yeah?' Danny was beginning to get fed up with all this hostility from the locals. Albie came puffing up the street behind him, grumbling indignantly, 'A dog like that and she knocks me back.' Pete continued to stare. The enmity was palpable. They turned for home. 'D'you ever get the feeling,' began Danny, 'that we're not wanted around here?'

'So.' Albie sounded contemptuous. 'Who else would do all the dirty work *and* romance the girls?'

FOUR

'Will you give the place a good seeing-to? Father Matthew's coming tonight. I don't want to be holding my head in shame.' Emma, eating toast with jam, tried to shut out her mother Bernie's ever-growing list of instructions. One of the worst things about being in limbo between school and university, she thought, was being treated like an unpaid skivvy, as if she had nothing else to define her. She was beginning to wish she'd gone straight to uni after A levels, instead of taking a year out. She was going to travel, see the world, work on a kibbutz, teach English as a foreign language, do Camp America. What happened to that?

'Start off with the bathroom. Give it a good go. Wash and dry the wee-mats. Rub everything down. A bit of bleach in the water.'

What happened to that was that I needed some money and we don't have any, Emma brooded. Mam's a waitress, Dad's a handyman, Granddad's only got his pension and Pete does bugger-all half the time and when he does work it's dodgy. Plus, it's hard to save enough being a chambermaid and that's the only job I could get. Then, of course, I didn't want to leave Robert. Funny how I used to think he was the bee's knees.

Her brother came in, got out a loaf and grabbed the jam from the table, where Granddad was also sitting, noisily slurping tea. Bernie stopped in mid-flow, although she still had hold of little Annie, Emma's young sister, whose jumper she was trying to sponge a stain from.

'Are you working?' This was a bone of contention between them.

'Yes.' He said it defiantly, without looking at her, and continued to pack a lunchbox.

She sighed, shook her head and returned to Emma's chores. 'I'm putting a piece of bacon on. Don't let it boil dry. You'll need to get a cabbage, the greener the better. Have you washed your face?' This was to Annie, who was fidgeting and wriggling.

'Yes.'

'You haven't. Go and wash it now.'

'I have.' She stamped her foot.

'Then wash it again.' Annie disappeared sulkily to the bathroom. Bernie straightened up, tucking loose strands of hair behind her ears. She was in her mid-forties and had once been a handsome woman – she still was, in certain lights, but looked careworn in the unforgiving clarity of daylight. 'If you get the time, Emma, you can do the landing and stairs for me.' She broke off again to observe Granddad, who was pouring himself more tea from the pot. He lifted the milk jug and sniffed, causing her to close her eyes in despair. She turned back to Pete. 'Look, if you're going to work on the side, do it without letting me know.'

'For God's sake, mother.'

'*I just don't want to know about it*. Right?' They were all surprised at this sudden outburst of anger. Bernie, barely pausing, continued to brief Emma: 'A hot soapy cloth all the way down the skirting board.'

Emma, too, had had enough. She pushed her chair back and got up. 'Give it a rest, will you, for Christ's sake.'

Bernie was taken aback. 'Don't you dare use that kind of language in this house. Do you hear me, young lady?'

'It's the company she's keeping,' chipped in Pete.

'You mind your own business,' retorted Emma.

'What company?' Bernie didn't know what he was getting at.

'It's got nothing to do with him.' Emma was furious.

'She's knockin' round with some scally from the bloody hotel.'

'I'm not "knockin' round" with anyone. He walked me home, that's all.' She stormed out of the room and grabbed Annie, who was hanging over the banisters, listening. 'Are you ready? Well, come on then. Get your coat.' And she slammed the front door.

'What's a scally?' asked Annie as she was half dragged down the street. Emma, grim-faced, ignored her. They reached the Thwaites' house, a pebble-dashed semi from which a satellite dish protruded like a single unblinking eye. Sheila was waiting for them by the gate, her hands resting on her daughter Paula's shoulders. She gave the little girl a kiss – 'Be good now' – smoothed her hair and dispatched her with a pat.

'I will,' she shouted gaily, skipping alongside Annie and Emma. Sheila waved at their departing backs.

The school was a good three-quarters of a mile away, on the outskirts of the village. Emma let the two nine-year-olds run on in front, shouting at them every now and again to stay on the pavement. Her mind was full of Danny. She smiled: he was a scally all right. He could charm the birds off the trees. Every time he looked at her – he seemed to have this special way of doing it that made her feel unique – her stomach flipped over. Whether he was the rogue Pete and Robert made him out to be, she couldn't say. He didn't back down from trouble, that much was clear, but his city background was partly what intrigued her; beside Danny, life in a Lake District village seemed very dull and uneventful.

Annie and Paula's yells brought her out of her musings. They were staring at a burned-out car on the road outside the school. Sergeant Eddie Slater, the local copper, was examining it, notebook in hand. He looked up, saw Emma and grimaced. 'Hotel workers.' She made a sympathetic face and ushered the kids into the schoolyard as head-master John Parr blew his whistle and called, 'Everyone form an *orderly* line.' He seemed tense, bawling the children out for chattering and making them stand perfectly still, even though some of them were shivering in the stiff breeze. Emma noticed that he kept glancing towards the classroom windows at his wife, Simone. She wondered if they'd had a row or something.

On the way home Emma stopped off at the village store opposite the hotel – which sold everything from groceries to guide books and offered photocopying and boot hire into the bargain – ostensibly to get the cabbage but really in the vain hope of bumping into Danny. She lingered, flicking through magazines. Their coverlines taunted her: 'Is He the One For You? Ten Ways to Tell' and 'Could You Fall For a Stranger? Read Our True Stories Inside!' This is stupid, she told herself, you're behaving like a soppy schoolgirl. The doorbell jangled and she looked up for the umpteenth time. It was Danny.

'Hi.' Now Emma felt embarrassed. She bought a bag of crisps – she didn't want to give Danny the impression she had been loitering around for him – and went outside to thumb through a display of paperbacks on a rack beneath the shop's awning. He followed her, unwrapping the cellophane from a fresh packet of cigarettes. 'Sunset over Hawksmere,' he read, turning over postcards.

'It isn't usually like that. Most of the time it rains.' Suddenly, she felt tongue-tied and awkward. 'Are you off work now?'

'Yeah, till tonight. Not much call for lunches yet.' Danny seemed equally nervous. He lit one of the cigarettes and offered her one. She shook her head. 'You doin' anythin'?' he asked.

'Mam's given me a heap of jobs. They can wait, though.'

'Want to go for a walk, then? Show me the sights?'

'OK.' I'm blushing, Emma thought. I'm actually blushing.

They strolled alongside the lake, following a footpath through some trees and clambering up a steep bank. Below them the water was glassily still, the lakescape reflecting the landscape in perfect symmetry. Barely a ripple broke on the shore. Two moorhens bobbed serenely past, nodding their heads in greeting. Danny and Emma stood side by side in silence, looking out across the tranquil water at the fells opposite. The green lower stretches were picked out in rectangles by dry-stone walls, becoming russet higher up where dead bracken covered the steeper slopes and fading to darkness where the rocky outcrops of the top ridges began. 'I think I saw a falcon the other day,' Danny began, but the rest of his sentence was drowned out by the sudden deafening scream of a low-flying jet, which had already vanished over the next crest while the painful noise continued to resound in their ears. 'RAF,' shouted Emma. 'We get them a lot round here. You never quite get used to them – they always seem to blast out of nowhere.'

The footpath cut through a nearby farm and they stopped to watch as the farmer, a taciturn man with a fierce ruddy face, dipped his sheep. 'Swaledales,' said Emma, 'You can tell by their black faces. It's the main breed around here now.' Watched by a sharp-eyed collie, the terrified beasts were creating a fearful racket, scrabbling over each other in their cramped pen in an attempt to avoid being caught by the farmer's long crook. Clad in protective green overalls, his sleeves rolled up above the elbow, the farmer grabbed a ewe by its shaggy fleece and hauled it into the deep bath to join two others, which were thrashing about wildly as a shepherd dunked them, using a long-handled wooden rake, holding the flailing sheep under until Danny thought they must be drowned.

The gasping animals surfaced, bleating pitifully, only to be submerged again and again beneath the murky solution. They were finally released to swim out, eyes swivelling, and join their dripping, bellowing flock in another pen. 'They get parasites in their wool. The disinfectant kills them,' explained Emma. 'Some farmers have stopped doing it. Health scare or something.' Danny, with a city-dweller's sensitivities, was beginning to feel discomfited by the scene. 'C'mon, let's go and find a pub.'

After that Emma saw Danny regularly but discreetly. She decided to keep it low-key, not because they were doing anything – unsure of her feelings, she was keeping him firmly at a distance – but because her family, who were friendly with Robert's, obviously disapproved. This was made clear when she found Danny waiting for her one Sunday after Mass, leaning against the wall that encircled the churchyard and holding a bunch of wild flowers. Her mother and father stepped round him like he was dog mess; Pete looked like he wanted to thump him. Danny said, 'Would you mind if I walked back to the village with you all, Mrs Quinlan?', to which Bernie had replied stiffly, 'You do what you like.' It was a frosty half-mile home.

'Windermere, Coniston, Rydal, Grasmere, Easedale Tarn. Morecambe Bay, right over there. You know Wainwright?' Emma and Danny were high up on the fells by a cairn, taking in the panoramic view. The landscape below them changed constantly, sunlit valleys falling dark as the shadows of clouds crept like sinister invisible forces across them.

'No,' said Danny.

'He writes these guides to the Lake District. He hasn't got a good word to say about here. I think it's the best place in the world.' A chilly breeze tugged at their clothes and whipped up their hair, though the sun was warm on their skin. 'Have you got a hanky? My eyes are streaming.' She turned to face him, her cheeks wet.

'Try this.' He proffered a bit of his flannel shirt sleeve and dabbed. She felt his breath on her face and suddenly, illogically, panicked. 'What are you doing?'

Danny, who had got to kiss her or burst, backed off. 'I'm sorry.' He was, too. Why? Normally he'd have tried it on ages before this. I must be losing my grip, he told himself, thinking of Julie. But that was different.

The next time they met, he took Emma out in a little rowing boat on the lake. She told him about the frustrations of life at home – Bernie had been giving her an even harder time ever since she came back off her shift to find the pan burnt, the bacon shrivelled and the bathroom untidy – and how she longed to live it up as a student in some cosmopolitan city. She did not, he noticed, mention Robert in her plans. In return, Danny told her the truth – edited – about his home life, leaving out the gambling but coming clean about being on the dole. 'Me mam's OK, really, though she nags me somethin' rotten, but me dad –' he broke off, looking out across the water's surface. For a moment he was pensive. 'One day we were walkin' back through the park. Me dad said, "We'll never get a bus; it's peak hour." I didn't know what peak hour meant but it was gettin' windy and the wind was making the lake go, y'know, peaky. So I thought that was peak hour, when the wind did that on the lake.' They sat in companionable silence, the boat rocking gently on the rise and fall of the swell.

'We'd better go back in, it's getting rougher,' she said eventually.

Back on the jetty, they kissed. It happened quite naturally. Danny was helping Emma out of the boat and he took her hand and pulled her up and she found herself in his arms. This time, when he bent his head and brought his lips to hers, she did not resist.

Robert was going to kill Danny. Pete Quinlan had told him that he thought his sister was seeing the Scouser from the hotel, but he couldn't quite believe it of Emma. Until today. He felt hot, furious tears starting at the back of his eyes. Emma was the girl at school all the lads fancied; she was the beauty, she was funny, she was vibrant, she was going places. People were drawn to her – she always seemed to have a gang of followers. A retinue, like a star. She was perfect. Until today.

He had glimpsed them together on the lake when he was out walking the dog – at least he thought it was them, that was why he had slipped down to the boat-landing, to make sure. He saw Emma – his girl – being kissed by that scally and she didn't fight it, did she? She kissed him right back. She put her arms around him. She gazed in his eyes. She smiled and laughed. She rested her head on his shoulder. She held his hand. She was a fuckin' traitor. And he – he was going to get it, good and proper.

Robert saw his opportunity that night, at the disco. He knew, with a sinking heart, that Emma would be there, flaunting herself with Danny. And that he, Robert, had to show her, and him, and all his off-comer mates for that matter, that he wouldn't take it, he wouldn't be made a fool of. He saw Danny head for the toilet outside the Ramblers Bar and pushed through the crowd to follow him. Inside the gents, a bloke was peeing at the urinals. It wasn't Danny. A cubicle door was shut. He bent and looked under it. Got him! He stood square outside the door, arms folded, and waited. After a few moments he heard Danny say loudly, 'I'm not coming out.' How did he know it was him? Robert was unsure of how to play this. Danny called again, 'I'm not into men, I'm into women. Right? Find someone else.' The peeing man

45

glanced round and looked at him questioningly. Robert realized why Danny had taken the cubicle. He fled.

Emma had never felt like this about anyone. Danny was a twin soul. He completed her. They spent all their spare time in each other's company, sneaking off to make love wherever they could, becoming more and more inventive in their choice of locations. One time it was in the lush undergrowth beyond the croquet lawn of the hotel. Another time they did it in a sheltered hollow up on the fells. Once they climbed up into the hayloft of an old barn and did it, gloriously naked, entwined in a patch of sunlight pouring through the missing slates. After Robert's pedestrian fumblings, which were all she had ever known, sex with Danny was a revelation and made Emma feel strangely liberated. He delighted in pleasuring her, allowing her to discover a sensual side to her nature that her Catholic upbringing had always denied. Occasionally they went to his place in the staff quarters, but there the cramped room seemed to close in on them. It made Emma feel sordid, whereas outside, on the hard earth with grass blades rasping against her skin, she felt grounded, connected by Danny to something elemental.

She had started out with the best of intentions, even – after a brief moral dilemma – tucking a packet of condoms in her bag, but somehow it never seemed right to produce them: fumbling with a ridiculous piece of pink latex was just too utilitarian for their kind of sex. Danny said he was clear and she trusted him. The other thing she shut her mind to. All she knew was that when their bodies touched they became supercharged and that once he was inside her they spun off into a universe all of their own.

As the days grew longer and high season brought the trippers in, choking the narrow roads and smothering the fells in armies of brightly coloured cagoules, Danny and

Emma were forced to tone down these alfresco liaisons and settle for walks and picnics instead. As Emma pointed out to him rather sternly – Danny, of course, revelled in the risk – she did not want to open her eyes to find an audience getting out their packed lunches and cameras.

'Local wildlife in the flesh? Go on, they'd love it,' he jested. 'They'd be able to tell people that although they didn't see a golden eagle they did see the beast with two backs.'

'Danny, I'm serious,' she said, trying not to smile but failing.

'So. You tell me, what could be more natural? How do you think primitive man got started? Natural selection would've ground to a halt if he'd gone all coy about doing it in the bushes.'

'That's rubbish. "Who made you?" God made me. "Why –"' she began, quoting the catechism.

'Bollocks.'

'"– did God make you?" God made me to know Him.'

'Evolution made you.'

'Explain eyesight.'

'It evolved.'

'How?'

'I don't know.'

'Exactly.'

'OK, explain piles.'

'What?'

'God made us, so he made piles as well. Sitting up there on his throne. "Oh, I know, I'll give them these little veins that swell up and pop out every time they have a crap. Itch like mad, bleed." What kind of sick, twisted brain would think of piles?'

It was a question Emma brought up with Father Matthew later that evening when she made a rare appearance at confession. The church was heavy with the cloying scent of lilies left over from a weekend wedding, making her feel nauseous and faintly swimmy. Father Matthew, a big-hearted Welshman with kind eyes, didn't seem to find it much of a conundrum. 'There are worse things than piles, Emma.'

'I know. It doesn't answer the question, though, does it?'

'No,' he admitted, waiting. There was a long silence. 'When in doubt, blurt it out,' he said encouragingly.

'I think I might be pregnant.'

FIVE

Emma sat on the edge of the bath staring at the indicator stick of the pregnancy testing kit, not sure if she was going to laugh, cry or throw up. How often had she seen girls from school mysteriously dropping out, only to reappear months later pushing a pram past the playground? She'd always thought they were stupid, getting themselves up the duff and then showing off their babies like they were some great achievement, a special award for not being bright enough to take GCSEs. They had no ambitions, no imagination; they still stood around like slags in tarty gear, blowing cigarette smoke across their buggies and talking about 'my old man', who was, in all likelihood, a spotty youth of seventeen who had been too slow to get away in time.

And now it had happened to her. Join the club. How could she go to university? What would her folks say? What would Danny do? He had never actually said, 'I love you,' but she thought he did, deep down; he just didn't like to show his hand – fear of commitment and all that. Did that mean he would scarper once the season was over? He'd told her he'd had relationships in the past, but no one special. Emma had assumed she was more than a fling but they hadn't discussed the future. Now she wasn't so sure.

There was no question of getting rid of it. The thought had crossed Emma's mind – guiltily – for a fleeting second after the affirmative blue line appeared in the little window, but it wasn't just her Catholicism that vetoed the idea. Emma had been brought up to believe that abortion was murder, and while she had never had cause to question that belief, it wasn't the stern negative imperative of the Church that compelled her response, but a positive, personal one. Of all the tumultuous emotions racing in her brain, the clearest was a voice that sang, 'My baby. My baby!' over and over again. She touched her belly tentatively. It felt no different – a bit bloated perhaps, but nothing to indicate the momentous changes going on inside. What did the baby look like at this stage? She imagined it as a little prawn, pink, curled and veiny with huge black eyes. That's how you were once, she told herself, and suddenly her body's capacity to create life overwhelmed her. There in the bathroom, surrounded by loo rolls and shampoo and drying socks and all the ordinary clutter of existence, she made a commitment to her unborn child: you'll come first, no matter what; I'll look after you. Already, her love for it choked her; it was of a different calibre to her love for Danny, something more intensely complete.

Her thoughts were interrupted by Pete hammering on the door. 'You'll never wash away all your sins, so get a bloody move on. I'm late.'

Emma could not begin to imagine how to break the news to Danny. 'Just tell him the truth, straight. If he's a responsible young man – and I'm sure he is – he'll be there for you,' Father Matthew had said. She tried to, later on in the pub that evening, but without some Dutch courage – Emma was on orange juice – she couldn't get the words out. Danny was playing the fruit machine in the corner, hitting buttons and staring fixedly at the three spinning drums. She swirled the ice cubes round in her empty glass. He had been at it for almost half an hour and seemed to have forgotten her presence entirely. The machine played a noisy victory tune and disgorged a handful of cash. 'Yesss!' Danny raised his arm in triumph. He looked over at her and grinned. Emma smiled and went over to join him.

'We've got a bit of a problem,' she began, but his back was already turned and he was feeding in more coins. She gave up on the idea.

It slipped out, the next day, when they were strolling past the school. Emma hadn't planned for it to come out the way it did; her mouth seemed to say something that her brain took no responsibility for. It was alarming the way your body could do that, she thought, simply react with no prior warning from head office. These days she found herself welling up at anything from adverts for baked beans to stories on the news. It was lunchtime and children were kicking up the usual din in the playground, scrapping, chasing and shouting, while others played hop-scotch on a big yellow snake marked out on the concrete. 'I used to do that,' Emma said, surprised it was still popular, as they stopped and looked over the wall. She waved to little Annie and Paula, who ignored her. They were in a huddle with two other girls, hatching some plot or other. 'Come on. I want to show you something,' she said on impulse, leading Danny into the schoolyard. John Parr was there, supervising the kids. 'I'm just showing him the plaque,' shouted Emma, pointing at the roll of honour on the wall, but he seemed not to notice them. She remembered the strained atmosphere between John and Simone the other day and wondered whether his distracted expression had anything to do with the fact that Simone had just driven past them on her way to the village. She looked quizzically at Danny. He shrugged. 'There's mine. Eight names down,' she said, returning to the plaque. 'I got a book on Wordsworth for it. Special presentation. Had to wear a frock. Susan Flaherty thought she'd win it. She was jealous as hell. I think I'm pregnant. She battered me after school. Tore my frock.'

A low-flying jet screamed overhead; a bolt from the blue.

*

Danny's impending fatherhood was the talk of the staff common room. Julie managed to ferret the information out of him after Danny staggered in looking pale beneath his recently acquired tan and slumped morosely on to the sway-backed sofa. Normally, Julie's fetchingly brief denim shorts and crop top would have provoked him to make some comment or other, but even Albie's news that he could now last for at least eighteen seconds without suffering grievous bodily harm failed to produce a response. Something was seriously wrong. 'Come on,' said Julie, sitting down beside him. 'What on earth's happened? It can't be that bad, surely?' She put a friendly arm around Danny's shoulders. Their one-night stand had been accepted by both of them for what it was, but she still had a soft spot for him.

'Can't it?' Danny buried his head in his hands.

'We're your mates. You can tell us. We'll look out for you.'

'No you won't. Not with this.'

'For God's sake, what have you done? Is somebody dead?'

''Ey! Even I'm not quite that bad.' He looked up and gave her a ghost of a smile. 'It's just that you'll take the mick.'

'Emma's pregnant,' she guessed. 'Is that it?'

'In a nutshell.' He flopped back and shut his eyes. There was a shocked silence. The door opened. 'Tharmy entered,' announced Joey. The others ignored him.

'Are you going to marry her?' asked Julie eventually.

'I suppose so, yeah.' Danny didn't sound enthusiastic about it.

'He scratched his head.' Julie glared at Joey warningly and continued gently, 'Where will you live?'

'I don't know.' Danny was reeling. He had been living for the present, doing what he wanted, glorying in his new-found freedom. No pressure, no nagging, no what-are-you-going-to-do-with-your-life. Even working in the kitchen was strangely satisfying: it defined his daily routine but did not ask of him any more than that he turn up and slip into automaton mode. He hadn't thought about the future, about what he would do when the season ended, and as for the past, it was a foreign country. They did things differently there and he didn't fancy revisiting it.

'He felt like picking his nose. He decided to leave it till later,' commented Joey.

Danny heaved himself up off the sofa. He had to sort out his head. 'I'm going outside. I may be some time,' he said with a touch of his old bravado.

'Add nappies to the list,' jeered Albie. Julie shoved him. Danny left.

He walked back up into the fells, pushing his body relentlessly, his breath coming in harsh gasps, sweat dripping into his eyes. At the summit Danny realized he had been there before – he was looking out over the same panoramic view as the day he first tried to kiss Emma. He remembered the wind-whipped tears in her eyes and how he'd mopped them dry. He remembered, guiltily, the tears in her eyes that morning, after she told him she was pregnant, and how he'd turned away and walked back up the road, leaving her standing outside the playground, sobbing.

Danny hadn't meant to abandon Emma like that; he just hadn't known how to handle the news. He still didn't. 'You could do a runner,' a sly voice inside his head suggested. 'You could pack your bags and find work in a different hotel somewhere else.' It wasn't said with any conviction: he knew he wouldn't because Emma was special. It was the longest courtship, the most sustained relationship he'd ever had. He wasn't interested in notching up conquests any more; he wanted to know what made her tick, what made her happy. He wanted to be with her all the time. When they weren't together, he felt as if something in him was switched off, as if he was existing rather than living. The truth slowly dawned on him: he loved her.

Would that be enough to see them through? If she wanted to be with him – and he wasn't sure that she did, not after how he'd just treated her – would she be prepared to live a different kind of life in Liverpool? A kitchen porter's wages would never sustain them and, besides, the work would dry up come October. He'd have a better chance of finding something permanent back home. But how could he ask her to swap the splendour of the Lakes for the squalor of a tower block in Everton Valley? Did she love him that much? Looking out across the sweep of fells, lakes and tarns below, he quoted Auden's 'The Shield of Achilles':

> 'She looked over his shoulder
> For vines and olive trees
> Marble well-governed cities
> And ships upon untamed seas.
> But there on the shining metal
> His hands had placed instead
> An artificial wilderness
> And a sky like lead.'

'Liverpool? Why there?' Bernie Quinlan was still getting over the shock of her daughter's unwelcome news. Unwelcome, but not entirely unexpected. That Scouser spelt trouble; she'd known it from the moment she set eyes on him. They had tried to put her off Danny but Emma wouldn't be told and carrying on had only made her more set on him. Bernie was the same at Emma's age, only she never dared to risk so much.

'Danny'll get a job there. We'll get settled there. When the baby's a bit older I can go to university there.'

'You won't go to university.' Bernie was a realist.

'I'll go.'

'Listen,' Bernie put her mug down on the table carefully and looked at Emma beadily. 'I know all about bringing up kids. I've had twenty years of bringing up kids and I'm telling you you won't go to university.'

'I'll go. It's put back a few years, that's all.' Emma and Danny had discussed this after he'd come round and apologized. Now that she knew how he felt, all the answers seemed simple.

Bernie sighed. Then she said something surprising. 'You don't have to marry him.'

'I want to marry him.'

'No you don't, you want to want to marry him. So there's no one left holding the baby, no whiff of scandal. Well, I couldn't care less about scandal. Or the neighbours. Let them think you're the biggest slut in the world. Fine. But for God's sake, don't let them think you're stupid. Don't let them think you've done one stupid thing on top of another. Don't marry him.'

Emma could hardly believe this was her devoutly Catholic mother speaking. If it hadn't been for the fact that it was so obviously provoked by her detestation of Danny, she would have admired Bernie for it. She opened her mouth to reply but at that moment the front door went and they heard Granddad and Annie in the hall.

'What?' Granddad shuffled in, carrying the evening paper.

Bernie looked harassed. 'How did I know you'd say that?' she snapped.

'What?'

' "What?" Because you always say it. Every time you walk into a room you say, "What?" ' She flounced out into the kitchen and started banging pots and pans around.

'If I were you I'd take cover, Granddad,' said Emma, relieved that Bernie's fire had been drawn elsewhere. It could have gone worse, she reflected. As for telling her dad, that was when the shit would really hit the fan. Danny had volunteered to be present and she had accepted his offer gratefully.

'What'll he say?' Danny asked, resigned.

'Not much. He'll be too busy kicking lumps out of you,' she warned.

There had been a certain amount of bluffing to Bernie. The details Emma and Danny had discussed were at best sketchy – they had spent most of the time making up. In her heart of hearts Emma was not as confident as she had made out. She needed to discuss her feelings with someone she could talk to without recriminations but it was hopeless trying to get an unbiased opinion from anyone in her family – or anyone in the village, come to that; they all mistrusted off-comers. There was only one person who would listen. She got her jacket and went to Father Matthew's house.

He did not seem particularly surprised to see her. 'Come in, come in,' he greeted her in his lilting Welsh accent. Inside, his house had the unkempt look of a bachelor pad rather than the spick-and-span domicile of a priest. He led her into the kitchen – 'Sitting room's a bit messy at the moment' – and put on the kettle. 'So how are you?' he asked, busying himself with tea things. 'Feeling a bit rough? First few months are the worst, I hear.'

'Not so bad. Tired, mainly.' Now she was here Emma wasn't sure what she had wanted to say.

'What are you going to do?' He put a teapot, a bottle of milk and a couple of mugs on the table and sat down opposite her. He looked friendly and concerned.

'I don't know,' she admitted wretchedly.

'Get married?'

'I don't know.'

'If you do get married, where will you live?'

'I don't know.' God, I sound stupid, she thought. I think I know what I want but the practicalities – I just don't know where to start. What must he be thinking of me? She stirred her tea. 'I might do better on the general knowledge round,' she said weakly.

It was dark by the time Peter Quinlan got home. He'd had a long, tiring day working outside in rotten weather reconstructing a dry-stone wall and then a couple of pints in the village pub – there was no rush; Bernie, he knew, was at choir practice, she would leave him a pie to reheat – he was ready to put his feet up and relax. He parked his rusty old van on the road outside their house and walked up the garden path. The sitting-room curtains hadn't been drawn and he looked in at the illuminated room, frowning. The Scouser was there, talking with Emma, Granddad and Annie. 'Hell's teeth. You'd have thought he'd have got the bloody message by now,' he muttered to himself as he unlocked the door.

'This is Danny Kavanagh,' said Emma as he entered the room. Thrown by the formality of the introduction – Danny had got up and was offering his hand – Peter shook it and grunted.

'I think it's time us young things went up the wooden hill,' Granddad said, taking little Annie's hand. 'Say goodnight.' She went on tiptoe and Peter stooped to kiss her.

'Night, love.' He threw himself into his favourite arm-chair. Danny and Emma remained standing, looking awkward. They glanced at each other.

'Do you want a beer?' she asked suddenly. 'There's a couple in the fridge.'

'No.' He sat up, suspicious. 'I want to know what this little charade is all about.'

'Don't get het up, now, Dad. It's just that there's some-thing we want to tell you.' She held on to Danny's arm for moral support. Peter got a terrible sinking feeling in the pit of his stomach. 'It's good news,' Emma insisted

57

brightly. 'Really. Danny and I are going to get married.'

'And?' Peter got up out of the chair, staring at Danny with a frightening glint in his eye.

'And . . . and . . . you're going to be a grandfather, too.'

Peter felt as if a switch had been thrown inside him. *You got my daughter pregnant? You Scouse bastard.*' He couldn't see them clearly for the mist in front of his eyes. 'I'm gonna kill you with me bare hands.' He was dimly aware of shaking Danny violently by the shoulders while Emma screamed, 'Stop it, Dad, stop it, you'll hurt him. It's not his fault, Dad, it's nobody's fault. We love each other, Dad.' She tried to prise him off Danny and Peter let go, his chest heaving with rage and anguish.

'What d'you mean, "It's nobody's fault"? It's your bloody fault and it's his bloody fault –' he turned on her instead. Just then the door clicked and Bernie ran in.

'Leave her, Peter,' she said firmly, walking up to him and taking his arm.

He was still in full flow. ' – or are you trying to tell me it's another immaculate bloody conception? Shall I take a walk up the fell and ask, "Excuse me, has anyone seen the angel of the Lord?"' He faced Bernie. There were tears in his eyes. 'She's pregnant.'

'I know.'

'*You know?* Since when?'

'Two days ago.'

'She told you two days ago?' He was incredulous.

Bernie sighed. 'Look, can we skip the next hour and a half, Peter? Can we just assume you've thrown –'

'Why didn't you tell me?' he interrupted.

' – all the usual tantrums and can we just get down to talking a bit of sense about what happens next?'

'*Why didn't you tell me?*' he bellowed, his anger building again.

'Because I knew you'd act like this,' she said quietly, and left the room.

Peter leant his hands on the table, head down, breathing hard. An awful silence descended, punctuated by Emma's stifled sobs. At last Danny said, 'I can understand y' bein' a bit, y'know, upset.'

The sound of his Scouse accent riled Peter so much that he was on the point of losing it completely. He said, through clenched teeth, 'You should leave this house right now, son. Unless you fancy the rest of your life minus your bollocks, you should leave this house right now,' and went out after Bernie. She wasn't in their room. He thought she might be checking on Annie and looked in, only to find his youngest daughter still up and plastered in garish make-up that she had obviously filched off her mother's dressing-table. 'Get that off and get into bed,' he shouted, thinking, Christ, she's only nine, I suppose she'll be giving us grief next.

He found Bernie in Granddad Toolan's bedroom, changing the sheets. 'What does he do?' Peter demanded, still ranting about Danny.

'Ask him,' she said calmly.

'I'm asking you. Apart from getting girls pregnant, what does he do?'

'Kitchen porter.' She folded the bedspread back, smoothed the pillow.

'A kitchen porter?' He should have known.

'There are worse things.'

'There's only one thing worse than a kitchen porter and that's a Scouse kitchen porter.'

Bernie seemed to have lost interest in the discussion. She bundled up the dirty linen, noticing, as she did so, a neat black hole right through one of the sheets. She made an exasperated noise. 'For God's sake!' Peter trailed after her as she bustled out and knocked loudly on the bathroom door. 'Dad!'

'They're talking about getting married.' Peter couldn't let it drop.

'Aye?' Granddad replied from the bath, making splashing noises.

'You're gonna have to stop smoking in bed,' she shouted through the door.

'I said they're talking about getting married.' It didn't seem to be registering with her.

'It's my house,' Granddad grumped.

'Where are they gonna live?' Peter persisted.

Bernie looked at him like she'd had a basinful of the lot of them. 'I'm going out,' she stated, stuffing the sheets into his arms.

'What? For God's sake, woman – where are they gonna live? What are they gonna do about money? What are they gonna do about the baby? Does she think we're gonna mind it?' Bernie was going downstairs. ''Cause if she thinks we're gonna mind it, she's got another think coming and if we don't mind it, what's she gonna do? I mean, she had a bloody future ahead of her, didn't she?' The front door slammed and Bernie disappeared into the night.

Father Matthew was rinsing coffee cups in the little alcove off the meeting room – a modern extension to the neat little nineteenth-century church, made possible by a generous bequest – when he heard organ music swelling in the choir. Wiping his hands on a tea-towel he walked through into the nave to see who it was playing at such a late hour. He guessed it was Bernie Quinlan – she had left choir practice early, looking anxious – and he was right. He sat down quietly in one of the choir stalls, listening, and his heart went out to her as she poured her troubled soul into the music. Maybe his thoughts reached her, for she stopped playing suddenly and glanced round.

'How long have you been there?' she asked in her soft Irish brogue.

'A while.' He waved his arm. 'Carry on, it's lovely.'

She pressed the keys again, softly, slowly. 'Emma's

pregnant,' she said, staring at the empty sheet-music holder in front of her.

'I know.'

'They're getting married.'

'I know.'

The music ceased, mid-phrase. Bernie swivelled round on her seat and looked at him with huge, sad eyes. 'Can you do it soon? I don't want it showing. And it's not for the reason you think. I just want her to look nice.'

'I'll do my best,' he promised. He left Bernie to be by herself and returned to his cups.

Despite his teddy-bearish appearance, Father Matthew was a passionate and committed man who was sometimes frustrated by the constraints the priesthood imposed. He came from a tough urban background and was used to rolling up his sleeves and getting stuck in. Hawksmere was very different from his previous parish: the problems here were not brought on by the environment – bad housing, drug-dealing, poverty, homelessness – they were internalized, deep-rooted problems that were hard to get any real access to. As the community's confessor he witnessed much suffering and pain, yet at the same time he frequently felt powerless to help in a practical way. On those occasions, the sanctity of the confessional became a double-edged sword and he would chew over the privileged information he held deep into the night. Emma Quinlan's situation – and more specifically, Bernie Quinlan's distressed reaction to it – was one such example. Chef's ill-concealed philandering was another.

Matthew was deeply troubled by one of his parishioners who had come to him one night and announced, 'Bless me Father for I have sinned. Well, I haven't yet, but I'm going to.'

'I can't absolve you for something you haven't done. And if you know you want to do it, that means you know

61

you needn't do it. Whatever "it" is,' he said reasonably.

'Oh, I am going to do it. No doubt about that. When the time is right, when I can be sure.'

'Well, can you give me a clue? We can talk about it. That's what I'm here for, to listen, to help.'

'You won't want to when I tell you.'

'Come on,' Matthew chided. 'Try me. Get it off your chest.'

'You won't stop me.'

'Thinking about doing something bad, fantasizing about it, it's quite common,' he said soothingly. 'We all do it – it's necessary, once in a while, to let off a little steam. You've got nothing to feel guilty about.'

'*I* haven't. *He* has.'

'Who?'

'Chef. He's got to be stopped. So I'm going to kill him.'

What was he supposed to do, Father Matthew tortured himself, when a parishoner told him calmly, rationally, and in confidence that he planned to commit a murder? He couldn't just sit back and watch it happen, yet he couldn't implicate the individual in any way, either. As it was, he wasn't at all sure who Chef was carrying on with these days or whether his parishoner had the right information. In the end, he decided it was his duty to deliver a non-specific warning and walked round to Chef's house – a long haul up a steep, unpaved road – to wait for him to return off duty. It was a long wait. He shivered in the lee of the house, beginning to regret his vigil. Finally he saw headlights bouncing up the track and a car pulled up outside the door. Father Matthew could just make out Simone Parr at the wheel. Chef got out and she reversed back down the road. Matthew stepped out of the shadows.

'Who's there?' Chef's fists bunched as he looked around at the sudden footstep. 'Oh, it's you,' he muttered, catching sight of the priest. 'What the hell are you doing lurking around up here at this hour?'

Father Matthew looked at him squarely. 'Someone's going to kill you,' he said, delivering it as a simple statement of fact.

'Who?' Chef looked disbelieving.

'I can't tell you that. But if you don't mend your ways, someone's going to kill you.'

Chef stared into the shadows, as if he expected another figure to emerge. Then he looked up at the bedroom window, where Ruth was visible, watching from behind the curtain, as always. He looked back at Matthew again and folded his arms. 'Bollocks.'

The following evening, Father Matthew found himself getting stuck in after all, albeit rather more profoundly than he would have wished. He was enjoying a nightcap in the crowded hotel bar when the kitchen staff poured in amid much ribald laughter. Albie pushed up to the front and, ignoring Robert, who was waiting to be served, ordered drinks for the lads. Robert appeared to be protesting and Matthew overheard Albie say, 'He's getting married in the morning,' pointing to Danny.

Danny's riposte sounded like, 'Cumbria – where men are men and sheep are nervous,' but Matthew couldn't be sure of this because all hell broke out. Robert punched Danny, Albie punched Robert, Tharmy swung out wildly and Pete Quinlan and various other locals piled in on top, glad at the chance of giving the off-comers a drubbing. 'Stop this at once!' Father Matthew shouted, wading into the melee. A fist shot out and smacked him right in the face, felling him like a tree.

Dressed in his best suit, which was tight across the shoulders, Peter Quinlan screwed a smoke alarm on to the ceiling outside Grandad's bedroom door. It was the day of the wedding and he was ready early and needing something to do with his hands – if only to keep them off

Danny Kavanagh's neck, he told himself grimly. Emma had been determined to see the wedding through and Bernie seemed to be supporting her – she had even managed to get them squeezed in on a Saturday at the height of the wedding season. At that moment, Bernie appeared at the top of the stairs in a lilac two-piece with her hair in large rollers. 'What are you putting it there for?' she asked, disappearing into a bedroom.

'Where do you want me to put it?' he snapped.

She reappeared, carrying the best tablecloth. 'Inside his room.'

'If he wants to burn himself to death, he can do,' Peter said dourly, checking the battery and making it bleep. 'I'm just making sure he doesn't take us all with him.'

She hurried downstairs and peered out of the window – 'Oh, my God, they're coming up the street' – and ran back up to extract the pink curlers.

'Who?'

'His bloody parents,' she replied through a mouthful of grips.

Pete emerged from the bathroom in his suit, his face battered and bruised. Peter got off the chair he had been standing on and surveyed his son. 'What happened to you?' He didn't require an answer.

The Kavanaghs seemed as ill at ease as the Quinlans. Over tea – the best china had been brought out too, as well as the best tablecloth – a delicate interview was being conducted in an atmosphere you could cut with a knife. 'So she's bright then?' Mrs Kavanagh remarked.

'Very. She was going to go to university. She'd just been accepted, as a matter of fact,' Bernie said, throwing down the gauntlet.

A tight-lipped smile. 'Oh. Where?'

Bernie looked distracted. 'Liverpool.' She had her eye on Granddad who was lifting the milk jug up. He wouldn't. She'd told him not to, only five minutes before they arrived.

'That's a coincidence.'

'Yeah,' Peter growled. It was the only word he'd contributed so far. Granddad sniffed the milk. Bernie flinched.

'Danny's very bright,' Mrs Kavanagh rallied.

'Really?' It was Bernie's turn to flash a false smile.

'Yeah, very bright. Isn't he, Dan?' She turned to her husband who, like Peter, had so far stayed out of the ring.

'Yeah. No bloody common sense but very bright,' he snorted.

'And decent. Well, that's obvious, isn't it?' Mrs Kavanagh added.

'Is it?' Bernie felt her face flush. What was she implying? she thought, angrily. That our Emma's a lucky girl or something? Does she think our Emma's at fault?

The door opened and Pete walked in, black and blue. Suddenly, Bernie wished the ground would open up and swallow her.

As it turned out, black eyes were the order of the day. Half the congregation seemed to sport one, including the groom – and Father Matthew. His, in fact, was the best of the lot, a real shiner, making him more panda bear than teddy bear. He acknowledged it with a wry joke as Emma – pale and, despite Bernie's hopes, visibly pregnant – took Danny's hand and stood beside him. 'Dearly beloved, bruised and unbruised . . .' Bernie clutched her Order of Service and slid a sidelong glance at her granite-faced husband. It had been an effort, she knew, for him to give away his beloved daughter – the daughter they had such high hopes for – under such inauspicious circumstances. We're all bruised, she thought miserably, though they might not show up on the outside. But touch us and it hurts like hell.

SIX

The coach that had delivered Emma from Liverpool and in doing so had sealed her fate was waiting to return her. As the driver climbed down and took her case round to the luggage compartment she hugged her family, who had come to see her off. 'If you need anything, phone,' Peter muttered hoarsely in her ear, holding her tight and feeling her huge bump rear up against him. 'I will,' she whispered, suddenly overcome. They broke apart and he looked at her tenderly. 'Take care of little one, now,' he said, patting her belly, and walked away. Emma kissed her sister Annie and turned to embrace her mother. 'Bye, love.' Bernie was brisk. 'Sure you've got everything?' The driver clambered back on board. Emma looked around for her brother and saw Pete, hands in pocket, kicking at loose clods of turf on the verge. 'Bye,' she called, but he ignored her.

'Go on, they're all waiting for you,' said Bernie, helping her up on to the coach. Emma found a seat by the window and waved at them as it drew away. She could see her mother having words with Pete. They all waved back.

The baby seemed to enjoy the journey. It always kicked when she sat still or lay down at night, only now that she was so big – eight months – there was no room for it to flail around any more; instead she could feel individual limbs pressing insistently on her abdomen or up under her ribs. Sometimes you could even make out the shape of tiny hands and feet. She rubbed her tummy gently to calm it; she was proud of her shape and had merely smiled when the pointed looks and stares from people in the village grew in direct proportion to her advancing pregnancy. It had taken her parents a while to calm down, but once the season had finished and Danny had returned to Liverpool to get a job and find the three of them a home, they had looked after her and stuck up for her to anyone who dared criticize. Now they seemed to be as besotted with the idea of a new addition to the family as she was.

The rolling green fells Emma had grown up with slid past the window, becoming endless unchanging motorway as the coach bore south. She felt different, this time, arriving in Liverpool; excited, grown-up. It was the beginning of a new chapter in her life; she had sloughed off the skin of the naïve country girl and was about to metamorphose into a mature adult living in a vibrant and colourful city. Her optimism remained undimmed despite the urban dereliction unfolding in front of her as the coach rumbled past disused docks.

Danny was waiting as the coach drew in to the bus station. Emma, clad in a pair of voluminous maternity dungarees – a stark contrast to the willowy figure that had initially entranced him – stepped down carefully carrying a small bag. She caught sight of him and smiled broadly. Danny was relieved: in his anxiety he had half-wondered whether she might have changed her mind and by the time the coach pulled in he had convinced himself she wouldn't be on it. They kissed and he put his arm around as much of her waist as he could reach. She looked up at him and asked impatiently, 'Is it nice?' She meant the flat. Danny hadn't told her much about the flat, only that he'd found them somewhere with a great view of the Mersey. Emma hadn't twigged.

She kept a brave face when she saw the grim high-rise block. It was surrounded by other, equally grim blocks, all poking up out of a lunar landscape into the grey, windswept sky like stacks of children's bricks, wobbly towers built to see how high they would go before toppling over. Puffing hard – the footpath followed a steep incline

– Emma stopped to catch her breath. Danny, lugging the case, stopped too. A swarthy unkempt man, his bare arms covered in tattoos, walked past, a huge German shepherd straining at the leash. 'Get yerselves a dog. A big one,' he shouted back over his shoulder.

Inside the empty flat there was nothing but terrible wallpaper. Emma walked from room to room, her footsteps echoing on the bare floor, saying nothing, feeling nothing. It smelt of stale fags and something else, something nasty that she couldn't put her finger on. Their neighbours' television could be heard clearly through the thin walls. She looked out of the window and the stomach-churning view – they seemed to be about a mile up – made her reel backwards. The attack of vertigo pricked the last little bubble of her dreams. She turned to Danny, who was watching her silently, and stepped into his open arms. They were the only place she could possibly feel safe and the only reason for being here at all.

Naturally, she didn't tell the family any of this. What Bernie received was a chirpy letter that Emma had written as much to try to convince herself as to inform them about her new home. 'The flat's lovely,' she wrote. 'It's not in a very nice area but once you're inside you can shut your door on everything else, can't you? I hope everything's well. I've heard nothing from the hospital yet but everything seems fine with the baby. Write soon. Lots of love . . .' Bernie glanced at Father Matthew, who she had given the letter to. He finished reading and handed it back. 'She sounds OK.' They were walking on the fells – it was his suggestion; he had realized, the minute he saw Bernie sitting in the empty church staring into space, that she needed to talk. He'd hoped a breath of fresh air might encourage her to open up, but so far she had said little. She didn't need to: he could sense her disquiet. Bernie seemed to have such a transparent covering that sometimes it was as if there was an open channel between them, that he could tap into her feelings telepathically. Matthew knew, for instance, she wasn't fooled by that letter.

A brutish, animalistic huffing noise disturbed his thoughts. It was the sound of someone having all the breath pumped out of their body, relentlessly, mercilessly, and was accompanied by a low moaning. Fearing that a murder was being committed (perhaps the murder that he'd been warned about?) Matthew was about to scramble up to the stone outcrop from where it was issuing when Bernie caught him by the wrist and shook her head. Slowly the truth dawned on him. She smiled at his embarrassed face – the first time he'd seen her smile in months – and pointed to a sheltered spot away to their right.

'You're worried about her, aren't you?' Matthew said, sitting down on the warm grass with his back against a boulder.

'Yes.' Bernie looked out at a tarn in a distant corrie, sparkling in the waning afternoon sun like a newly minted coin, and wondered what 'not a very nice area' translated as.

'Phone her.'

'They're not on the phone.'

'Well, go and see her.'

'I'll wait till she has the baby.' Bernie sighed. 'I don't want to play the interfering mother.'

Two figures were approaching, the woman twitching her grass-stained skirt and tucking in her blouse. The couple did not see Bernie and Matthew until they were almost upon them, by which time it was too late for Chef and Simone not to acknowledge them. Simone, in agonies over what the priest – the priest, for God's sake, what was he doing up here? – must have heard, could only nod dumbly; Chef, who didn't give a fuck, grunted.

'The whole village is talking about her,' said Matthew as they disappeared from view down the track.

'They're jealous of her,' replied Bernie.

'She's married!' Matthew was astonished at her candour.

'She's *bored*.' Bernie stated this with an emphasis he found even more surprising. Their eyes met. She flushed.

'Either that wallpaper goes or I do. Who was it said that? Wilde? I know how he felt.' Emma attacked a particularly stuck-on patch of the vile brown-and-yellow wallpaper with her scraper, revelling in the sensation of stripping away the layers of grot and starting again with a clean, blank surface, hers to make her mark on. After the initial shock of the flat's awfulness had worn off, she was determined to appear cheerful. Emma had a streak of her mother's gritty perseverance – it hailed from the old country, she reckoned; all that getting down on your knees and scrubbing – which manifested itself in intensely practical ways. Getting rid of the wallpaper was the first step towards turning the dump into a home. Considering her enormous size – her feet seemed almost as far away as the ant-like people they could see from their window – she felt full of energy, fired up by a force fizzing inside her. Nesting, that was what it was called. Women did that before a birth, they cleared out cupboards and hoovered madly. Only a fortnight to go now.

'Yes.' Danny had hold of a piece of wallpaper that was promising to ease away in one long, satisfying strip. It began to peel back, strands of glue stretching and letting go of the wall as he pulled. 'Yes, oh yes!' It was nearly at the bottom. 'Can he do it? Oh yes!' The entire strip came off in his hands. He scrunched it up into a ball and threw it in the corner, trying hard to ignore the racing commentary on the portable TV in the kitchen. The sound of Peter O'Sullevan's familiar voice and all the images it brought back – the thrill of the race, the adrenalin pumping through his body, the euphoria of winning, walking away with a wad of instant cash – was getting to him. 'I'll make us a cuppa,' he said. It wouldn't hurt him just to see who was running in the 2.45. He filled the kettle, keeping one eye on the screen. Several of the horses he'd seen out before and knew their form. The starting prices came up. Watching was torture. Emma's purse was on the counter in front of the television, sending out siren signals to him. He couldn't steal from her. But it wouldn't be stealing, would it? He'd just borrow some money, slip off, nip down the bookie's. He could be back in half an hour with double, triple the amount. Even more maybe: there were some good odds. Think what they could buy! They needed all kinds of baby stuff. And she'd be so pleased. He came to a decision and opened the purse. There were two twenties in it. He took them out, then put one back and stuffed the other in his pocket. The kettle came to the boil noisily, clouds of steam pouring out of the spout. He used it as cover but Emma heard the door open and called from the other room, 'Where are you going?'

'Out,' he said. The door slammed.

She returned to her scraping, thinking he'd gone to get milk, or teabags, and hoping he would remember to pick up bread and a tin of beans or something for later. The shops were so far away; going out for anything was a major expedition, particularly for her. The baby weighed down so heavily in her pelvis that it felt as if it was about to plop out, added to which her lower back had been aching dully all day. A sudden cramp of pain gripped her belly, causing her to catch her breath. She hadn't been organized enough to go to any classes but it hurt enough to be a contraction and seemed to last for ever before subsiding. She sat down shakily on an upturned box. I'm in labour, she thought. Where the hell's Danny?

The spasms continued to come – every fifteen minutes at first, then every ten minutes, then every five minutes, lasting for longer each time and becoming more and more painful. Still no Danny. Perhaps he'd gone to the pub? Outside, the dreary afternoon was closing in; she could see headlights whizzing along the wet roads far below. She knew she couldn't leave it any longer. Fortunately, for once the lift was working.

The first taxi she hailed wouldn't take her – 'Sorry love, it's against the regulations' – leaving her standing wretchedly in the rain. Emma had never felt so abandoned and frightened. Her body had taken over and was sweeping her along on its own momentum. Another huge contraction swamped her and she clung to a railing, sobbing. A middle-aged woman in a plastic rain bonnet dropped her shopping bags and asked, 'Are you all right, pet?' and when Emma shook her head and gasped 'Baby,' she stepped out into the road and commandeered a cab, bundling Emma inside. 'Fazakerly Hospital, maternity entrance, and no messing about. Here's a tenner, you can keep the change.' She patted Emma's arm. 'You'll be fine, love. Just keep breathing deeply and don't panic.' And she bustled off into the night.

The hospital was busy. Emma, blitzed by pain and disorientated by the bright lights, the staff rushing about and the numerous arrows pointing to different departments, tried feebly to ask a technician in a white coat for directions but he did not seem to notice her. She spotted a sign marked 'Admissions' and went up to the desk. 'Excuse me.' The woman behind it was rifling through files and did not look up. 'I'm having –' The next contraction hit and she screamed, letting go of all her agony, anger and frustration. The woman looked up. A porter stopped. A nurse ran over. After that, things happened quickly.

'Not yet, not yet. Don't push now or you'll tear. Wait, wait . . . good girl, good girl, you're doing really well.' The midwife in the delivery suite had taken charge while

Emma's bottom was apparently attempting to turn itself inside out. She was entirely focused on the woman's voice; it was a beacon guiding her through the storm racking her sweat-soaked body. 'Slowly, slowly – the head's crowning. It'll soon be over now, love.' There was an intense, hot, burning sensation so acute it was unbearable. 'Just get it out of me,' she heard her voice shout from somewhere across the dark waves. Another nurse gave her the gas-and-air mask and she sucked on it greedily, a drowning woman thrown a lifebelt. 'It's coming! The head's out! Almost there, Emma. Another push now – bear down hard. Harder! You can do it!' Marshalling every ounce of strength she had left, Emma clenched her chin to her chest and expelled the baby with an almighty yell. 'Yes! You've done it, Emma. You've got a lovely baby girl,' the midwife congratulated her. Suddenly, all the pain was gone. She heard a tiny cackling cry and opened her eyes. 'Give her to me. Please give her to me.' A squirming, living, breathing, slippery little bundle was placed on her tummy and she folded her arms around it. She found herself looking down into Danny's blue eyes.

Danny had gone to the dogs. He was up after betting on the horses – not by much, but enough to know he was on a roll. It was a sign. He couldn't stop now. Tonight, finally, was going to be his night. The dogs broke from the traps. The crowd roared. Danny was aware of nothing but his dog, number six, as it pelted round the bend on the outside and inched up towards the leaders. He leaned forward, willing the animal on, and saw it flash past the field and hurtle first over the line. A grin as wide as a Hallowe'en lantern split his face. There was one more race to go. If he staked the lot he could make £600. They could furnish the nursery, buy a pram, the lot. Someone was putting round the word that number nine was pure dynamite. It could be dodgy, but the form wasn't too bad.

Danny closed his eyes and tried to conjure up some sort of psychic feeling for the dog's chances, focusing all his energy on the number. It had good vibes. His hands were shaking so much he could barely fill out the betting slip. He pushed his way down to the track and stood by the railings. The greyhounds were led in. The floodlit stadium fell silent. The hare shot away, the traps burst open and the dogs flew out in an indistinguishable blur of legs and bodies. Danny couldn't make out the numbers as they passed, couldn't hear himself screaming above the screaming crowd. They were all bunched up, it was impossible to tell which one was winning. He was beside himself, sinews straining, urging his dog forward with every fibre of his being. Two dogs broke into the lead and crossed the line together. Neither of them was his. The crumpled betting slip dropped from his fingers. He had put on all he had to win.

He got home late, expecting grief from Emma, knowing he deserved it but dreading her disapprobation all the same. How could he possibly tell her they had barely enough money left to eat, let alone pay the rent, the bills or buy anything for the baby? He unlocked the door. There were no lights on. She must be in bed, he thought, praying she was asleep. He crept down the hall and pushed the bedroom door. It swung open with a creak. Their bed was empty. Was she sitting up in the dark, waiting to ambush him with the wallpaper scraper? He peered cautiously into the living room. 'Emma?' No sound. Danny switched on the light. The room was bare, save for the tray of congealed takeaway and mugs of scummy coffee that were there earlier. 'Emma?' he called louder, really worried. Had she noticed the cash was gone from her purse and left him? Then he saw the writing on the wall. Daubed in paint in large red letters it said, 'Baby's coming!'

The hospital corridors had an air of unreality about them at 2.00 a.m., as if he had fallen through into an alternative universe where night-time didn't exist. Danny, following signs for the delivery suite, heard his trainers squeaking on the shiny red linoleum as he hurried along wondering whether she'd had it yet, whether she was all right. A porter pushing a young woman in a wheelchair cuddling a tiny baby passed him. There's one, he thought. I wonder what ours looks like? Then the penny dropped. He swung round. 'Emma?'

'Danny?' He ran back and there was his wife holding their child. The baby had a thatch of dark hair and a reddish complexion and was sleeping with its eyes screwed tight shut, its little mouth open like a fledgling's beak. 'Isn't she lovely?' Emma whispered, rocking the baby gently. He stroked the soft chubby cheek with the back of a finger and looked up into Emma's radiant face. 'Yeah,' he replied, suddenly choked. Kneeling on the floor he embraced them both, burying his head on her breast and breathing in the scent of the newborn skin. His love for them both, and his responsibility for them, overwhelmed him.

SEVEN

Danny had to get hold of some money. Fast. Fortunately Emma and the baby – they had decided to call her Samantha – were staying in hospital for a few days, buying him a little time. Emma hadn't asked why he'd disappeared for as long as he had and she didn't seem to hold it against him, but then she had been too wrapped up with the baby. She was as high as a kite when he left, sitting up in bed drinking tea and devouring toast with Samantha in a hospital cot beside her. The thought of taking the baby home to their dismal flat had obviously not yet occurred to her. Danny, on the other hand, surrounded by its peeling walls and bare floorboards, could think of nothing else. Drastic measures were called for.

He remembered a scam Nick, an unemployed mate of his, had once boasted about when they were out drinking. Nick had been caught not long after for doing over a video shop, so it was safe to assume he hadn't been pulling this particular ingenious stunt for a while. It involved a deal of brass neck and brashness to pull off successfully, both of which Danny possessed, besides espousing a Robin Hood-type philosophy that he approved of. It was also, now he came to think of it, a good gag. He set off into town, heading for the plush hotel by the station. The Apollo was the best for fat cats: they had big, boozy expense-account lunches there and then staggered half-cut on to the train.

Danny walked in purposefully, striding across acres of burgundy carpet and jogged up some stairs as if he knew exactly where he was going. Spotting a corridor marked 'Staff Only' he went along it, whistling a jaunty tune, and stopped at the first set of doors he came to. They opened to reveal a vast airing cupboard stacked with towels and linen. It wasn't what he was looking for. The next cupboard was full of soaps and sachets and loo rolls. Not quite what he wanted, either. The coast was still clear but he was beginning to lose his nerve. Third time lucky, he told himself, going on to another set of doors. Bingo! It was a porter's cupboard. He shrugged on a liveried jacket, picked up a polishing kit and tucked a small pair of steps under his arm. Stage one completed.

Still whistling, he retraced his steps, doubling back past reception and through a palatial ballroom with marble pillars and glittering chandeliers. A flunky was putting out gilt-backed chairs ready for an evening bash. 'OK, la?' he said in broad Scouse. Danny gave him the thumbs up and went through more doors and into the gents toilets. Once inside, he propped the steps up against the wall and, hearing the outer door click, set to polishing the mirror above the basins. A fat, well-dressed businessman entered, nodded to him and disappeared into a cubicle. Silently, Danny stole across the floor and placed the stepladder sideways on to the door, tying it to the handle with string. He climbed up and peered over the top at the fat man, who was sitting in bare-kneed splendour enjoying a satisfying bowel movement. 'Nice and comfy are we, sir?' he asked smiling, before snatching the man's jacket from the hook on the back of the door and disappearing again. ''Ey!' the man bellowed, tugging at the door. Danny knew it wouldn't be long before someone released him. He slipped off the porter's coat, donned the expensive jacket and sauntered out, feeling for the wallet. Gotcha! He extracted a thick wad of notes and deposited the rest in the middle of a luxuriant floral arrangement. A doorman touched his hat as he bowled confidently out of the building. Stage two completed.

He went straight to Mothercare. Inside the shop he

simply asked, 'What do I need for a new baby? The essentials, I mean?' and stood there helplessly as the assistant reeled off a long, long list. Having ordered a cot, he came out again half an hour later, pushing a pram loaded with baby clothes, feeding bottles, nappies, rattles and toiletries. The jacket he off-loaded on to an alky who was begging on a street corner. 'Armani, I hope,' the old boy said, cheerfully, raising a can of Tennants Extra to him. Danny winked and wheeled his booty home. Stage three was about to start.

Emma and Samantha came out of hospital four days later. The post-birth elation had worn off and Emma was feeling vulnerable and confused. Although the nurses had been kind and patient and had taught her how to feed, change and bath the baby, she was terrified at the thought of how little she knew. And not just about tiny Samantha. There was a lot, she had begun to realize, that she didn't know about Danny. Where had he gone off to that afternoon? Why hadn't he appeared until it was all over? He'd only been to see her twice since, claiming he was busy. He didn't say with what. Somewhere at the back of her head an alarm bell was ringing. She slapped it off. Everything would be fine.

'Look, there's Daddy.' Emma bounced the baby in her arms and pointed. Danny had arranged to meet her by the hospital gates and she could see him crossing the road ahead. At least, she thought it was him. This man was pushing a pram. He came up to her, grinning broadly. It was Danny. It was a pram. A brand new Italian model with matching accessories. Emma found she could not smile back. 'Where d'you get it?' she asked anxiously. Her reaction took the wind out of his sails. He did not meet her eyes. 'Bit of luck on the horses,' he muttered. The alarm bell sounded in her head again. This time it went off louder.

The lift wasn't working. Emma carried Samantha while Danny heaved the expensive pram up the dingy, stinking staircase, banging and crashing the wheels unnecessarily hard against the concrete steps as he hauled it up each flight. It was a laborious process. 'What's wrong?' Emma inquired, trying not to burst into tears herself. There were pools of urine in the corners and she'd seen more than one syringe on the floor, along with what she hoped were dog turds. Everywhere, graffiti spelt out dire and very specific threats. 'I didn't want it to be like this for you,' he said angrily. They carried on up without speaking.

Outside their flat he fumblingly took the baby from her. 'Close your eyes,' he instructed, unlocking the door. 'OK, go in. Keep walking straight ahead. That's it. Now stop. You're not lookin', are you? Turn to your right. Stop. All right, you can open them.' Emma thought she must be seeing things. The baby's room had been done out like a proper nursery, painted in soft pastels with a pretty border running round it, cheerful curtains at the window and a big fluffy rug on the floor. There was a rocking chair in the corner for her to sit in and feed the baby and a chest of drawers with a changing mat on it. Best of all, there was a beautiful cot, all made up, with toys and a mobile hanging over it. 'It's lovely,' she whispered, her face glistening with tears. She was unsure what, exactly, she was crying about.

'Samantha Ann Kavanagh, I baptize you in the name of the Father and of the Son and of the Holy Spirit. Amen,' intoned Father Matthew, pouring water over the baby's head. She let out a surprised squawk at the shock of the sudden drenching, which turned rapidly into a full-bodied scream, echoing round and round the rafters of Hawksmere's church. Bernie, little Annie, Peter and Granddad – Pete was conspicuous by his absence; 'She's married a scumbag,' he said, refusing to come – watched as Father Matthew introduced Samantha informally to the congregation, walking her up and down and calming her crying. Mr and Mrs Kavanagh were also there, having come up on the coach with Danny and Emma, while Albie, Joey and Tharmy were standing stiffly by the font. Albie clutched a long, fat candle, unsure of what to do with it. Afterwards there were photographs and congratulations, people crowding round to see the baby and exclaim over how bonny she was. As a rematch, thought Bernie, remembering the plethora of black eyes, it went some way towards compensating for their first outing. She looked at her daughter's blissful face as Emma bent and kissed the baby. Father Matthew caught her eye and smiled.

The christening party adjourned to the local pub, which was soon packed out with guests. Bernie and Peter had put £100, which they could ill afford, behind the bar and the volume levels were increasing with every round. Emma, bottle-feeding Samantha on a bench by the open door where it was less smoky, cocked one ear, amused, as she overheard Father Matthew being put on the spot by Albie. 'Are you allowed to have a wank?'

'Pardon?'

'Is that against the rules as well – a sly wank?'

Father Matthew didn't appear to have a reply for that. 'He rolled his eyes to the heavens,' Joey remarked. As you would, thought Emma. I suppose you have to forgo all sexual temptations whatever form they take. It must be hell being a priest.

Danny, meanwhile, had been buttonholed by Peter, who had four whiskies inside him and was spelling out his problem with off-comers generally and Danny in particular. 'You know what the difference is, Danny? Between us and you, people from the city like you? A sense of guilt. Of shame. You can do anything – steal, take drugs, fall over pissed in the gutter. And no one's to know; the city's anonymous. Up here it's different. If you're an idle bastard, content to sign on the dole and live in a shit-heap for the rest of your life, everyone knows – and you soon mend your ways.' He glared at him. Danny held his gaze. 'I'm looking for work,' he insisted. Peter's face was disbelieving. Danny shook his head and walked away.

They had been surviving on benefits, but barely. Even with the extra allowances for the baby it wasn't enough to live on and Danny felt a nagging sense of inadequacy about not being able to provide for his small family. Emma had been understanding – she could see for herself what the job situation was like in Liverpool; few of their neighbours worked, and those that did weren't declaring it – but Peter's words had touched a raw nerve in Danny. Previously he would have laughed in the face of such moralizing; now it was too accurate. He didn't want to be responsible for Samantha and Emma living in a shit-heap, yet he was.

You didn't get work by going down the Job Centre or looking in the paper. Vacancies went too quickly for that. You heard about jobs on the grapevine: if someone was recruiting, word spread around the estate as if blown in by the wind that swirled the litter on the landings. So when Danny heard that one of the big warehouses was taking on workers he hit the ground running. Literally. Along the docks road, past container lorries grinding out of depots, past steel girders and wire fences and factory gates he jogged, blowing hard. He vaulted a barrier, ran across a dispatch bay and headed for the warehouse. Then he saw the queue. The line of men stretched all the way to the corner. When he reached the corner, he realized that it went back all the way along the wall. He followed the wall and saw the queue disappearing around the next corner. The line didn't stop there, either. It ran all the way around the building, so that by the time he got to the end of the queue his back was turned to the man who was first in line. They were still joining in behind him, shuffling their feet and craning their necks to see how far it went. Danny had five hours to think up something really good.

'I've never missed a day's work in my life. I've never been late. I'm honest, trustworthy. Above all, I'm loyal. I've had the same job ever since I left school: Webbs, 6 Thirlmere Road,' he pitched the two personnel officers when his turn eventually came.

'Thank you. We'll be in touch. OK, Geraldine, love, send in the next one.' The queue inched forward. Danny still couldn't see the end of it as he left.

The following three mornings he rose early and waited in the boarded-up doorway of number 6 Thirlmere Road (Webbs, a grocers, had long since closed, but the name was still etched faintly on the wall). On the fourth day, the postman stopped, a letter in his hand, double-checking the address. 'Thanks.' Danny stretched out his hand. The postman gave him a dubious look, hesitated, then passed him the envelope and walked on. Danny ripped it open gleefully and sped home.

'Should my character be "impeccable" or just "excellent"?' he asked, as he filled out the reference form. Emma, playing with the baby, who was trying to grab a bunch of brightly coloured plastic keys she was dangling in front of her, looked up. 'You won't get away with it.'

'Impeccable,' said Danny, writing furiously.

His scheme worked. A week later he was back at the warehouse along with twenty-nine others, trying on over-alls. 'Danny Kavanagh,' called a man, who was registering the new recruits. 'That's me.' Danny went over and collected his timesheet. The man put a tick by his name. 'Excellent references, by the way.' The group was led through the huge warehouse to a loading bay, where they were all assigned duties. Danny was put in charge of moving and stacking heavy boxes of tinned pet food. Driving the forklift loader was fun but humping the cartons was hard work. By the end of the day his body ached, his shins were bruised and he was coughing from the thick dust that seemed to hang suspended in the air.

For a short – very short – time they existed in a state that was as near to domestic bliss as you could get in a high-rise block on a notorious estate, what with doors banging, dogs barking, people coming and going at all hours, their neighbours' audible rows broadcast through the walls and the occasional, unidentifiable scream that seemed not to perturb any of the other residents. Cocooned in their little flat – made bearably sunny with a few pots of paint, some posters and cheap furniture – Danny, Emma and the baby lived high above the world as if in an eyrie. Emma rarely went out; the lift was untrustworthy, the stairs were too much hassle and she was intimidated by the kids that hung around the estate looking for trouble. Instead, she gave a delighted Samantha her full attention, reading to her, playing games and watching TV, and used the times when the baby slept to pick up one of the academic textbooks she had brought back with her after the christening. Currently she was on *Social Problems and the Sociological Imagination* ('I'll wait for the film,' Danny had said when he saw it), about which she was developing some interesting new theories of her own. She had not given up on her plan to go to university, although they hadn't discussed it since the day Danny had asked her to marry him. As for the happening, cosmopolitan lifestyle she had anticipated them leading, that was also on hold, at least until Danny could earn more money and they could get somewhere better to live. Emma did not allow herself to think for one moment that this was it; that this was her adventure in the big city, avoiding crackheads on the landings and counting the number of patrol cars that appeared outside nightly. She switched on the radio and shut all that out. And then the roof fell in.

They had been lying in bed – she was squeezing a blackhead on Danny's back; he liked that, 'exquisite pain' he called it – when water started dripping on them. A few seconds later the drips became a massive gush as gallons of it broke through the ceiling and drenched them. They leapt out of bed, Emma screaming in fright – fortunately the baby was asleep next door – and Danny ran upstairs to investigate. He found the empty flat above them had been vandalized, fittings ripped off the walls, broken pipes pumping water into an overflowing bath. By the time a council workman arrived to fix it everything in their room was sodden. The carpet in the flat took a week to dry out, Samantha developed a chill and Emma became noticeably withdrawn. Danny felt more useless than ever.

Finally, it was pay day. Finally, something to make a week of humping boxes of cat meat and dog biscuits worthwhile. Finally he could take his wages home to Emma and she would smile again and maybe they would have a couple of cans of lager or a cheap bottle of wine and then she would write home to her parents and tell them that Danny had a job and was looking after them both really well. He signed for his pay packet, whacked it on the palm of his hand and then stuffed it in his pocket.

Temptation. Danny knew all about temptation. Today it wore a friendly face. As they walked away from the wages office one of his new workmates, Graham, said, 'We're going for a pint and a game of cards. Poker. Want to come?' Danny nearly caved in: it would be good to have a night out with the lads, to forget about the baby crying and his own weariness and their hopeless circumstances for once. He wrestled with his conscience and, surprisingly, it won. He was astonished to hear himself reply, 'Nah, I'm gettin' off.'

Winning. Danny knew a lot less about winning than he did about temptation, but he knew it felt bloody good. He was on a high as he strolled down the docks road, having beaten himself at his own game. But the thing about winning, as any footballer will confirm, is that it can make you careless. While you're still celebrating scoring, the opposition is slipping one into the net the other end of the pitch. Which was why, when Danny passed a small, shabby-looking, independent bookie's – one of those popular with poorer punters because it gave quarter odds as well as paying up on disqualification – he wasn't on his guard. The thrilling sound of a race commentary spoke to him through the half-open door and while his conscience rallied half-heartedly, it was a feeble effort this time. He was less astonished than before when his feet walked into the shop.

Emma was putting the baby down when he got home later. Danny stood and watched as she drew the covers over Samantha's small sleeping form and kissed her gently on the forehead. She turned and saw Danny, put her finger to her lips, and crept out on tiptoe, leaving the door ajar. 'Your wages,' he said, handing her the small brown envelope as she passed him. She went into the living room but he stayed where he was. He did not want to see her face. The guilt that he felt about failing her – again – lay like a stone in his stomach. Eventually, he could stand it no longer and followed her in. Emma was standing under the bare light bulb, gazing at the cash in her hand. 'There's only fifty,' she said dully.

He swallowed. 'I lost the rest.'

She shot him a look. 'Horses?'

'Yeah.'

There was a long, painful silence, during which she simply stared at him as if she had never seen him before in her life. Emma, who, unlike everyone else, had never criticized him, who had always stuck up for him no matter what, finally cracked. 'You've worked hard all week for that money.'

'I know,' he said defensively.

'And we depend on it. Me and . . .'

'I know.'

She continued to give him that look, that strange, new look. Then she squared her shoulders and said, 'Promise me you won't do it again.'

He exhaled in relief, realizing he'd been holding his breath. 'I promise. I'll get paid through the bank. It won't happen again.'

EIGHT

Bernie Quinlan's walks with Father Matthew had become more regular. He was a good listener and she was beginning to find that she could talk to him more freely than she could to anyone else, including her own husband. She was also – though she wouldn't admit it, even to herself – flattered that he made the time to see her. There was a bond between them which, as far as she could tell, he didn't have with other parishioners. Bernie felt she was special. She liked having him to herself. Was it wrong to feel that way? Was she guilty of covetousness, pride? Shameful thoughts, even? It was true that, out in the open air, as they were today, walking round the lake, she saw him more as a friend than a priest, more as a man than a moral authority, but that wasn't wicked. Was it?

She returned her thoughts to Emma. Bernie was convinced her daughter was in trouble. 'She phoned last night, asked for money, said she'd lost her purse,' she confided.

'Poor girl,' he said sympathetically.

'I didn't believe her. She talked too much, went into all kinds of details.' They were standing looking out across the lake. Hawksmere looked small and insignificant from their vantage point, thought Bernie, feeling suddenly disconnected from her troubled life there. Peter seemed to take her for granted – when he could be bothered to speak to her, that was; often he was taciturn or withdrawn – while their son, Pete, was alternately sullen and aggressive. Granddad was driving her mad with his ingrained habits, while little Annie – well, Bernie was getting too old to go running around after a demanding youngster. But, of course, they all expected her to be there for them, to have dinner on the table and organize their lives. She was the linchpin: remove Bernie and the whole lot would collapse around their ungrateful ears. Sometimes she was tempted to walk out and leave them to it, to go off and do something madly exciting and irresponsible, just once, just for her. But . . .

'Why would she lie?' asked Matthew, studying her profile as she stared out across the water, deep in her own thoughts. He wanted to reach out to her, to connect with this extraordinary woman. It was not a purely altruistic emotion: he realized, with a jolt, that he wanted to touch her physically. He struggled against an overwhelming urge to stroke her thick, dark hair.

'I don't know,' said Bernie, still looking at the village in the distance. Matthew's hand was stretching forward. 'I'm worried about –' She turned round and broke off, seeing him so close, his hand hovering an inch from her head. He didn't move, simply stood stock still, his eyes on her face boring into her with such intensity that she too was frozen to the spot, as if caught in their beam. Neither of them spoke. The faintest of breezes stirred the leaves on the trees behind them, blowing a few strands of Bernie's hair across her cheek. As if in slow motion Matthew extended his fingers and caught the silken strands between them, combing them gently back off her face. He leant forward and brushed her lips with his and felt hers respond, opening to receive him. They kissed like awkward teenagers, bodies held stiffly apart, mouths searching to fit, and his inexperience and clumsy passion ignited a spark in her that took her back nearly thirty years to the thrill of her first, fumbling kiss. Bernie hadn't thought she would ever feel like this, so alive, so utterly *now*, but even as her nerve endings screamed for him to touch her, her mind interceded and screamed just as loudly that this was a sin, a terrible sin, and that she would be punished for it. They broke apart, both of them shaking. Even if she had been able to talk, Bernie would not have known what to say. She turned and walked away, fast, back the way they had come.

When she got home she was still so flustered that she had difficulty getting her key in the lock. Bernie entered to find the house full of noise: the smoke alarm was blasting out, the TV was on loud – Granddad must be watching it – and the sound of raised voices was coming from the living room. She went in to find her husband and son rowing.

'You wouldn't get out of bed for three-fifty an hour,' Pete was saying, belligerently.

'I would if I didn't have a job.' Peter looked riled, his hair was roughed up and his complexion had gone a familiar ruddy colour.

'I get jobs.'

'On the side.'

They didn't seem to have noticed that Bernie had come in. Or that the house was apparently on fire. 'The smoke alarm's going,' she said.

Peter turned to her. 'There's a job going at the boat-landing.'

'Why is the smoke alarm going?' she insisted.

''Cause *he*'s just made toast,' chipped in Annie, pointing accusingly at her brother.

'I'm not working on the bloody boat-landing,' stormed Pete.

Bernie found a newspaper. 'Wave that under it,' she said to Annie. Annie played dumb; she was enjoying the entertainment. 'Go on! Wave it under the smoke alarm.' Bernie swatted her with the paper and pushed her out of the room.

'I'm in the building trade. Right? I'm not in the tourist trade. I'm not bowing and suck-holing to a bunch of bloody tourists for three-fifty an hour.'

Bernie's mind was still reeling as she went out to the kitchen. She heard Peter reply, 'Beggars can't be choosers,' and closed her eyes, leaned back against the sink and tried to let it all wash over her, remembering Matthew's expression as he bent his face to hers. Peter ranted on. 'You're too proud to do this, too proud to do that, but you've got no problem living here under our bloody roof, eating our bloody food.' He was a priest, thought Bernie. She would be damned. She would go to hell and tongues of flame would scorch her body just as they had only two hours ago.

For some reason – it was perverse to go there, she knew – Emma chose to use the cashpoint in the university quarter. She wheeled the pram across the precinct, catching sight, as she did so, of a young couple sitting on a bench, necking away oblivious to all around them, a pile of books and folders at their feet. The man whispered something in the girl's ear and she giggled and Emma felt a sudden pang for something she had lost. It was more than one thing, she thought, jiggling the pram to keep Samantha happy as she inserted her cash card and tapped in her PIN. They didn't get time to laze around together in the sun like they did back up in the Lakes. Things were different since the baby had come along and Danny had started working. Emma and Danny were perpetually exhausted and they didn't seem to have a laugh like they used to. Two more girls, also students, judging by their eccentric dress – long fringed skirts, Doc Martens and men's jackets from the Oxfam shop – passed by, talking about some gig they were going to that night, and Emma remembered the teenage mothers with the buggies outside her school playground looking in at the rest of them and pretending they'd got something better. Now she knew how left out they really felt. The machine beeped sharply and she switched her attention to peer at the message flashing on the little screen: 'We are unable to authorize this transaction'. She blinked, staring at it hard. They had only opened the account five days ago; she knew there was money in it. Unless . . . The baby started to cry. Emma set her jaw.

'And they're off.' Danny's monochrome world had come alive on the green green grass of Haydock, where the going was officially good to firm, the skies were blue and the stands were a sea of colour. The riotous shades of the jockeys' silks and the glossy coats of the horses as they flashed past worked on him like a shot in the arm. He stood rooted in front of the bank of TV screens, feeling the adrenalin flow through his veins as the commentary gathered pace until he was there; he was riding his horse for the jockey, he was lifting its feet up over the fences, he was the great heart pumping its blood. He showed it the whip and the horse edged past the leader and he was the harsh air in its flared red nostrils as they approached the last. Danny jumped it for him, a huge leap, too huge – the horse pecked and fell on landing before Danny could rescue his flying hooves and the rest of the field swept past them. The horse did not get up. Danny was powerless to help. He was too winded.

Once again, he lost everything in a frenzy of betting, betting to dig himself out of the hole that he was digging himself into, deeper and deeper. When he got to the bottom and there was nothing left and he knew he could not go home with empty pockets, he made a decision. He would try the hotel scam one more time.

Knowing where the porters' cupboard was made it easier. He put on the gear, took a bucket and ladder and went into the gents. The trick worked as sweetly as it did before and he left another irate businessman bellowing in the toilet, minus one expensive jacket. He crossed the lobby, relieved, and went to push open the heavy swing doors when a man materialized in front of him from behind a potted palm, grabbed him and said harshly, 'You're goin' nowhere.'

Danny struggled violently, kicking and flailing. 'Get off me.' The man held fast so Danny headbutted him instead, giving him a bleeding nose, but two more men had appeared and they slammed him on to the floor, splitting his gum and pinning his arms behind him. A warrant card was held close to his face as the first man yanked his head back by the hair and spat, 'I'm a copper, son. I'm a bloody copper.'

Down at the station they took his details and put him in a line-up. He saw someone enter the room out of the corner of his eye and knew he was doomed. It was the fat man. The guy wheezed cursorily down the line: he had spotted Danny straight away, too. He stopped in front of him and smiled broadly. Danny wouldn't give him the satisfaction. He stood up, touched the fat man on the shoulder and said, 'It's him'.

Two uniformed officers led Danny to an interview room. One of them sat down opposite him, the other stood across the room, saying nothing. 'Would you like to make a statement?' asked the first.

'I think blood sports should be banned.' Danny folded his arms.

'A comic, eh?' The copper looked amused.

'I'd like to see a lawyer, please.' It was as desperate as waiting to see if a jockey weighed in, and he'd done that before, too.

'Ken Dodd's?' The silent policeman by the door joined in with the other officer's chuckles.

Danny was charged and bailed to appear before magistrates the following week. He had no money for his bus fare home, so he used his one phone call to ring Emma. He didn't expect her sympathy, not after this, and he didn't get it. Her cat's eyes were hard, narrowed with tiny pupils, and her teeth were bared in a snarl. 'What about the rent?' she snapped, cornering him on a landing in the police station.

'I haven't paid it for yonks but that's all right 'cause they couldn't put us anywhere worse.' Her lip curled contemptuously. This strange, frightening Emma appalled him. 'Don't look at me like that.' Her expression did not change. 'You've had your share,' he said defiantly, 'Whenever –'

'You don't gamble for me, Danny. You don't –'

'– I won, I boxed you off.'

'– gamble for me or the baby. You do it for yourself.' It was as effective as a slap around the face, and as painful.

'I know,' he admitted, at last. He had always known, really, but the other voice inside his head, the insinuating, persuasive one, had always tried to kid him otherwise. He preferred to listen to that one.

Emma said, calculatingly, with her head on one side, 'Shall I borrow off my mother again?'

He realized she had no respect left for him at all. More than that, she wanted to make him suffer. 'Shall I bring you a knife? A nice, sharp knife? You can stick it in and twist it around a bit,' he retaliated, defeated.

She started walking away from him down the stairs, then turned and looked back at him through the metal banisters. 'If it was just me, Danny, I'd stay. But I'm not gonna let you take the food out of my child's mouth and give it to some bloody bookie.' She opened her purse, got out a pound coin and tossed it at him. 'There's your fare. Try to make it last you home.'

All the way back up to the Lakes, Emma could think of nothing else but how stupid she'd been. Somewhere in her heart she knew she still loved Danny, but she couldn't trust him. How could she, when he couldn't trust himself?

That was the real problem. Yes, she'd thought him reckless and irresponsible when he lost half his wage packet and, looking back, she'd been concerned when he disappeared off that time, but she had never understood that Danny's betting was out of control. It was hard, with gambling, to pinpoint when exactly it became a harmful addiction: there were no physical signs. It wasn't like living with an alcoholic who woke up sweating and shaking and needing booze for breakfast. The body didn't deteriorate like a drug addict's, the lungs didn't seize up like a smoker's. Danny looked OK and most of the time he acted OK. Unless he had money in his hand. That was the dangerous thing about it: there was nothing to warn you – until the police came knocking on your door, anyway. Not only that, it didn't seem to be taken very seriously. People used harmless terms like 'having a flutter'. The national lottery gave gambling an acceptable social gloss. There were no posters saying 'Gambling Costs Lives'.

Emma got off at the stop where she'd waited so optimistically just a few months earlier to begin her new life. The driver pulled out her folded-up pram from the luggage compartment and the bus drew away, leaving her standing there like a refugee, surrounded by bags and clutching the baby. It was colder than it was in Liverpool and she shivered, wrapping her coat around Samantha, who had woken up and was grizzling pathetically. The baby needed feeding and changing but it was almost a mile to her parents' house. There was nothing for it but to load up the pram and walk.

She kept her head high, but she could feel the curtains twitching, she could hear the gossip going on behind closed doors. 'That Quinlan girl, got herself pregnant, married a scally, always knew it wouldn't last.' As Emma neared her own street, a neighbour walking by on the opposite pavement cast a curious look at her, confirming Emma's suspicions. Unable to bear the humiliating homecoming, she veered off in the opposite direction and went to Father Matthew's instead.

'Is it pride? You can't face going home because that's admitting you made a mistake?' he asked gently, after she had seen to the baby and was once again drinking tea in his untidy bachelor kitchen.

She listened to the clock ticking on the wall. Its metronome precision was hypnotic. 'Mainly, yeah,' she said, eventually.

'There's something else?' he persevered.

'I don't want them to hate him.' Emma felt completely wretched. It wasn't just the nosy neighbours she was dreading: Pete's sneers, her father's rant, little Annie's inquisitive questions, her mother's grim-faced silence. 'Will you drive me up there?' she whispered tearfully. 'I don't want to walk up the street.'

Bernie, though, welcomed her with unexpected warmth, as if she was relieved to have her back under her wing. Other than asking, 'Is something wrong?' – to which Emma could only nod miserably – she did not inquire what it was or start issuing recriminations, but merely took the baby and went on into the house, while Emma thanked Father Matthew for the lift. Bernie entered the living room carrying Samantha and fixed Peter and Pete with a stern look. 'Not one word. No I-told-you-sos.' Emma came in red-eyed and said a subdued, 'Hiya,' but before either of them could answer, there was a commotion along the hall and Sheila Thwaite bustled into the room, gushing. 'Can I see her? Will you let me hold her? She's grown, hasn't she? Oh Emma, she's absolutely gorgeous.' Surprised, Emma found herself smiling.

Being banged up in Walton Prison had given Danny a good long time to think. It didn't stop him betting though: the inmates bet on anything and everything – what was for dinner, what tie the Guv'nor would be wearing that day, how many sparrows would squabble over a crust of bread in the yard. Little money changed hands – the main currency was cigarettes – but it added a flicker of interest to an otherwise dull existence. Danny missed Emma terribly. He fantasized constantly about how he would make it up to her when he got out and spent hours lying on his bunk reliving their carefree courtship. So when he was told that he had visitors he could hardly contain his excitement. It must be Emma with Samantha. She had forgiven him.

He shuffled forward in a line with the other cons, all of them wearing the kind of blue vests he'd last seen years ago when he'd been sneaking a look at girls' netball practice. The screw checking their names off mispronounced his – probably deliberately; they liked to get a rise out of him – but he ignored it. He just wanted to see her. In the visiting room he found Joey, Albie and Tharmy waiting for him. Danny's face fell. 'I thought you were Emma.'

'She's back in the Lakes,' said Albie, champing on gum.

'I know,' he replied quietly.

'You look like shite.' Albie never had been one for smooth talking.

'I'm not sleeping.'

'Why not? I mean, no one's gonna break in, are they?' Albie seemed much tickled by his joke, looking around to see if the others were laughing. They weren't.

'His heart went out to his old comrade,' Joey muttered.

'What's the food like?' Albie persisted.

'Shite. The chef needs locking up.'

'Tell him if it doesn't improve, you'll go somewhere else.' He grinned widely.

'D'you see her?' asked Danny, ignoring Albie's grating attempts at wit.

'Who?'

'Emma.'

'Yeah.'

Danny brooded, chewing his nails, forgetting the lads for a moment. Eventually Albie said, 'How long are you in here for?'

'Another five and a half weeks.' It felt like eternity.

The massive grey steel door slid back and Danny stepped out, a free man. After two months inside, even the carbon-monoxide-choked air tasted good to him, though the darting, blaring traffic and the crowds of scurrying pedestrians threatened to overwhelm his senses completely. It was as if he were learning to see and hear again after being rendered temporarily blind and deaf. It was almost too much. Feeling agoraphobic, Danny beat a hasty retreat to the relative safety of their high-rise flat.

It was eerily quiet without Emma and Samantha. The furniture had all gone – taken in lieu of rent, he supposed – and his footsteps sounded on the bare floor as he walked into the empty rooms. He tried to remember how they'd arranged things but it was difficult to recall his and Emma's colourful life in these drab surroundings. The baby's room was most poignant of all: he found one of Samantha's squeaky toys fallen behind a radiator and covered with dust, the only reminder – along with the wallpaper border with its animal motif, now coming unstuck from the damp walls – that his tiny daughter had been there. He closed his eyes and heard Blake's 'The Sick Rose' in his head, a recriminating commentary:

> 'O rose, thou art sick;
> The invisible worm
> That flies in the night
>
> In the howling storm:
> Has found out thy bed
> Of crimson joy;
> And his dark secret love
> Does thy life destroy.'

Danny turned and walked out of the flat and kept walking until he was on a road heading out of Liverpool that connected with the M6. He stuck out his thumb and waited.

NINE

Danny arrived at the Ullswater Hotel in the middle of the night and gave Albie the fright of his life by tapping on his bedroom window. 'Bloody 'ell, Danny, where d'you spring from?' he said blearily. 'You on the run?'

'I'm out, you daft fucker. Told you last time I'd be back. Let me in, will you?'

Albie padded through the darkened common room in a singlet and underpants and opened the door. 'Good to see you, mate.' He swung an arm round Danny, giving him a whiff of his armpits.

'Don't get fresh with me, you bugger. I'm hopin' to share your bed for a night or two – if it's not already taken?'

'I should be so lucky,' Albie replied gloomily. Danny filched a couple of cushions from the sofa and followed him back to his room, positioning himself at the other end of the bed so that Albie's feet were level with his nose. As with all the staff bedrooms, the damp walls were papered with tattered posters – Albie favoured Jimi Hendrix, though he had Ministry of Sound on the ceiling – and the air smelt fusty and masculine. Over a shared joint, Albie proceeded to recount his most recent sexual experience, which did not show much improvement on his previous attempts to stop himself coming prematurely.

'She said try this: next time you're screwing, sing that song from *The Sound of Music*. Y'know, "Do, a Deer".'

'Yeah?'

''Cause it's not easy,' said Albie, propping himself up on his elbows. 'You've got to think, what's next? Is it "me", is it "ray" or what? And it takes your mind off the fact that you're screwing and you can hold back a bit, y'know what I mean?'

'Does it work?' Danny asked, amused.

'A bit, yeah. I've got as far as "fa".'

All the hotel positions were filled – Archer had a new intake of workers, although most of the old gang had returned, too – and at first Danny was in despair. Having made it this far he needed to stay put in Hawksmere if he was to have any chance of winning Emma back, but the season was well under way and none of the other hotels had vacancies either. It was Don, the elderly groundsman, who tipped him off about a job. Danny had got up early – Albie's feet had become unbearable – and was watching the mist rise off the lake when he smelt pipe smoke and turned round to see the old man standing behind him. 'Thought it was you. I said to meself, "That's that bird-lover who was 'ere last year." Only I ent seen you this season so I weren't sure.'

'Yeah, that's me. How're you doin'?' Danny wasn't sure how he had earned himself such a title: Don must have seen him conducting the dawn chorus that time with Julie. Or maybe he just sloped around the grounds and kept an eye on people's nocturnal comings and goings.

'You stopping here then?' inquired Don closely.

'Not officially. I'm looking for work but they're full.'

Don sucked on his pipe. 'There's one going up at the boat-landing – *if* you'll do it for the money.'

Danny knew the boat-landing; it was where he and Emma had first kissed. Maybe that was a sign? 'Ta, Don. I owe you one, pal,' he said, encouraged.

He headed off after breakfast carrying his stuff, following the footpath by the lake. Half a mile along it he passed John Parr, who was out on the steamer pier, looking through a pair of binoculars at a point on the shore further round the lake. He seemed totally engrossed in what he was watching. Wading birds perhaps, or waterfowl? Funny, didn't have him down as a twitcher, Danny thought. It certainly didn't look like he was enjoying his hobby: Parr's face was suffused with a manic expression and he was muttering 'Bitch' over and over again, as if it was some kind of mantra. Later, Danny saw why: Chef and Simone were emerging from a coppice, brushing twigs off their clothes and laughing.

The boathouse wasn't like the other, rather twee little boathouses, owned mainly by businessmen with flash yachts, that were dotted around the lake like miniature Swiss cottages. This one was large and imposing and shaped rather like a Dutch barn, and was built of wood, not slate, painted in camouflage green. A narrow slatted jetty ran out into the lake and wooden rowing boats were pulled up in a line on the shingle beach. There was a grassy area outside the boathouse set with picnic tables and benches which a harassed-looking woman in jeans and an apron was clearing of drinks cans and crisp packets. She looked up as Danny approached.

'I've come about the job,' he said, putting down his case. 'Danny Kavanagh.' He held out his hand.

'Juliet Bray,' she replied briskly. She stood back and studied him, unsmiling. 'It's waiting on these tables. Pushing the boats out, bringing them back in, rowing out to get them now and again. Can you do that?'

'Yeah.'

'And keep your hand out of the till?' she continued, going into the boathouse, which had a small shop at the front selling postcards, shrimping nets and ice-creams.

'Yeah.'

'What would you do if a gang of Hell's Angels came – we get them now and again – and started causing trouble?'

'I'd shit meself,' he said truthfully.

She half smiled, caught herself doing it and put on her strict employer's face again. 'Three pounds an hour.'

'I heard three-fifty,' he protested.

'Three-fifty for locals. Three pounds to anyone else. Do you want it or not?'

'I'll take it.'

'You've brought your things, I see. There's a bed made up in there. You want to move in straight away?'

'When do I get paid from?'

'Here's a cloth. You can finish these tables.'

The smoke alarm was really getting to Bernie. Its din clamoured in her brain as she grilled bacon for breakfast, trying to shut out the unholy thoughts that kept coming back, unprompted, whenever she least wanted them to. Apart from when he dropped Emma off, she hadn't seen Father Matthew since he'd kissed her, but her mind was no clearer now than it was then. The situation was making her tense and bad-tempered; little things were taking on huge proportions. Like Granddad, sniffing the bloody milk. He was at it again, even now, and if he did it one more time she would throttle him.

'Have you used this grill?' she threw accusingly at Peter as he passed her to get to the sink.

'No,' he said, surprised at her anger.

Bernie shouted above the racket of the radio, projecting to the whole house, 'When you use this grill, wash it after you. Either that, or move that bloody smoke alarm.'

Peter didn't like being given an ultimatum. Especially when he hadn't done anything to make her go off at him in the first place. 'It stays where it is.'

Bernie rounded on him. 'It's always going off.'

'There's always bloody smoke.'

In the hall, Emma was getting ready to go out with Samantha and little Annie, who she was walking to school. 'Byee,' they shouted, putting on coats.

'Be good,' Bernie called from the kitchen.

'I will,' Annie sang out as they closed the door behind them.

They picked up Paula from the Thwaites' on the way. 'Be good,' Sheila echoed automatically, as the two little girls squabbled over who should push the pram. 'We'll all push,' Emma told them, smiling and pulling a face at Sheila, who laughed and said, 'Rather you than me,' as they made their way down the street. The playground was deserted when they got there, so Emma took the girls inside. She immediately wished she hadn't: the Parrs were engaged in a row that was audible from the corridor.

'Till half-past one in the morning,' John was shouting. 'What the hell did you find to do till half-past one in the bloody morning?'

'What are you suggesting?' Simone replied coldly.

'Just answer the bloody question. What did you find to do till –'

Emma coughed conspicuously and entered with the children. John shut up, looking embarrassed. Simone turned her back and started cleaning the blackboard. 'Yes?' he said.

'I'm sorry to bring them so early but I've got to take the baby to the clinic,' Emma faltered.

'That's O K.' He looked equally ill at ease.

'I can leave them here?'

'Yes,' he said brusquely.

'All right then. Bye, kids.'

She shot off hastily, bumping the pram across the schoolyard, then slowed as she reached the gate. Standing outside, leaning against the wall with his back to her, was a familiar figure. She halted abruptly. It couldn't be – he was still inside, wasn't he? She had tried to forget about Danny, tried not to imagine what he was going through in prison, tried not to envisage what he'd do when he got out. There was nothing she could do for him; he had to sort his problems out for himself. And there was nothing he could offer her until he did. That was what common sense told her, anyhow, and that was what she told her family, although secretly she always hoped that he still cared enough to come up and find them. Now it seemed that he had. Danny hadn't noticed her yet; he was staring down at the ground as if he was lost in thought.

'Hello, Danny,' Emma said, hesitantly. He skewed round and, seeing her there, was at a loss for words. He looked different: thinner, certainly, but there was something else – as if his confidence had been pricked and had shrivelled up like a balloon. 'What are you doing here?' she asked, when he did not reply.

'Waiting for you. You're early.'

Of course – he'd remembered her old routine. 'I'm taking her to the clinic,' she explained, tucking in the blanket round the sleeping baby.

'Why?' He looked in at Samantha, concerned, and touched her cheek tentatively.

'A check-up. It's just routine, there's nothing wrong.'

Another awkward pause. He stared at the pram, then up at Emma, meeting her eyes for the first time. 'You didn't know I was up?'

'No.'

'I'm working on the boat-landing.'

'Oh.' Emma didn't know what else to say. After all her dreams of seeing him again, now that he really was there, in the flesh, she couldn't cope. She started to go.

'It gets quiet in the evening. We could talk. Or if it's raining . . .' But Emma continued to walk away from him, her eyes blinded by tears.

At the clinic, Dr Sarah Kilbride pronounced Samantha a fine bonny lass. 'But,' she added, 'I'm worried about you, Emma. You look very pale. Are you feeling all right?'

Emma gave her a wobbly smile. 'Yes, I'm fine, doctor. Just a bit tired. She's not sleeping through yet.'

'Well, take it easy. Be kind to yourself. It's hard work raising a child alone.'

Outside, it had started to rain lightly, fine soft rain that fell straight down; typical Lake District weather. Emma put the pram's hood up and deliberated for a moment before setting off for the boat-landing. By the time she reached it the rain had become a torrential downpour. Danny was at one of the picnic tables under a large umbrella, smoking. He stubbed his cigarette out as she parked the pram and sat down. Then he smiled his old smile and said, 'I used to love rain like this, watching it hit the ground, ricochet.'

Emma didn't know why she'd come – it was something to do with what the doctor had said. At last she asked, 'Where are you living?'

'In there.' He nodded at the boathouse. She was quiet. He leant forward and put his hand on her arm. 'Come round tonight. Please.'

She wanted to. She wanted to give in and lie with him wrapped around her, holding her close, his lips nuzzling the back of her neck. But how could she tell if he'd really changed? The fact that he seemed less sure of himself wasn't any proof. The only proof she could possibly have was to see him walk past a betting shop with cash in his wallet and not go inside.

She got up again, clicked off the brake and left him staring out at the splashes of the raindrops as they pitted the lake's steely-grey surface.

All was not entirely lost then, thought Danny. The steady drumming on the umbrella seemed to beat out a new resolution in him. She was interested, but wary. He could understand why. He needed to make it up to her, big time. Back in the boathouse he made himself a cup of coffee and did a few calculations on the back of an envelope. Juliet was due to drop by with his first week's wages.

It was still chucking it down when he walked round to the Quinlans', so that he arrived looking as if he'd swum across the lake, not walked around it. Pete opened the door. He did not invite him in. 'Is Emma there?' Danny asked, as Pete glowered at him wordlessly.

'Emma,' Pete shouted back up the hall. He continued to stare Danny out.

'Is this contemptuous silence or d'you just need a bit of time? "Piss off and die," that's always a good one. Monosyllabic, three short vowels, and a long one to finish. Poetic,' Danny said, riled.

'Yeah?' Emma appeared behind Pete. Pete shoved past her and disappeared.

'I've just been paid.' Danny, his wet hair dripping into his eyes, offered her £80.

'Ta.' She took it and looked at him curiously. He held her gaze for a moment, then turned and walked back up the garden path, water squelching in his sodden trainers. At least she hadn't thrown it back in his face.

That night he lay awake, smoking and reading on his narrow bunk – a customized shelf surrounded by bits of boating equipment – listening to the thunder as it rumbled round the encircling fells and bounced off the crags like some meteorological pinball game. It was muggy and he couldn't sleep. His skin felt clammy and the rough blanket beneath him was itchy. He swung his legs over the side and got up to open the window. Better the rain come in than be suffocated to death. The air was stifling. He was just about to undo the catch when, in the stillness that followed the next clap of thunder, he heard footsteps outside. He tensed. There was definitely someone walking on the shingle outside. He felt around and picked up a length of lead piping and weighed it in his hand. It would do as a cosh. The footsteps were getting closer. Whoever it was wasn't messing about. Danny felt isolated and vulnerable in his hermitage. What if there was more than one of them? He stood to the side of the door, his muscles taut, ready to strike. His heart was hammering so loudly that it was hard to distinguish it from the rap on the door. Would an intruder bother to knock first? He reached out and flicked off the lock with one hand, nudging the door open a few inches with his foot. A vivid flash of lightning splintered the sky, illuminating the dark trees in silhouette, and in the weird blue light he saw Emma, soaked to the skin, as pale as a ghost. Danny opened the door wide and she stumbled in and they fell into each other's arms, clinging together as the next crash of thunder exploded overhead. They kissed, his lips devouring her feverishly as if he could never, never get enough, but she broke free suddenly. 'Here. Take it back,' she said shakily, pulling the cash he had given her earlier out of her jeans pocket.

'No.' Danny was stunned. 'Why?'

Emma tossed it on the table by the window. 'I don't want to depend on it. 'Cause I know I *can't* depend on it.'

'I don't gamble any more.'

She started to leave. 'Stay away from the house.' The door slammed.

Danny was left standing there, stunned. One moment he thought she'd come back to him, the next she'd gone again. How could he convince her that he'd changed? 'Wait!' he cried, running after her into the rain. Emma was trudging along the footpath beside the lake, her shoulders hunched. 'Wait! Emma, please listen to me.' She carried on walking, ignoring him. 'I know you're angry and you've a right to be,' he said, grasping her shoulder.

'Let go of me, Danny Kavanagh. I don't want you to have any kind of hold on me ever again.' She shook his hand off, brushing away the rain – or was it tears? – from her face. He fell in beside her. 'You've got every right to hate me. I don't blame you. I blame meself for everythin'.

But I've learned my lesson the hard way. I don't gamble any more.'

Emma stopped abruptly. 'How do I know that? You've said that before. You promised me you wouldn't do it again. "I'll get paid through the bank. It won't happen again." Then you empty our account, blow it all gambling and get yourself arrested. The bailiffs come. And Samantha and I have to flee with our tails between our legs. Do you know how that feels?' She glared at him furiously.

'I'm sorry. I'm really, truly sorry,' he said, trying to stop her walking off. 'Just give us one more chance, Emma. I promise I won't gamble. I'd do anything to prove it to you.' He dropped on his knees in the mud and clutched hold of her hands. 'Please?'

There was another rumble of thunder. She looked down at him and said, 'Get up, Danny. I don't want dramatics. I don't want your money. The only thing that will convince me you've altered is time. Actions speak louder than words.'

Father Matthew didn't expect any comers that evening with a storm so intense: he had been sitting in the confessional and praying – well, trying to; his thoughts kept wandering – so when he heard the church door creak and a blast of rain blow in, he assumed the latch had come undone. He had been preoccupied with the nature of his vocation. In truth, and only the bishop and a few other priests knew this, Father Matthew's posting to Hawksmere was not accidental. It had been decided that he should be removed from his urban diocese, where it was felt that he was becoming a little too actively involved in the community. He was a friend to single mothers, druggies, prostitutes and down-and-outs and had been known to put them up *on Church property*. As the bishop acidly remarked, having a priest's house as a haven for hookers trying to come off crack was one thing; getting himself arrested on anti-government demonstrations was another. Both had generated headlines in the local press and on television. The Church did not need that kind of publicity. He was to go somewhere quiet for a while and keep his head down.

In other words, thought Matthew, shivering in the draught, three strikes and you're out. And if he wasn't careful, he was going for the hat-trick with Bernie Quinlan. Unlike other priests of his acquaintance – he knew a lot of hypocrites – sex was one thing he hadn't, so far, been tempted by. He'd been attracted to women, certainly, but it was something his principles had always provided him with a defence against. The passion that he espoused in his causes stemmed, above all, from his passion for the Roman Catholic faith. Or so he had always believed.

He was just about to leave the ancient wooden confessional to close the door when the wind sucked it shut again with a resounding crash. Footsteps rang out on the stone-flagged floor, echoing in the empty church. Someone entered the adjacent cubicle and sat down. Bernie looked at him through the grille.

'Bless me Father, for I have sinned. It's been almost two weeks since my last confession.'

Father Matthew held his breath. He had been waiting for this moment since that day by the lake; waiting for it and wanting it and dreading it. How could he absolve her for a sin that *he* was guilty of? A sin he still thought about, a sin his flesh still wanted to commit? He had longed to see her again, to talk to her – she had virtually ignored him that time he took Emma round, and he hadn't seen her in church since – if only to beg her forgiveness. He tried to compose himself.

But Bernie wanted to talk about something else: Danny's reappearance in the village and the way it was affecting

Emma. Matthew couldn't take it in at first, he was so sure she had come about what had happened between them. He heard himself saying, reassuringly, 'He had the chance to stay in Liverpool, footloose and fancy-free. He didn't take it. He followed his wife and child back to here. That proves something.'

'I know,' she replied quietly.

'Rest of the family OK?'

'Yes.'

'You?'

'No.'

'Oh?'

She paused and sighed. 'I've been married a long time, Matthew. Not a lot of passion there any more. Sex once a week. His day off. But only when he's finished the racing page.'

What was she really saying? He fumbled for the subtext but was unsure whether this was an opening or not. 'There's more to marriage than sex,' he answered finally, kicking himself for falling back on the standard priest's response.

Bernie was silent for a long time. Then she said: 'There's another man. There *could* be another man. I'm *tempted* by another man.'

So. He decided to play it her way. 'Do I know him?'

'He's my priest,' she whispered.

The conjunction of images – potential lover, priest – momentarily stunned him. At last he managed to say, 'And him. Is he tempted?'

'I think so.'

Matthew shut his eyes and prayed silently. 'You've got to avoid seeing him. Can you do that?'

'He's the only priest for miles. Do I stop coming to Mass? Do I stop taking the sacraments?' Her voice rose slightly.

'Then you've got to make sure you're never alone with

this man. He's not worthy of you. He's beneath contempt.'
Was it him speaking, or was it God? He began the words
of absolution . . .

TEN

John Parr stood in the playground watching parents deliver their kids to school and wished Chef, who was dropping off his eight-year-old, Thomas, a painful and undignified death. It wasn't enough that he was being cuckolded by the man. As his son's teacher, he was supposed to maintain a veneer of professionalism and politeness towards him while he did it. Chef, who knew – and didn't care – that Parr suspected something was going on between him and Simone, merely returned the look with a belligerent stare he normally reserved for out-psyching kitchen porters and the occasional whinging diner.

The morning's lessons included some elementary physics demonstrations. Parr quite liked doing these, they brought out a touch of the entertainer in him; not just because of the surprise element – although he got a kick out of the dramatic build-up, too – but because it gave him the opportunity to explain how life's mysteries worked, and that they weren't really mysteries at all. In the end, everything had an explanation, often a simple one, and it gave him pleasure to demystify things, to show that the universe was rational. The class gathered round as he stood, holding a jar of water and a card, with little Paula Thwaite, his guinea-pig, standing apprehensively in front of him. 'You think it's going to spill out if I turn it upside down?' he said.

'Yes, sir,' she replied waveringly.

'Right, I'm going to do it right over your head and drown you,' he proclaimed, upending the jar with a flourish.

'Sir!' Paula ducked and covered her head with her arms. The card stuck to the mouth of the jar and she was saved a drenching. The class gasped, then broke out into an excited babble. 'Right, hands up if – ' he hesitated, spotting Simone out of the corner of his eye as she got into her car. 'Hands up if you can explain it.' Simone reversed out of the drive. The children clamoured for his attention, jumping up and down. 'Sir, sir.'

'No shouting out,' he bellowed sternly. He watched as the car disappeared off up the road in the direction of the village. Something in him snapped. This time he would catch them at it; he would prove what the dirty little bitch was up to with that, that – monster. That disgusting, offensive, cocksure brute. He'd probably confirmed today's assignation with her this morning when he came up with Thomas. That was why he'd given him that baleful look. He thought John was chicken. If he didn't stop it, right now, they'd be at it in his bed before long. They'd make him watch. Chef would say, 'This is what your wife needs, look,' and screw her right there in front of him. And Simone – Simone would – she would enjoy it. She was practically flaunting it at him now. Parr walked to the door and turned to face the increasingly unruly class. 'Nobody's to leave this classroom until I get back. Understood?' Silence. '*Understood?*'

There were a few quiet 'Yes, sirs'.

'Tessa, you're in charge,' he said to a plump girl with plaits. 'If anyone misbehaves, I want their names, OK?'

'Sir,' she said dubiously.

Lucy Archer was playing with Tharmy like a cat toying idly with a mouse it couldn't be bothered to kill.

'Look, just leave me alone,' Tharmy pleaded, his adam's apple going up and down frantically in his thin neck.

'I just want to know where you're from,' she said with a killer smile.

'You don't.'

'I do.' She had him cornered in the deserted kitchen.

Tharmy tried to say 'Birmingham' but got stuck on the 'B'. Lucy moved in close, swaying her nubile body in front of him, taunting him with it. 'B-B-B-B-B-B.' He was confused, aroused, helpless. Putty in her hands. She put her face even closer, running her tongue around her lips, staring, fascinated at his contortions. 'B-B-B-B-B-B.' He thought he would explode with frustration. The proximity of her breasts made it even worse. The word would never come. 'Leave me alone,' he said miserably, pushing past her. He heard her laugh ringing and ringing off the white-tiled walls as he stormed out.

Tharmy took refuge in the staff quarters. From up the corridor he heard Albie's voice, singing gruffly, ' "Do, a deer, a female deer. Ray, a drop of golden sun. Me, a name I call my" . . . oh, *shit*.' At least I can keep it up, Tharmy consoled himself. Sex wasn't a problem for him; it was the prelims that he had difficulty with. He went to open his bedroom door and found it locked. Puzzled, he rattled the handle. It was yanked from his grasp by Chef, who stood framed in the doorway wearing nothing but a gold chain round his neck and a leer. 'Take a walk for half an hour,' he ordered.

'But I live here,' Tharmy protested.

'Half an hour,' barked Chef, slamming the door.

Tharmy wandered off disconsolately, deciding to find Joey for a game of pool. As he crossed the yard, he caught sight of a figure outside the staff quarters, peering into windows in a state of obvious agitation. It was John Parr. He stopped outside Tharmy's and stared for a very long time before turning round and picking up a hefty rock from a nearby wall. Tharmy's jaw dropped as John brought his arm back to throw.

John made himself watch. It was like a scene in a movie, one of those awful, visceral close-ups of raw red flesh that you couldn't bear to look at, yet you couldn't tear your eyes away from. He saw his wife, naked except for a pair of silky French knickers, lying on her belly, crying and clawing at the blankets on the bed as Chef, standing behind, thrust into her with deep, deliberate strokes. One of her slender white thighs was gripped in one of Chef's hands and with the other he was forcing her head back by the hair so that her delicate body was bowed. Parr thought her spine would snap in two. Her face was contorted in an expression he'd never seen before. Agony? Ecstasy? Both. What wild shore was she on? One that he'd never taken her to, that much was clear. One that he knew he *couldn't* take her to, however hard he tried. He didn't know this woman. It wasn't his Simone. She never would be his again. She wasn't the gentle, mild, middle-class intellectual he had married, the one that went with him to art-house movies and smart dinner parties. She was a feral creature who would risk everything for bestial sex with a grunting thug. He felt his guts dissolve in a meltdown of jealousy and rage and looked around blindly for a missile. His fingers scrabbled hold of a rock and he hurled it with all his strength. Glass shattered everywhere. He heard Simone scream. It gave him a stab of pleasure.

Chef paced out of the staff quarters rolling his eyes. His barrel chest was heaving and the veins in his thick neck stood out like ropes. His almost-naked body – he had pulled on a pair of boxer shorts – reeked of sweat, which matted his hairy pelt and glistened on his bulging forearms. He thrust his face into John's and said, through gritted teeth, 'Smashing.' John tried to hold his stare but was cowed by Chef's formidable physicality. With his neat hair, his sports jacket, his collar and tie, he felt hopelessly weedy and inadequate. He looked away and saw Tharmy watching, mouth open, from across the yard.

Simone came out, half-dressed and barefoot, carrying

the rest of her clothes. She walked up to John and said, 'I'm sorry.' He smacked her across the mouth. Simone stood still for a second or two, her hand to her face, then turned and walked to the car. Chef continued to eyeball him contemptuously: his expression left John in no doubt that he considered him the lowest form of life for hitting a woman but not having the balls to go for him. John cast around for a weapon, spotted a spade against the wall, and grabbed it with both hands, holding the steel blade out in front of him.

'This could seriously damage your health,' Chef spat, as John advanced, brandishing the implement. Even though he wanted to bludgeon his brains out, John knew he was right. He couldn't win this fight. He couldn't even compete. The spade clattered from his hands as he dropped it and walked off to the car. Whatever dignity he might have hoped to retain was utterly crushed: Simone, as always, was in the driver's seat.

Neither of them spoke on the way back to the school. Simone disappeared into his office and when he came in to collect the register he found her examining her mouth in a mirror. Her reflected eyes met his, as if she couldn't bring herself to look at him directly. 'I'm sorry you found out like that.'

'Stop looking in the mirror.' He could feel his anger beginning to build again.

'You chipped a tooth. Caught it with your wedding ring.' The irony of it pleased him. His face wore a sick grin as he went back out to the class.

The children were running wild, dodging round the desks, screaming, shouting, throwing things, drawing rude pictures on the board. John yelled at them to sit down and, once they were back in their seats, began to call the register.

'Abbot.'

'Yes, sir.'

'Bates.'

'Yes, sir.'

'Burns.'

'Yes, sir.'

'Charles.'

Silence. He looked up. 'Susan Charles?' Her chair was empty. 'Where's Susan?' he demanded. Some of them fidgeted. None of them answered. 'Come on, she was in this morning. Where is she now?'

'She went out at break, sir,' Pauline Burns piped up.

He sighed heavily and banged the register on the desk in front of him. 'What did I tell you? What did I tell you all?'

'Not to go out, sir,' she whispered tearfully.

'Ex-actly. Well, she's in trouble. OK? Susan Charles is in serious trouble.'

Simone entered the room and started putting out art materials on a table. He stared at her treacherous back, seeing again her naked body pulled whiplash tight as Chef drove into her. He closed his eyes for a second. A murmur went through the class. John struggled to pull himself together. He refocused on the register.

'Cormack.'

'Yes, sir.'

'Davis.'

'Here, sir.'

'Eccleston.'

'Sir.'

'Fraser.'

'Here, sir.'

'Graham.'

No response again. There was another empty chair. 'Where's Lisa Graham? Is she with Susan? Pauline, is Lisa with Susan?' It was then that he noticed two more vacant seats. 'And Paula Thwaite? And Annie Quinlan?' Pauline nodded reluctantly. 'Well, they're in trouble. Every one of them. *Serious* trouble.'

Danny had meant what he said to Emma about giving up gambling. At the time. He still did, although he was finding it much easier to say than to do. Being so isolated and not watching the racing on TV or reading the results in the paper was almost impossible. He hadn't actually promised not to look at a horse again, Danny reasoned. Just not to bet on one. So he tuned in out of habit and it was torture. Living miles away from the nearest betting shop helped, but going cold turkey overnight was sending him up the wall. For that reason he had decided to wean himself off the habit gradually. In the process of easing the withdrawal symptoms he had struck up a telephone relationship with a bookie in Penrith, where he kept an account.

That morning he had been up early and was enjoying a mug of tea and his first cigarette of the day when he heard, not Beethoven's Fifth, but a snatch of Italian opera floating across the lake in the grey dawn. He put down his tea and walked out to the end of the jetty, straining to see who was on the water. A faint but unmistakable 'plop' of oars punctuated the aria. As far as he knew, the lake wasn't haunted by the spirit of any jolly boatmen but it was, none the less, a surreal experience. Danny could feel his scalp pricking. Just then a boat bearing two ghostly figures, one tall, like a figurehead, slid out of the smoky blanket of mist. He held his breath. As it drew nearer, he could make out the portly corporeal form of a fat tenor – Italian, presumably – wearing, rather bizarrely, full evening dress, who was standing and belting out the song while Albie, of all people, rowed. 'Vesuvius. First race today. He owns it,' Albie panted, hauling on the oars. He flashed his wide-boy grin at Danny – 'Twenty quid an hour I'm on' – before disappearing back into the mist.

Which was what prompted Danny to dial his mate in Penrith. How often did you get a God-given tip like that, after all? It hardly counted as gambling. The scene had been too weird not to be significant, he reasoned. It was a sign. He went back and forth over it all morning and by lunchtime he had convinced himself. He went into the boathouse and picked up the phone. It rang for a long time before being answered. The shop must be busy, he thought, picturing punters filling out their betting slips, gathering round the television screens, shouting, cheering, waving their arms. Danny ached to be there, to feel the current that ran through him as if he were wired up directly to the pulse of the racing horses. He took a long drag on his cigarette to try and quell his agitation. At last someone answered the phone. 'It's Danny Kavanagh, Harry. Can I have twenty on Vesuvius? First race.' He paused. Harry put him on hold while he served another customer. He drummed his fingers impatiently. 'Yeah, I'm still here. I'll pay the tax. Twenty-one eighty, OK.' Harry started telling him about a punter he'd had to eject earlier for causing trouble and Danny rubbed a clear patch on the grimy window while he listened, peering out to check on the boats. The wooden one on the end was missing. His eyes scanned the lake and he spotted a bunch of schoolgirls in it, some distance out. 'Cheers, pal, gotta go,' he said hurriedly and slammed the phone down. He ran outside, cupped his hands and shouted, 'Back in. Right? Back in, right now. Back in, right now,' at them.

Footsteps crunched behind him on the shingle beach. He turned and saw Lucy Archer. She drew her long hair back from her face and fixed him with a wanton smile, aware of the effect her curving lips and seductive beauty spot – a small brown mole à la Marilyn Monroe – usually had on men. 'Hello, Danny.' Danny, however, was impervious to her charms. As far as he was concerned, she was a slag. Last season he had found her reclining on his bed in a tight sweater and Capri pants, smoking dope. She had practically pushed her breasts in his face. He had resisted her then and it was even easier to resist her now, even though he and Emma were estranged. There was more to sex than sex.

'You're working here now?' Lucy purred.

'Well spotted.'

'Why?'

'I didn't have what it takes to wash dishes. Drive, ambition, a lobotomy.' He turned back to the lake and squinted at the kids, cupping his hands once more. 'Don't mess about. Straight back in. Now.' The girls were about 200 feet from the shore. They dipped their oars, as if they were taking notice. He looked at Lucy again. 'What d'you want?'

'Nothing.'

'No?' He raised an eyebrow. It wasn't a boat ride she was after.

'No.'

Like hell. 'Right, go in there, get stripped off. If I'm not there in ten minutes, start without me,' he said dismissively, walking away.

Lucy pouted. 'I hardly know you.'

'Oh, piss off,' Danny flung over his shoulder, annoyed. Lucy's pride was severely hurt. She was accustomed to getting what she wanted. She had wanted Danny. A bit of Scouse rough. He had a scent of danger that really turned her on.

Just then a low-flying RAF jet rent the sky directly overhead like a crack of thunder. Danny heard screams of fright and saw the schoolgirls, two of whom had been clambering about to swap places at the oars, jump up and overbalance in the small space. They fell against one side of the old-fashioned skiff, causing it to list heavily. Scrabbling in panic to regain their footing, they weighed it over still further so that slowly, agonizingly slowly, it tipped right up and began to fill with water and sink. He saw small arms flailing, heard the girls' desperate cries as they were thrown into the lake, and was suddenly galvanized. Racing to the end of the jetty, he yanked off his trainers and dived in. Lucy, who had also been frozen to the spot, ran stumbling in her clumpy sandals to the boathouse and dialled 999. 'Ambulance,' she panted in response to the operator's query, then hesitated. 'And police.' She stood on tiptoe and squinted anxiously out of the window. Danny had disappeared.

Juliet Bray's car bumped up the stony track to the boathouse in first gear. It was a beautiful, bright, clear day and she hummed a tune to herself as she drove. Business was quiet, she observed, noticing the empty tables and chairs on the grass. And where was that slacker, Danny Kavanagh? She'd have to have words with him. Juliet parked, cut the engine and got out. A young girl – she looked familiar; it was Lucy Archer from the hotel – came running towards her. Something was wrong. Her face was awash with tears, great streaks of black mascara running down her cheeks. 'Where's Danny?' Juliet shouted, alarmed. Gulping, Lucy turned and pointed at the lake. Juliet stared. There were no sounds at all. The lake was utterly quiet, utterly still.

ELEVEN

John Parr ran his finger down the list of names and numbers and decided to ring the hotel first. Kill two birds with one stone and all that. It wasn't the first time the girls had skived off school but it was a little embarrassing to have to inform their parents they'd gone AWOL again. It made him look careless. He dialled the number and waited.

'Ullswater Hotel. Good afternoon,' Doreen Archer fluted.

'John Parr here. Can I speak to Mrs Quinlan and Mrs Thwaite, please? It's about their children.'

Doreen bustled into the kitchen, incurring a wrathful look from Chef, and beckoned to Bernie. 'Phone,' she mouthed above the din of clattering dishes and bubbling pans, signing by making her thumb and little finger into a handset. 'It's the school,' she hissed as Bernie passed her, wiping her hands on a tea towel.

Bernie picked up the phone lying on the desk at reception. 'Mrs Quinlan.'

There was the sound of someone clearing their throat. 'It's John Parr, Mrs Quinlan. Your Annie's gone missing, I'm afraid. Along with three other girls.'

'She promised me she wouldn't do it again,' Bernie sighed.

'Well, she has, I'm afraid.' He sounded formal, uptight even, she thought.

'I'll have a word with her tonight. More than a word.'

'Thanks. Is Mrs Thwaite there?'

'She's coming.' Sheila was trotting down the hall, twisting her sleek pony-tail back into its scrunchie.

'Headmaster,' Bernie whispered, her hand over the receiver.

'They've bunked off again?' Her sister nodded. 'I'll kill her,' Sheila said.

'Murder's way down the list of options.'

Sheila took the phone. 'Hello?'

Bernie hurried back to the kitchen where things were hotting up. The lunchtime rush had turned it into the usual hellish madhouse. A huge basket of chips was frying in a vat of seething oil, while under the grill a spitting tray of steaks had caught, giving off a lick of fire. Steam taps blasted by the wall, vegetables were boiling on the rings and Chef was flambéing crêpes Suzette, igniting liqueur in a copper frying pan with a whoosh of blue flames. As always, the radio was on full volume, porters were chopping, dicing and slicing, and other waitresses were swinging in and out with orders. Everyone was working flat out – apart from Albie, who was standing in a corner, singing softly and timing something with his wristwatch. ' "Do, a deer, a female deer. Ray, a drop of golden sun. Me, a name I call".' He stopped mid-phrase, peering at the second hand. Disappointment was writ large on his face.

The door banged and Sheila came back in, her arms full of dirty bowls, and shouted over to Chef, 'Table five's complaining about the soup.'

'There's nothing wrong with it,' he snarled.

'They're saying it's cold.' Bernie, who was loading up plates to go, gave her a sympathetic look.

'It's not cold. It's just not hot. Good soup's not supposed to be hot,' Chef ranted.

'I've told them that. They want it hot, said "Some like it hot".'

'They're not getting it hot.'

'Will you tell them that?'

'Charlie's the head waiter.'

'Charlie couldn't serve Mass,' she snorted. Bernie grinned at Sheila as she backed through the double doors into the dining room bearing her orders.

The calm surface of the lake was broken by a head exploding into view, gasping for air. Lucy clutched hold of Juliet Bray as they watched a swimmer strike out for the shore, apparently towing a body. Long moments passed before it became clear that the sleek seal's head was Danny's. Eventually he touched bottom and waded waist-deep through the shallows, staggering under the weight of the inert child in his arms. Juliet ran to help. They laid the girl on the bank and Danny started pumping at her thin chest, his own breath coming in strangled sobs, lake water and tears raining down on her mud-covered body. 'Let me do it. I've been trained,' Juliet said urgently, taking over.

'There's more out there,' he panted, scrabbling to his feet and heading back towards the line of boats. Lucy stood some distance away, watching in horror.

'Have you phoned the doctor?' Juliet shouted at her. Lucy was chewing the neckline of her top. She didn't answer. '*Have you phoned the doctor?*' Juliet yelled again.

'Ambulance.'

'The doctor'll be quicker. Phone her. Now.' She stopped pumping, tipped the girl's head back and began to give her mouth-to-mouth.

'What number?' Lucy was still standing there, her legs wound round each other awkwardly.

Juliet watched the bird-like chest of the little girl fall. '5683.' It did not rise again. She blew in another breath.

'What?'

Juliet reared up again and glared at her furiously. '5683.' Lucy took off back to the boathouse, repeating the number to herself over and over again.

Dr Sarah Kilbride arrived twelve minutes later in her

four-by-four, blue light flashing on top. She saw a figure kneeling by the shore and sprinted over, carrying her bag, reaching Juliet just as she drew a towel over the bedraggled body of a young girl wearing the distinctive burgundy sweatshirt and grey skirt of the village school. 'She's dead,' said Juliet, looking dazed. They regarded each other in silence.

At the school, the afternoon's lessons were under way. Grouped around John Parr in a semi-circle, the pupils were reciting Aesop's 'The Ant and the Cricket'. Most were wearing the regulation uniform, but one of them was dressed in a leotard and green tights with matching deely-boppers on her head, while another was kitted out similarly in black. Solemn-faced, they chorused:

'A silly young cricket accustomed to sing
Through the warm sunny months of gay summer and spring
Began to complain when he found that at home
His cupboard was empty and winter had come.
Not a crumb to be found on the snow-covered ground
Not a flower could he see, not a leaf on a tree.
"Oh, what will become," said the cricket, "of me?"
At last by starvation –'

Simone entered and walked over to John's side. 'Father Matthew's here. And Sergeant Slater.' The tone of her voice told him that something was wrong. They've probably caught the kids playing truant, he thought. Well, who's fault is that? He ignored Simone and continued to mark the beat, mouthing the poem at the children, who chanted obediently. Simone didn't know how to break the news. She moved round in front of John into his eyeline, demanding his attention. 'There's a boat gone down on the lake.' The children's voices faltered and stopped.

The local policeman, a WPC and the priest were waiting for John in the headmaster's office. Simone went in with him. Sergeant Eddie Slater stood up and removed his cap, revealing a receding hairline, and said, without formalities, 'We've recovered the body of Susan Charles. We need to know who else is missing.'

John felt as if he had been thumped in the solar plexus. He couldn't speak. There was no air in his body. Eventually he heard himself croak, 'Oh my God.' It did not sound like him at all. His brain had stopped functioning. They were all looking at him, waiting for him to do something.

'John. The register.' Simone nudged him, bringing him back.

He groped on the desk and picked it up. 'Susan Charles, Lisa Graham, Annie Quinlan, Paula Thwaite,' he read out.

'Four?' queried Slater, jotting down the addresses Simone handed him.

'Yes,' he replied numbly.

'We think there were only three in the boat.'

'They're all friends, all four of them.'

'Will their mothers be at home?'

'Susan Charles's, yes. Lisa Graham's works at the Lion. Mrs Quinlan and Mrs Thwaite work at the Ullswater.'

'Thanks.' Slater snapped shut his notebook, put on his cap.

John hesitated. 'There's no point in sending them home? The rest of them, I mean.'

'No,' Slater said. He paused in the doorway, looking uncomfortable. 'I'll get back to you. As soon as I can.' The three of them left. Simone walked over to John and put her arms around him. He stood, unmoving, in her embrace, then broke free abruptly. Back in the classroom the children were messing about. They quieted as he entered. He resumed his stance in front of them like a conductor and gave them their cue: 'At last by starvation and famine made bold.'

'All dripping with wet and all trembling with cold . . .'

*

The police had arrived at the boathouse, too, bringing a couple of inflatable launches and a team of frogmen. The first boat's engine roared into life, the harsh noise echoing across the lake. Danny watched it bounce through the water leaving a trail of white foam as it sped out towards the spot he had indicated. 'I'd've got there in time if I'd had one of them,' he said bitterly to Dr Kilbride, who was standing next to him. Shock was beginning to set in. The sight of Susan Charles's body – the doctor had identified her – being loaded into a parked van emblazoned on the side with 'Williams, Carpenters and Joiners Since 1894' was a detail that upset him unreasonably after all he'd just been through. His teeth were chattering uncontrollably. She studied him closely. 'Have you got any dry clothes?'

He jerked his thumb at the boathouse. 'In there.'

'Go and put them on.'

Inside, Juliet Bray was sitting on his bunk with her head in her hands. She watched as Danny peeled off his wet shirt and started to dry himself with a tea towel. At last, she said, 'Did you let them go out on their own?'

Danny couldn't believe that she could ask such a question. 'What?'

'If you let them go out without an adult, Danny, we're finished.'

He went up to her, shaking both with cold and rage. 'For God's sake, what do you take me for?'

Juliet did not reply.

The police car drew up outside the hotel, followed by Father Matthew's battered Fiat. He and Sergeant Slater exchanged glances, their faces grim, as they got out. 'I'll tell Mrs Quinlan,' Matthew said. Slater nodded.

Bernie was setting tables in the dining room, folding napkins and polishing silverware in preparation for the evening meal. She looked up at the sound of the stiff rustling of the weatherproof jackets the two police officers wore and caught sight of Father Matthew standing behind them. The colour drained from her cheeks. 'What's wrong?'

'Where's your Sheila, Bernie?' Slater asked.

'In the kitchen. What's wrong?' she cried again, alarmed by Matthew's grave expression. Slater and the WPC went through the archway leading to the other half of the dining room. Father Matthew took her arm and led her towards a table that had not yet been laid. 'Shall we sit down?'

Bernie's huge brown eyes scanned his unfathomable grey eyes. 'What's wrong?' she repeated, twisting her hands in her lap.

'There's been an accident on the lake,' he said softly in his lilting Welsh accent. She looked confused. 'A boat sank,' he explained. 'There – there were children in it.'

'Annie?' Pure horror spread across her features. Her face seemed to crack and fall apart as tremors broke across it.

'We don't know yet. But she's missing from school,' he began, unable to go on. Bernie could not contain her grief. She rocked backwards and forwards, her head in her hands, sobbing in loud, shuddering gusts. Father Matthew wanted to take her in his arms and hold her tight, so tight, but Sheila was coming towards them with the police officers. She ran over to Bernie, knelt down in front of her and tried to take her sister's clenched hands. 'What's happened?' she pleaded, looking round at the others.

'There's been an accident,' Slater said, letting the words sink in. 'Shall we sit down?'

Sheila got to her feet slowly, holding on to the edge of the table. 'Paula?' she asked, her voice quivering.

He paused. 'We think so.'

'And Annie?'

'Possibly, yes.'

She put her hand over her mouth and ran out of the room. The WPC followed her. Sheila barged into the lounge, where her husband was drying glasses behind the small bar. Several of the residents, who were resting in comfortable chairs, stopped talking abruptly. 'Oh, Arthur,' she wailed.

Peter Quinlan was sawing up a fallen tree at Birkitt's Farm, high on the fells. The deafening chainsaw bit through the bark and into the white trunk like butter, sending wood chips flying all around him. Sawdust stuck to his hair, his clothes and his ruddy, sweat-streaked face. He was wearing ear protectors and goggles and didn't notice the farmer gesticulating at him until he put the still-running chainsaw down to roll the log on to the pile. He switched off, pushed back the goggles, and jogged over. 'Telephone call for you. Your wife. She sounds upset, like,' Birkitt said, leading the way into the kitchen. Peter picked up the phone, his heart thumping.

Five minutes later he screamed out of the yard in his ancient van, jolting over pot-holes on the rough single-track road. He had his foot flat to the floor, accelerating down the hill, barely slowing for the corners. The sheep stood no chance. It was dithering in the middle of the road and Peter didn't see it until he was virtually upon it. He jammed on the brakes, the tyres screeched and there was a sickening thud that knocked the van on to the opposite verge. Fortunately, there were no other cars about. Shaken, he got out and walked round to where the bloodied pile of fleece lay, unmoving, blocking the narrow road. He caught hold of it by the legs, pulled it to one side, then thought better of it and dragged the sheep round to the back of the van. He opened the doors, stuffed the dead animal inside and continued his journey.

*

'This is God punishing me,' Bernie said, biting her lip, as Father Matthew drove fast along the switchback road beside the lake.

'Why should he punish you?' Matthew replied, looking in his mirror at the police car following with the Thwaites.

'You know why.' She looked at him accusingly.

'We've done nothing wrong,' he insisted, keeping his eyes on the kinks and bends in the road. 'We've been tempted, but that's all. We didn't succumb. You've got nothing to feel guilty about, nothing whatsoever.'

A terrifying thought dawned on Bernie. 'You think she's dead,' she said dully.

'I don't.'

'You think she's dead. You're talking as though I'm bereaved. You're easing my conscience. You think she's dead!' Her voice rose unsteadily.

Matthew's knuckles whitened as he gripped the steering wheel. He could not answer her.

Slater flicked a glance at the speedometer and sucked in his cheeks. Father Matthew was driving far too fast. He hoped they would all arrive at the boathouse in one piece. But arrive to what? He dreaded to think. He had a daughter himself; older, true – she was at a different school – but no less precious. His eyes flicked to the white-faced couple in the back. Arthur was holding Sheila's hand, staring straight ahead, saying nothing. Sheila babbled desperately, 'She's a good swimmer. Best swimmer in her class.' No one else spoke.

The two cars drew up behind a haphazardly parked collection of vehicles – the police van and trailer, the doctor's Jeep, Juliet Bray's little Toyota. Bernie leaned back against her seat and shut her eyes. The Thwaites got out and started walking tentatively down the track towards the edge of the lake. Out on the water they could see two police divers working off a rescue launch. A grey one with several officers in chequered jackets hovered close by. Sheila looked away and buried her head on Arthur's shoulder. He put an arm round her and they turned back towards the car. There was one more vehicle she hadn't noticed initially: a carpenter's van, the makeshift mobile morgue, waiting, doors open, ready to receive more bodies. Beside it, Susan Charles's mother was crying her eyes out. Sheila was unable to go on. She did not know where it was safe to look.

Bernie left the car and went inside the boathouse. She found Danny, wearing dry clothes, rubbing his hair with a tea towel. Juliet Bray was sitting motionless nearby. Danny raised his eyes to Bernie's. 'Have you told Emma?' she asked. He shook his head. Bernie went to the phone. She glanced at Juliet. 'Can I?' Juliet nodded. Bernie dialled home.

'All right, I'm coming!' Emma hurried down the stairs trailing an armful of washing and dumped it by the hall table to pick up the phone. 'Hello?' No one answered. 'Hello?' she said impatiently, preparing to slam down the receiver if it was a crank call. She heard a muffled sob, then Danny came on the line. 'It's me,' he said. His voice sounded strange. 'I'm at the boathouse. Your mam's here too. I think she needs you.'

Emma didn't know what to feel. Her mind seemed to empty as he told her what had happened. She replaced the receiver slowly and walked into the living room, where Samantha was kicking happily in her playpen. Tears welled in her eyes and she scooped up her child and cuddled her, breathing in the soft, sweet scent of her skin. The baby patted her face with a chubby hand and smiled. Emma smiled back and kissed her, then carried her upstairs to change and dress her. She had to hurry.

Robert was the only person she could think of to turn

to for help. She wheeled the pram up the path to his house and banged on his door. 'Will you mind the baby?' she said rapidly as soon as he opened it.

'What?' Robert looked bemused.

'Something's happened, Robert. Will you mind the baby?' she repeated urgently. He could see her desperation. 'What is it?'

'A boat's gone down on the lake.' Robert peered dubiously at Samantha, who was gurgling contentedly. Emma was already backing away. 'Thanks Rob. There's a bottle and some nappies under the covers.'

Peter's van bumped up the track, which was now crammed with cars. A crowd had gathered by the boat-landing; worried parents, friends and neighbours, all waiting anxiously by the shore, watching the police frogmen as they dived and surfaced and dived again into the deep, cold water. The van screeched to a halt and Peter leapt out and ran over to where Bernie and Danny were standing. She clung to him, weeping. Peter stroked her hair and said softly, 'They haven't found her?' He did not add 'yet', though it was on the tip of his tongue.

'No,' Bernie whispered. She looked up at him with bloodshot eyes. 'There were only three in the boat, four missing from school.' A ray of hope.

'Three?' Peter checked with Danny.

'I think so.'

'You think so?'

'Yeah.'

'You saw them?'

'Yeah.' He looked uncomfortable.

'Was Annie with them?'

'I don't know.'

Peter let out his breath slowly. 'You don't know?' he repeated deliberately.

'No.'

'You saw them out there on their own?'

Bernie interrupted him, sticking up for Danny. 'He did everything he could.'

Peter ignored her. 'You saw them out there on their own. A bunch of kids? You left them out there?' His tone was incredulous.

'They were heading back in,' Danny protested. 'If they hadn't been heading back in I'd've gone out to get them.'

'Heading back in?'

'Yeah,' he said, stung.

'Heading towards y'?'

'*Yeah.*'

'You didn't see them side on?'

'No.'

'So how d'you know there were only three?' Peter said loudly. People turned and stared at them.

'I don't. I *think* there were only three.'

Bernie laid a restraining hand on Peter's arm. 'He did everything he could. He went in there after them.'

'You let them go out there.' Peter wouldn't let it drop.

'For God's sake,' shouted Bernie. She walked away, shoulders shaking. Father Matthew saw her distress and moved towards her.

Danny stood his ground and said, 'They took a boat out when me back was turned,' but Peter stalked off in disgust, obviously disbelieving. He got to Bernie first and Father Matthew veered away, making it look as if he was going to talk to Sergeant Slater instead. Danny was left on his own, swaying. Emma appeared and ran across the grass to him. They hugged each other tightly, tears coursing down the other's neck.

Suddenly a diver broke the surface, his arm signalling to the crew in the grey police launch. A murmur spread through the crowd. Sergeant Slater's radio crackled into life. He listened intently. 'Any ID?' he asked.

'No, nothing,' the tinny voice on the radio replied.

Slater looked at Father Matthew and headed towards the waiting parents. He stopped in front of the Quinlans first. 'They've found a body. They're bringing it in.' Bernie trembled. Peter looked stony-faced. The police launch was chugging in towards the shore. Slater went over to the Grahams: 'They've found a body. They're bringing it in.' The woman, a redhead, paled. Her husband put his arm round her protectively. Slater moved on to the Thwaites. 'They've found a body. They're bringing it in.' Arthur, who was cradling Sheila against his chest, looked at him over her shoulder. Eddie Slater had never seen such pain in a man's eyes.

TWELVE

The policeman at the tiller cut the engine and the launch glided in soundlessly through the shallows. A hush descended over the crowd. All eyes were on Father Matthew as he walked over to it. He spoke to the officer, who pulled back a cover in the bottom of the craft. Father Matthew looked in and made the sign of the cross.

Bernie Quinlan watched as he straightened up and came back towards them. 'Let it be someone else's child,' she prayed, reciting the Hail Mary over and over again, her chanting becoming louder and more desperate as Father Matthew approached. 'Hail, Mary, full of grace, the Lord is with thee. Blessed art thou amongst women and blessed is the fruit of thy womb, Jesus. Holy Mary, Mother of God, pray for us sinners now and at the hour of our death. Amen. Hail Mary, full of grace. . . .'

Matthew did not meet Bernie's eyes. Instead, he walked past the Quinlans, his face impassive. A tremendous wave of relief swept over her as she realized her prayers had been answered. She looked up at Peter and saw the same expression reflected back, the tension momentarily leaving his rigid features. His eyes were bright with unshed tears. She leaned her forehead against his and a long, shuddering sigh escaped from him. 'Thank you, thank you, Mary. Thank you, Lord,' her soul sang. She heard a stifled sob behind her and a second wave, a huge dark wave of guilt, immediately towered above her and came crashing down. She turned.

Father Matthew was standing with her sister. Sheila had her knuckles pressed into her mouth, as if to prevent herself crying out. 'I'm sorry, Sheila. I'm sorry, Arthur,' he said. Sheila closed her eyes and moaned, 'No, no, no, no, not Paula, not our Paula, no, no, no.' Her knuckles were bleeding. Arthur tried to comfort her but she broke away and tried to push past them both, screaming in a strange, crazed voice, 'Let me see her, I've got to see her, let me see my little girl.'

Father Matthew restrained her gently. 'Let them clean her up a bit.' Sheila struggled to get free. 'Please, Sheila, let them clean her up a bit,' he begged, but she wrenched his hands away and started walking blindly towards the launch. Arthur glanced at Father Matthew, then chased after her. All Bernie could think as she watched her sister go was, 'Better hers than mine. If that's the deal, that's the deal. Thank you, God. Better hers than mine.'

The van was a premonition. Somehow Sheila had known, the moment she saw it waiting, doors open, that the next small body to be loaded into it would be Paula's. The mud-slathered corpse with the unseeing eyes and the weeds tangled in her clothes and hair did not look like her daughter. It was Paula Thwaite, but it was not her daughter, this bedraggled creature fished up from the bed of the lake. Seeing Paula quieted her and she allowed Arthur to lead her away. The crowd parted sympathetically to let them through. Police officers followed with a blanket-covered stretcher. The respectful silence was suddenly shattered by a noise like a thunderclap that seemed to rip open the heavens and vibrate the air as a jet appeared, apparently from nowhere, and flew low above the water.

Granddad Toolan and little Annie were walking the Quinlan's dog, a rangy hound called Godiva, along the road by the lake when a carpenter and joiner's van turned out from the track leading to the boathouse, followed by a police car. Annie stared in curiously and saw, in the back, her uncle and aunt. Aunty Sheila looked back at her. Her face was weird. She did not wave. 'What's going on?'

grumbled Granddad, who had noticed, too. He took Annie's hand and they crossed the road, following the footpath down to the boat-landing.

There was a crowd of people standing looking out at the lake. Annie squinted into the sun. She saw a diver jump over the side of a rubber dinghy type of boat and a similar one floating close by. Everybody had their backs to her. They were talking in low voices. She tried to find someone she knew and made out her parents. Dad had his arm around Mum's shoulders, which was unusual because they got mad at each other so much these days. Annie scampered up behind them, leaving Granddad to stumble after her with Godiva. 'What's going on?' she asked brightly. Her mother seemed to freeze. At first she did not move, then she turned round ever so slowly. 'What's going *on*?' Annie persisted, feeling as if she'd been left out of a big secret. Her dad had spun round too. They both looked at her oddly – a bit like Aunty Sheila, only her look had been different somehow – and then her mum's face sort of crumpled up and she started bawling and fell on her knees and grabbed her and kept going on about her being lost to them and other stuff Annie didn't understand. 'What's wrong?' she whined, trying to wriggle out of her mother's suffocating grip. She was holding on to her so tight that Annie thought all the breath would be squeezed out of her body. Even her dad was crying. She'd never seen *that* before. 'What's going on, Mum?' Annie started to grizzle herself, overwhelmed by their reaction. People were all gathering round them, the buzz of voices getting louder and louder. Father Matthew pushed his way through the crowd and looked shocked when he saw her. Emma ran over, her face all blotchy and puffy, and hugged her too. It was as if she'd come back from the dead or something. Like when Jesus performed a miracle.

*

Arthur Thwaite poured himself a large scotch, the neck of the bottle knocking against the side of the glass in his trembling hands. He wanted to drown himself in the drink, to numb all feelings and slip into unconsciousness so that he wouldn't have to keep on seeing Paula drowning in the lake. The sight of her shoeless, staring corpse, one plait matted and undone, the other still tied in its neat plastic hair bobble, would not go from his mind. Worst of all was the memory of her open mouth, full of leaves and gunk and mud. The very thought of her lungs filling up with water made him feel like retching. He downed half the whisky in a gulp. Dr Kilbride was watching him. And Sergeant Slater. Arthur didn't care. He tipped more scotch into the glass.

'I could prescribe you something,' the doctor said. Arthur shook his head. 'Sheila?'

Sheila was standing by the sideboard, Paula's school photo in her hands. 'To put me out?' she asked edgily.

'To ease the pain.'

'That's the last thing I want,' she snapped. She drew a deep breath. 'When can I see her?'

Slater looked at his watch. 'Another hour or two.'

'Why?' she demanded angrily.

'There's things we have to do,' he explained mildly. 'I'll give you a lift when it's time.'

'I'll drive,' Arthur said, but his eyes had a glazed look already.

'I'm giving you a lift, Arthur,' Slater said firmly.

The Quinlans were also back home, drinking tea and trying to take everything in. Bernie felt cold, chilled to the marrow, despite putting on two bars of the electric fire. A terrible inertia had taken her over; she felt she might never manage to stand up again. Annie was sitting on her lap, her thumb in her mouth, the other arm around Bernie's neck – she had been glued to her side since finding them at the boat-landing, knowing instinctively that her mother needed to keep a physical contact with her. Granddad was struggling into his coat. 'Are you ready?' he said, impatiently.

'I can't go,' Bernie replied quietly.

'She's your sister,' he shouted. 'She's lost her child, your niece.'

'I can't face her just yet,' Bernie said into Annie's hair.

He stormed over to them. 'For God's sake, get your coat on.'

Peter intervened, shouting back, 'She said she's not going.' He laid hold of Granddad's arm and pulled him away roughly. 'Take it easy, Dad.' Pete jumped up too, but his father turned round and glared at him. 'You keep out of this.' Pete shrugged and went out of the room, banging the door. Peter still had hold of Granddad's coat and yanked it hard. 'How dare you lay down the law, you stupid Irish bloody peasant. Have you any idea what you've put us through? We thought she was dead. We thought she was dead as well.'

'I'm just asking her to comfort her sister,' Granddad mumbled, his eyes bleary.

'You knew she should've been in school. You knew they should've *all* been in bloody school, so why the hell didn't you make them go *back*?'

Bernie, recovering, said, 'He's lost his grandchild, for God's sake.'

There was a pause as Pete burst back into the room, looking peculiarly animated for once, and announced, 'There's a sheep in the fridge.'

'What?' Bernie was stunned.

'I'm chopping it up for later,' Peter said briefly. He continued to tear a strip off Granddad. 'I don't think you're in any position to lay down the law to my wife. Not after what you've done. OK?'

Granddad sniffed loudly. He pulled a large cotton

handkerchief out of his pocket and wiped his eyes. He looked over to Bernie, pleadingly. 'Will you come with me, please?'

She gripped the arms of the chair, as if panicked. 'I can't.'

The lake looked tranquil in the fading early evening sun. The police launches had gone and in their place jaunty sails were tacking across the calm blue water. At this time of the day in the summer months the lake was a place of recreation: it was the hour when wealthy boat-owners drew up in their smart cars at the marina and donned cable-knit sweaters and took their slinky yachts out and afterwards drank large gin and tonics in the bar. Arthur Thwaite, looking out of the police car's window at the familiar scene, knew all about that. He had been a steward at one of the clubhouses before he got the hotel job. The boat-owners were rich bastards with loud voices and that well-groomed, well-fed look who thought they had some sort of claim over the lake with their money. Didn't they realize, he thought, that no one had any claim over it? Not even the locals. It was the lake that had a claim on them.

The car pulled up outside the hospital entrance and the Thwaites, accompanied by Slater, got out. He led the way to the hospital chapel, a small, modern room with plain white walls, several rows of chairs and a wooden crucifix above a simple altar, which was unadorned apart from a vase of flowers and two candlesticks. The lights had been dimmed slightly. In the centre of the room was a hospital trolley. Slater walked over to it. He looked back at the couple and Arthur swallowed and nodded. Slater drew back the sheet. Sheila stepped forward hesitantly. The body had been cleaned up; the child in front of her looked like her daughter now. She noticed how Paula's golden freckles stood out on her pale skin and the contrast of her coppery hair against her white forehead. The little girl looked peaceful, lying there, her eyes closed, long tresses combed out, like a pretty princess who was merely asleep. Sheila touched her cheek and felt its marble coldness. 'What were you doing on that lake? Hmm?' she admonished softly. 'I sent you to school. Why didn't you stay in school? Hmm? Why didn't you stay there, Paula?'

The sound of his wife talking to her daughter as if she was still alive was almost unbearable to Arthur. He looked at the tableau, watched her smooth Paula's hair as she did last thing at night when she popped upstairs to look in on her. Tears welled and he blinked them back, noticing Slater glancing at him. Arthur could not bring himself to touch Paula or even stand too close. He half turned away, looking down at his feet and biting his lip, as Sheila, her voice rising, carried on addressing Paula. 'Can you see what you've gone and done? Can you see what you've gone and done to us?' Arthur's shoulders shook and the tears dripped silently down his face.

In a nondescript hospital office with a few dried-out spider plants dangling from grey filing cabinets, Sheila Thwaite signed her daughter's life away. Slater read her statement back to her. '"At 6.30 p.m. on Tuesday 18 September at the Cumbrian Royal Infirmary I identified the body of my daughter Paula, aged ten." Is that OK?'

'Yes.' Her lips made the word, although no sound came out.

'Could you sign there, please, Sheila?' He indicated on the paper with a cross. Sheila took the pen and watched it scratch out her name on the form. 'And just below,' Slater said, pushing the paper towards Arthur.

'She's not my daughter. She wasn't my daughter. She was my stepdaughter,' he replied gruffly.

Slater paused, thought better of it. 'One signature will do, anyway. I'll drive you back.'

The two men were left alone in the room while Sheila

went to fix her blotchy face in the ladies. Arthur lit a cigarette and began pacing up and down. He felt the urge to explain his stark disclosure to Slater. 'We're both divorced. Sheila's was O K. Mine was a bit messy. Found out she was carrying on. Came home by train. Our house backed on to the line. I pulled the communication cord, climbed over our back wall, caught them at it. I gave him a bit of a pasting. She called the police. I dug myself in, in the front garden, watched them all, dozens of coppers, coming and going, talking about me. I gave myself up in the morning.'

'What did you get?' asked Slater.

'Twelve months. Did eight. I've got a kid, you see. A boy. But he's by her, the first wife. So I never see him. So Paula was – I know all kids are precious but we can't have one of our own so Paula was, well, a bit special.' He shook his head wretchedly, unable to go on.

Slater drove them home. By the time they drew up outside the house it was dusk. They could just make out Danny Kavanagh waiting on the porch. He was sitting on the step, his head bowed, a bunch of flowers on the ground beside him. At the chink of the latch on the gate he scrambled to his feet, snatching up the bouquet. 'All right,' he said to Arthur as he approached.

'All right,' Arthur grunted. He unlocked the door and waved Danny in.

Sheila turned to Slater, who had got out of the car with them. 'Thanks.'

'I'll be round tomorrow,' he said. She looked exhausted, thought Slater, who felt drained himself. He wanted to keep an eye on them both, especially Arthur: he was like a bomb that could go off at any moment.

'Bye.' She followed the others inside. Danny was standing in the living room, looking awkward. 'Thanks for all you did, Danny,' she said, meaning it. She had heard all about him swimming out there and retrieving Susan

Charles, and then going out again to look for the rest.

'If I'd had a motor boat –' he began, uselessly, his voice catching. Sheila went over and hugged him. He hugged her back, fiercely. Arthur, watching, caught Danny's eye over her shoulder. Arthur's expression was inscrutable.

Lucy Archer's bedroom was part boudoir, part sweet-teen's fantasy. Two sides of it were taken up by floor-to-ceiling wardrobes with mirrored sliding doors. Mirrors featured prominently. There was also a large, angled one on her dressing-table on the third side of the room. All that was missing to turn it into a sex den was another one on the ceiling. Lucy, a complete narcissist who enjoyed watching herself masturbate, was working on that. Those mirrored tiles might do, she thought. The rest of the pink and white room was cluttered with make-up and decorated with pop posters and pin-ups from teen magazines. Her sleeping companions were, as yet, a small army of teddies and fluffy toys. The Barbie dolls (Lucy had the collection) sat on a shelf all of their own.

Lucy checked her appearance – front, sideways and rear – twisting and admiring her reflection in the mirrors. ' "Because you're gor-geous",' she sang, leaning forwards so that her cleavage showed and practising a pout. She flicked her long hair over her shoulder, gave her reflection a smouldering look from under lowered eyelashes and jiggled her hips as she sang it again. Her love affair with the mirror was interrupted by her mother knocking on the door, calling, 'There's a policeman wants to see you'. Lucy did not seem particularly fazed. She undid another button on her blouse and sashayed out.

Doreen Archer gave Sergeant Slater the chair with the best view of the lake, which looked at its most glorious in the morning sunshine. Her upwardly-mobile pretensions had ruled out living in a slate-built bungalow like most of the locals. Instead, she had commissioned an architect to build them something 'original and stylish'. The architect, having sat through several tedious lunches presided over by Doreen, came up with a mock Swiss chalet with an integral garage which, he told her, 'was designed to suit her exceptional personality'. Doreen loved it and Archer didn't seem to care as long as his wife was happy. The house had a first-floor living room with a balcony and huge windows looking out over the lake, an outlook of which Doreen was most proud. Hence the chair in which Slater was sat, nervously balancing his cup and saucer on his knee, was known as 'the visitor's seat'. Lucy and her father sat on a green leather sofa opposite the policeman while Doreen, ever the gracious hostess, fussed about offering him things.

'What school do you go to, Lucy?' inquired Slater, putting down his cup and saucer on the floor – Doreen immediately whisked it on to a side table – and getting out his notebook.

'Ellergreen,' said Lucy, crossing her legs and admiring her tight-fitting knee-high boots.

'What's it like?'

'It's OK.' *Boring.*

'A thousand pounds a term, it should be,' interjected Archer, who was in his casuals and slippers.

'But you were off yesterday?' quizzed Slater.

'Exams.' She rotated a foot.

'Sorry?'

Lucy sighed. 'They're all doing exams. If you're not doing one you can stay off.'

'You're in the upper sixth?' Slater was writing all this down.

'Lower,' said Doreen.

'My daughter's in the lower sixth and –' he broke off, looking intently at Lucy. The Archers exchanged a glance.

'And?' repeated Doreen.

'She was in today.'

'In Ellergreen?' Her tone implied surprise, doubt.

'No, she goes to the local comp.'

Doreen relaxed visibly. 'It'll be a bit different in the local comp. They've got to keep them off the streets.'

'Probably, yeah.' Slater seemed not to notice the snub.

'Nuts?' inquired Doreen brightly, jumping up and bringing over a cut-glass bowl of mixed salted nuts from the drinks cabinet.

Slater drew in his breath with a hiss. 'I never touch them now. I read that survey. Analysed an average bowl of nuts, found thirty-four different types of male urine.' He had, of course, felt Doreen's snub and decided to lob one back. The Archers blinked at each other but said nothing. He turned to Lucy again. 'Will you tell me what you told Julie?' She looked taken aback, unsure of herself for the first time. 'About Danny Kavanagh,' he prompted. Lucy looked down at her hands, spreading out her fingers. She scratched at a patch of flaking polish but did not answer. Slater pressed again. 'You told her that Danny Kavanagh let those girls get in the boat and then he pushed it out on to the lake?'

'Yes,' she said, eventually, still not looking up.

Sergeant Slater glanced across at her parents, who were leaning forward, perturbed. 'You're sure?' asked Archer, disbelieving.

'Yes.'

'Did they pay him?' Slater was scribbling furiously.

'Yes.'

He straightened his back, fixed her with serious eyes. 'I can't stress enough how important this is, Lucy. You're saying Danny Kavanagh took money off those children?'

'Yes,' said Lucy, decisively.

THIRTEEN

Sheila looked into the haggard face of the old man sitting opposite her, a face, she realized, she'd never noticed changing, ageing, crumbling, because you didn't when you saw the person almost every day. It was the face of the man who had raised her; a man she trusted and loved and respected. It was the face of her father. The face of the man who had let her daughter drown.

Granddad looked little and old and frail. He had arrived the morning after the accident with Bernie, Emma, Annie, Samantha and Father Matthew, saying they needed to talk to her. *He* needed to talk to her. Arthur took the two young ones into the kitchen and fed them milk and biscuits. The others, at Father Matthew's suggestion, sat around the dining table. He asked them to join hands and they did, and prayed. Then Granddad spoke his piece, telling them how he'd met the truants when he was out walking Godiva.

'Age grants you licence. A licence to indulge,' he said, looking at Sheila with watery blue eyes. 'I knew the girls were being naughty, sagging off school, but I wanted to show them I was on their side. That's what granddads are for: to be on their side. But I had the dog. And Annie loves the dog. So I took Annie. I let Paula run off.' His whiskery chin quivered.

Surprisingly, Sheila felt her heart go out to him for the burden he had to bear. Even though he could have stopped her. She knew how headstrong Paula could be. 'You're not to blame for that,' she said, her own voice trembling too.

'I am,' he insisted. 'I should've sent them all back to

school. I remember what I said to them. I said, "Going to the lake's nice. But sagging off school to go on the lake, that's not just nice, it's an adventure."'

There was silence while they all took that in. Even Bernie didn't know it had been Granddad's idea. She hardly dared to look at her sister. Granddad blew his nose loudly. After a while, Sheila said, her voice steadier, 'I know I've got Arthur. And Arthur's a good man. But I want my father and my sister, too. And you've got nothing to feel guilty about. But even if you had, even if you were as guilty as sin, it shouldn't stop you coming to me when I need you.' Her hands tightened on Father Matthew's and Bernie's, who were sitting either side of her. There was another, long silence. Father Matthew cleared his throat and said, 'Emma?' but Emma was too choked to speak. Bernie couldn't, either; she was sobbing softly, her chin on her chest, her eyes screwed shut. Sheila turned to her. 'I want to say this now, Bernie, before it gets too difficult. I'm not jealous or bitter or . . . you don't have to hide Annie away, apologize for still having her. I want her to grow up and be the happiest girl in the world and live to be a hundred. I really do.'

Bernie's sobs became louder; they seemed to bubble up from a well deep inside that she hadn't known existed. Sheila, who had remained so calm, broke down and cried too, her arms around Bernie's neck. Across the table, Granddad wept a pool of tears that dripped down his seamed and lined cheeks and fell on to the polished surface unchecked. In the kitchen, little Annie, who was holding the baby, looked up at Uncle Arthur and saw that he could hear the chorus of weeping, too.

Doreen Archer felt they should do something, 'show willing', as she put it. It was only proper – the Thwaites were their employees, after all, and the Archers were involved, too. Hadn't Lucy witnessed the appalling tragedy? She'd even played a part herself, getting the doctor and the emergency services there so swiftly. (After a few initial reservations, she had decided to support Lucy's version of events entirely. How could it have been otherwise? Doreen argued. There was no earthly reason for Lucy to make up such a story.) Which was why, after the sergeant had gone, Doreen had insisted that they pay the Thwaites a visit that very afternoon. True, it meant risking the BMW on the council estate, but it needn't take long and she was sure Sheila and Arthur would appreciate the thought. She made her husband put on a sombre suit and spent a considerable amount of time choosing her own outfit. It needed to strike the right tone, she decided; not funereal (not yet, anyway – she would save the hat for later) but in keeping with the sad occasion. She decided on a matching navy skirt and jacket with a soft pink scarf and a rather nice brooch she'd bought recently. They tried to get Lucy to come along, but she said she was too upset, claiming the sergeant's visit had made her relive it all and she needed to rest.

They timed their visit for 3.00 p.m. – an acceptable hour for calling, Doreen judged – and parked in front of the house. She rang the bell, glancing at the scruffy gardens either side, littered with children's trikes and plastic toys. Sheila answered. She had dark circles under her eyes and her hair, usually so neat, was all over the place. Doreen wondered briefly whether she had overdone it with the scarf. She put on her concerned face and handed Sheila a lavish bunch of flowers. 'We're so-o sorry,' she enunciated. Sheila smiled – a rather strained smile, Doreen thought, but then she must be worn out – and took them, saying, 'They're lovely.' Arthur hovered behind her in the hall, looking equally tired. He had a day's stubble growth and his shirt was hanging out. 'Will you come in?' he said. Doreen picked her way into the hall on her high heels as delicately as a cat. Wordlessly, Archer followed.

'Tea?' asked Sheila, falling into the hostess's role despite her grief.

'If it's not too much trouble,' Doreen replied graciously.

'Go in.' Sheila gestured to the living room. Arthur followed her into the kitchen, went to the cupboard and got out the scotch. He poured himself a large measure and downed it in one, while Sheila stooped and got out the best cups and began dusting them off with a tea towel. He patted her shoulder and went through into the other room. Doreen was reading a sympathy card from the mantelpiece. She looked thrown, for a second, as if she'd been caught snooping. Arthur held out his hand for the card, saying, 'Kettle's on.' Doreen, recovering herself, gave it to him and said with a sociable smile, 'They're comforting, aren't they?'

'Yeah.' Arthur thought they were a pile of crap. He knew people meant well, but what did they really know about what he and Sheila were going through? 'Thinking of you at this sorrowful time' didn't even begin to scratch the surface.

Sheila entered with tea things on a tray and put them on the table. She stood up and pushed her hair self-consciously behind her ears. 'How are you feeling?' asked Doreen, solicitously. Sheila tried to answer honestly. Like Arthur, she was already tiring of the hollow phrases used to express and sympathize with grief. 'Empty.' She wanted to say, 'As if I'm tumbling down and down into this great dark hole,' but she knew they wouldn't understand.

'She was a lovely girl,' Doreen said.

'Thanks.'

'Don't worry about work. Take as much time as you want.'

'Thanks.'

Doreen nodded at the card Arthur was still holding and said, in a scandalized tone, 'I don't know what he was thinking of.'

'Sorry?' Sheila was baffled, thinking Doreen meant Arthur.

Archer, who had also read the card before Arthur entered the room, chipped in warningly to his wife, 'Lucy could be mistaken.' Arthur, mystified, opened the card to see who it was from.

'Mistaken about what?' asked Sheila, looking concerned. Archer shot Doreen a look, which she chose to ignore. 'Please tell me,' Sheila begged.

'This is from Danny Kavanagh. Is it something to do with him?' growled Arthur.

'Lucy says he allowed them out on the lake.' Well, Doreen thought to herself, returning her husband's look with an equally steely glare, they have a right to know.

'She was there?' Arthur said.

'Yes,' said Archer. It would have to be a united front.

'She saw it?'

'Yes.'

'So how could she be mistaken?' Arthur was beginning to lose his temper.

'I don't know,' Archer said cagily.

'You think she's lying?' Arthur walked over to him. 'You think she'd lie over a thing like that?'

'No.' Archer took a step backwards and glared at his stupid, witless wife. They left without drinking their tea.

Arthur went into the kitchen and retrieved the scotch. He poured himself another large glass, downed it swiftly, then brought the bottle into the living room and poured another shot. Sheila was sitting with her head in her hands, trying to make sense of what they'd just heard. Arthur slumped down in a chair. Neither of them spoke. The sympathy card stood on the coffee table between them; the grossest insult possible, framed by a border of gilt. Or guilt, thought Arthur. No wonder Danny had been round so damn quickly yesterday. He took another swig of the whisky and stood up. 'Where are you going?' asked

Sheila, who had been eyeing him, waiting for this. He shrugged on his coat. 'Where are you going?' she insisted. Arthur didn't answer: he knew she'd try and stop him. He dug in his pockets for the car keys. They weren't there. He spied them on the table, but Sheila was quicker than him and snatched them up. 'Give me the keys,' he shouted.

'Where are you going?' Sheila was edging away from him.

Arthur pursued her. 'Just give me the keys.'

'No.' She backed into the hall.

'Sheila, I don't want to hurt you but I need the keys.' He lunged for them but she stepped out of range, feeling for the front door knob with one hand. 'You're gonna *have* to hurt me 'cause you're not getting them,' she said, determined.

'Give me them!'

'You're going to see him, aren't you?'

'Who?'

'Danny Kavanagh.'

'No.'

'You're lying.' She kept them behind her back, found the door knob, turned it gently.

'*Give me the keys!*'

'For God's sake, aren't I suffering enough?' Sheila began to sob. She opened the door and backed out of the house. After the bright start to the day it was pouring down now. Tears and rain streamed down her face. 'I'm just gonna talk to him,' screamed Arthur, who had followed her out and was also getting soaked.

'You won't be able to keep your hands off him. I know you. You'll kill him.'

'*Give me the keys!*' he caught hold of her arms and shook her.

'You'll get put away. I'll have to go through all this on my own. For God's sake, think about me for a change, will you?' Sheila cried, holding on to the keys as if her life depended on it. Her lank hair was plastered to her skull, giving her a strange, desperate appearance.

'*Give me the bloody keys.*'

'No,' she screamed at the top of her voice, wrenching herself free and hurling them high and long into the bushes and long grass at the end of the garden. He looked at her, shocked, then turned and ran down to where she had thrown them and fell on his hands and knees in the torrential rain, scrabbling about for the keys.

'What good will it do?' Sheila was screaming in his ear, tugging fruitlessly at his coat. 'It'll make you feel a lot better but what good will it do me? What good will it do Paula? We don't even know he's to blame. We've only got her word for it.' She got down on all fours in the mud beside him, trying to force him to look at her. 'Some stuck-up little tart's word for it. He went in after them. He did everything he could to save them and now you're gonna beat hell out of him.'

'He's to blame.' Arthur wasn't listening to reason. He was driven by a blind need to act, to avenge Paula's death, and the Archers had given him something concrete to fix on. Something he could do. He got up, abandoning his search, and decided to walk.

'Arthur,' Sheila sobbed, still on her hands and knees. He shut his ears and went out of the gate. 'Arthur.' She fell on her face in the mud, utterly beside herself with despair.

Down at the boat-landing, Danny Kavanagh and Sergeant Slater were also standing in the rain, looking out across the grey water. The third body – that of Lisa Graham – had been found several hours after Paula Thwaite, but the police divers had returned to look for the boat. 'They still haven't recovered it?' Slater, who had just arrived to interview Danny, looked surprised.

'They think they will soon,' Danny said, kicking at the wall that ran out along part of the jetty.

'Where was it moored?'

'Over there.' He pointed to a line of boats pulled up on the shore.

'Would you mind showing me?'

Danny wondered where all this was leading. He jumped off the duckboards on to the shingle beach, Slater following. As they walked, Danny pulled out a piece of paper from his pocket and handed it to him. 'That's the council certificate. The boat was checked a month ago. Nothing wrong with it.'

Slater studied it. 'Can I keep this for now?'

He nodded. 'We've got a copy.' They came to the row of boats. 'It was here,' he said, indicating a space near some reeds.

'Right on the end?'

'Yeah.'

'Why?'

He stared at Slater, trying to read his mind. 'It's wooden. The fibreglass ones are more popular.'

'And safer?' asked Slater, writing something on the pulpy paper in his damp notebook.

'No. More popular.'

Slater stuffed the notebook in his top pocket and said, 'Let's go inside.'

Back in the boathouse, Danny offered to make him tea, but Slater said no, thank you, he was awash with the stuff already. Danny lit up a cigarette and stared out of the window at the rain lashing down with a sense of *déjà vu*. Was it only yesterday that he had looked out of the same window and seen the girls on the lake? He felt as if he'd lived a lifetime since then. Emma had had to stay with her family – Danny understood, he was just thankful that, for all the horror, he and Emma had been reconciled – but that night in the boathouse was the longest he'd ever known. Danny had gone over and over the events in his head and, by the morning, had come to a decision. A decision he intended to stick to, come what may. He breathed out two streams of smoke through his nostrils and tried to focus on what Slater was saying about the number of girls in the boat.

'How could you be so sure?'

'I wasn't.'

'You seemed to be. You told the Thwaites there were three, you told the Quinlans –'

'I said I *thought* there were three. Look, the first time I saw them they were heading back in. If they'd been going out, I'd've gone out to them. If they'd been going *across*, I'd've gone out to them. I didn't go out to them because they were heading *back in*.'

There was a long pause, then Slater said, 'I'm going to have to ask you to come down to the station, Danny.'

'No way.'

'Just to make a formal statement.'

'No way,' he said again, turning round, eyes blazing. 'I can see what's happening: they're looking for someone to blame. Well, it's not going to be me.'

'I've spoken to Lucy Archer.'

'Yeah?'

'She says you let them out on the lake, you took money from them.'

Danny was stunned. 'She's lying.'

'Why would she lie?'

'I don't know,' he replied. The mundane truth had not yet occurred to him.

'Come on, get your things and lock up.' Slater put on his cap and walked out to the car. Danny found his jacket and followed him, holding it over his head as he ran through the rain. He got in the back and Slater switched on the wipers and the blower, waiting for a minute because the windscreen was fogged up. A clear patch spread up from the bottom, revealing, as it got bigger, the hulking figure of Arthur Thwaite standing doggedly in front of the car. Slater wound down the driver's window. 'What d'you want, Arthur?'

'Nothing,' he said, glaring at Danny. Slater glanced back over his shoulder. 'I didn't know they were out there,' Danny appealed to Arthur. Slater revved the engine and started to move off. Danny wound down his window too and hung out of it, shouting back at Arthur, 'I didn't know. Right? *I didn't know.*'

Being in an interview room with a tape recorder rolling brought back memories Danny had been trying to forget. The spartan room, the bare table, the policeman at the door – he'd been there before and he vowed then never to go back. That time in Liverpool he deserved what he got, but this time he was being made a scapegoat. He remembered the numerous lectures he'd been given about off-comers in general and Scousers in particular since he'd been working in the Lakes. As far as people like the Archers and Arthur Thwaite and Peter Quinlan were concerned, he might as well be hanged for a sheep as a lamb.

Sergeant Slater asked Danny to go over for him exactly what had happened the day before. Danny tried to recount the events – seeing the girls out on the lake, their frightened reaction to the low-flying jet, watching as the boat tipped right up on its side, as if in slow motion, and sank, taking them with it – without experiencing it again, but it was hard. Hard, especially, not to remember how he himself had nearly drowned, the strange other-worldliness of being under the water, the seductiveness of the impulse to let go, to stop fighting for breath, to succumb to the deep. He did not tell Slater about that. No one else could possibly understand, except the drowned.

'I got her out of the water, carried her to the shore, tried to do all that –' Danny mimed his actions, feeling Susan Charles's brittle ribcage, her unformed chest, feeling also his own inadequacy at being unable to save her.

'Cardiac massage.'

'Yeah, but I didn't know what to do, I was just copying what I'd seen on the telly. Then Juliet came and she knew what she was doing so I went back on to the lake. But I'd lost me bearings, couldn't tell where the boat had gone down, but I went in anyway and started looking. But it was deep, y'know what I mean. And the deeper I went, the darker it got. And colder. I carried on doing that for – I don't know, it's hard to judge the time – about twenty minutes. Then I gave up.'

He paused. Slater looked at him intently. 'You deny taking money from the girls?'

'Yeah. Can I go now?'

'How did they get into the boat without you seeing them?'

'I was in the boathouse.'

'What were you doing in the boathouse?'

Danny hesitated. At last he said, 'Making tea'.

'Who for?'

'A customer.'

'But you've already told me there was no one on the boat-landing apart from Lucy.' Slater's eyes were as hard and cold as the pebbles on the bed of the lake.

'I don't know *what* I –'

'You're lying, Danny,' he snapped.

'– was doing in there. I'm not lying,' he replied angrily, pushing his chair back. 'Can I go now, please?'

'Interview terminated at 14.57,' said Slater, switching off the tape recorder.

Sergeant Slater had said he would report back to the Thwaites, but he wasn't looking forward to telling them his suspicions. When he pulled up outside the house he found Bernie, Emma, Granddad and Father Matthew waiting on the path and the front door ajar. He called 'Hello' and stepped inside, to find the Thwaites in the hall getting ready to go out. He was surprised when Sheila didn't react to what he told her – she was putting her coat on, fussing with her collar – but she said that the Archers had already let slip Lucy's version. 'One of them's lying,' she added, looking in the mirror and adjusting her hair.

'Yes,' he replied grimly.

'Which one?'

'That's not for me to –'

'Which one? Danny or Lucy?' She swung round, making the demand with such vehemence that he was momentarily taken aback.

'I think Danny might be lying,' he said reluctantly.

She looked troubled and glanced back at Arthur, who was also shrugging on a jacket.

'I don't want you to come, Arthur.'

'What?' He looked amazed.

'He'll be there.'

'I won't do anything. I won't *say* anything,' he said, pulling up the zip.

Sheila obviously did not not believe him. She walked over to him, rested her hands on his shoulders and looked down at her feet, biting her lip. Then she gazed up into his eyes, holding his, and pleaded, 'Look after Annie and the baby. Please don't come.'

Arthur turned, wrenched off his jacket and stomped back into the living room.

Sheila couldn't bear to have her communion with Paula ruined by harsh words or brawling. She wanted their little ceremony on the lake to be a special, sacred moment. Arthur was entitled to be there, she knew, but he was still spoiling for a fight and couldn't be trusted not to lash out at Danny. Today was for her and her daughter. She shut the front door and joined the others in Father Matthew's car. They drove in silence to the boat-landing.

Danny was waiting for them by the water's edge. Father Matthew got into the boat first, followed by Bernie. For a second or two Sheila thought she wouldn't be able to go through with it and stood petrified with fear, but then Father Matthew reached out his hand and she stepped cautiously into the varnished wooden skiff. The boat rocked alarmingly as she did so, causing Sheila to panic and cling to the priest until he guided her gently to a seat next to Bernie. He sat down too, picked up the oars and nodded at Danny, who was waiting to push them off. Sheila found herself staring straight into Danny's expressionless face as he waded out into the shallows. This morning she did not want to think about the implication of Sergeant Slater's words, about whether Danny had pushed Paula and the girls out on to the lake as he was doing for them now. Sheila shut her eyes.

She kept them shut while Father Matthew rowed out to the spot, so that it felt as if she were gliding on some mysterious journey – being transported to the afterlife, perhaps – with only the slight swell of the waves and the wind in her hair and the peculiar weedy smell of the lake to tell her where she was. Then she heard him praying with Bernie, 'Our Father who art in Heaven, Hallowed by thy name. Thy kingdom come, Thy will be done on earth as it is in Heaven,' and opened her eyes.

Danny Kavanagh watched from the shore and saw Sheila Thwaite strew flowers on the water. Granddad and Emma were drifting nearby in another boat, their heads bowed as Father Matthew prayed. Danny had never been so utterly exiled: he bowed his head too and prayed for – what? He wasn't even sure he could articulate what he felt or what he wanted. The scream of a low-flying jet shattered his meditation, making him jump out of his skin. Instinctively, he glanced across at the two boats. Everyone was looking up, startled, but the jet, as usual, was already out of sight.

FOURTEEN

Word got out two days after the drowning. Danny, who had, until then, been fêted for his courage, instantly became an outcast. The tourists didn't know he was a pariah: they wandered to the boat-landing in their sun-hats, ate ice-creams and took boats out on the lake, keeping him busy. No one else visited him. Emma, Danny's only ally, had been banned from seeing him by her parents. Juliet, his boss, was also conspicuous by her absence, although he was half expecting her to turn up at any moment and sack him. He was living on a diet of crisps, choc ices, Coca-Cola and coffee because he couldn't face the hostility in the village. At night he lay awake, lonely and not a little afraid of Arthur Thwaite turning up to exact retribution. He had been stripped of his wife, his child and now his reputation, when all he wanted to do was make a fresh start. It was time, Danny decided, to clear his name.

First on his agenda was John Parr. Danny visited the school and found the playground deserted: it had been closed temporarily as a mark of respect for the three girls and their families. It was strange, seeing the school without kids; normally he'd be dodging small boys ricocheting like bullets around the yard. He shaded his eyes and peered through the window. The Parrs were there in the classroom. The door was unlocked and he went inside. 'Why did you leave the kids on their own?' he demanded, without formalities. John Parr, dressed as usual in his sports jacket and polished brogues, glanced up briefly from his pile of exercise books and said, 'I've made a statement to the police,' before returning to his work.

'Yes but *I* need to know. Why?' Danny walked over to Parr's desk and stood in front of it. Parr kept his head down, ignoring him. Finally, when Danny did not budge, he glared at him and snapped, 'Look, I've got rather a lot of marking to do,' and blanked him out again. Simone looked at them from the other side of the room where she was tidying up.

'There's three you needn't bother with.' The head-master's red pen hovered and stopped several inches above the paper. Danny planted his hands heavily on the table and leaned forwards. 'A feller from the *Gazette* turned up. I played it all down, like you're supposed to. Said I only did what anyone else would've done. But it's always there at the back of your mind, no matter what's happened, no matter how many's dead: yeah, I'm a bloody hero. But all of a sudden, I'm *not* a bloody hero. I'm the cause of it all. And that's not on.' He breathed out harshly. 'Why did you leave those kids on their own? Please.'

John Parr still wouldn't meet his eyes. Suddenly, Simone, who Danny hadn't noticed listening behind him, said quietly, 'I'm having an affair with someone.'

He spun round. 'Chef.' This time Parr did look up, wincing as if someone had slapped him.

'Yes,' Simone replied.

'And?' Danny couldn't see the relevance.

'John followed me, caught me with him.' She fiddled with a box of crayons. Danny stared at them both, realizing what she was saying. He opened his mouth to speak, shut it again and headed for the door. It slammed shut with a bang, making a display of artwork pinned to the wall flutter in the draught. They both jumped. John Parr got up and went into his office. He retrieved a bottle of whisky from the back of a filing-cabinet drawer and poured a large measure. Simone, who had followed him in, watched in silence.

'He knew,' John growled.

'Yes.'

'So you didn't try to hide it.'

'Not particularly, no.'

He knocked back the glass and went to pour himself another one. Her hand snaked out to whisk the bottle away but he was too quick and clamped his hand over hers. 'I don't honestly know what hurts more,' he said in a choked voice, his fingers tightening vice-like round Simone's wrist, causing her to gasp in pain. 'Three children dead – or my wife and that man.'

Danny needed a drink himself. He went to the pub halfway up the hill where they'd had Samantha's christening bash – it seemed a lifetime ago – and considered his next move. It was quiet, midweek, although a few walkers who had made an early start had begun to drop in for a pint and a sandwich on their way back down. He sat outside in the sun, nursing his ale and decided: Chef.

Chef was in his garden, stripped to the waist, tending his roses. He straightened up when he heard the gate and rested his forearm on a fork stuck in the ground. Keeping a healthy distance between them, Danny said, 'Lucy Archer's telling all kinds of lies about me. You've got a bit of clout with her old man. I want –'

'It's got nothing to do with me.'

'– you to talk to him. I want him to get the truth out the lying bitch.'

'It's got nothing to do with me,' Chef repeated, stony-faced.

'It's got plenty to do with you. You're carryin' on with Mrs Parr, the headmaster's wife. Right?'

'Right?'

'Her husband caught you at it.'

'Yeah?' Chef picked up the fork and stabbed it down into the grass in front of him.

'He left the kids on their own. Four sloped off. Three drowned.'

Chef's colour was deepening. He twisted the fork. 'I'm not to blame for that.'

'Bollocks,' Danny said, disgusted.

Chef looked murderously at him. 'Does wonders for the roses, the odd pint of blood.'

Danny stood his ground. 'There'll be an inquest. It'll all come out. I'll make sure it all comes out 'cause I'm not takin' the blame.'

'So?'

'You're *married*.'

It was a shock to see Chef smile. Unnatural. Leer, yes, but grin in this horrible fashion – Danny had never witnessed that before. 'Ruth,' Chef bellowed. 'Ruth'. They heard her answer faintly from the house. Chef fixed him with one of his belligerent stares. 'I like screwing other men's wives, Danny. Other men's girlfriends. You've been safe till now: I've only ever seen you with slags. And a local girl, a local girl with a bit of sense so, naturally, that didn't last long. But you cop off with anyone decent and I'll be there, sniffing around.' Danny held his gaze. Ruth came out of the house. 'Who have I been screwing for the last few months?' Chef demanded.

Ruth ignored him and turned to Danny. 'Would you like a cup of tea?'

'Who have I been screwing?' he thundered again.

'Mrs Parr, the headmaster's wife.' Snap. She brushed this humiliation off as lightly as a fly and repeated, 'Would you like a cup of tea?'

'No thanks,' Danny replied, dumbfounded.

'Extra-curricular activity I think it's called,' Ruth said casually, walking back towards the house. Danny couldn't believe what he'd just witnessed. How could she not mind? What kind of a relationship did those two have? He returned to Chef, who had picked up the secateurs and was dead-heading his roses. 'This is Wordsworth Country. Millions come here, Danny.' Snip, snip, snap. 'All looking for Nature. They clog up our roads, stomp all over our fells, pack our bars, buy up our houses. Hotels and restaurants spring up; the mines and the quarries close down; farms get turned into timeshare complexes. So for people like me, Danny, local people like me, there's nothing else to do but look after this urban filth. We get to *depend* on this urban filth.' Chef stopped and wiped his forehead on his forearm. He squinted past Danny, looking out at the vista of fells encircling the village. 'Well, OK: they've come here looking for Nature; I'll give them a bit of Nature; I'll give their wives and their girlfriends a bit of Nature. Just the tourists, I mean, and outsiders like you, urban filth like you. Nobody local. If they're local, they're safe.' And he decapitated a few more drooping heads, trampling the petals into the flowerbed.

By mid-afternoon John Parr had made substantial inroads into the whisky, all pretences of work forgotten. He had taken his jacket off, his tie was unknotted and he was slumped over the desk in his shirt sleeves. Simone, acting as if nothing was going on, busied herself with administration duties. He watched her balefully as she dialled a number and spoke into the phone. 'I just thought you'd like to know the school's open tomorrow as normal. Despite what's happened.' A pause. 'Thanks, I'll pass that on. Bye.' She ran her finger down a list, crossed out a name and dialled again.

'"Having an affair",' John slurred, swilling the dregs in his glass around.

She looked up. 'Sorry?'

'You said, "I'm having an affair." Not, "I had an affair." "Having an affair." Present tense. Ongoing.'

'Yes.'

'So it's not over?'

She hesitated. The phone was picked up. 'Simone Parr here, Mrs Quale. I just thought you'd like to know –' John glowered at her and tried to tip more whisky into the glass, spilling half of it on the desk and soaking the register. ' – that school's open tomorrow as usual, despite everything that's happened,' Simone continued.

'You think you can go on seeing him?' he roared drunkenly, standing up and swaying in front of her. Simone was listening to the voice on the other end of the line. 'We think so too. Bye.' She consulted her list and dialled another number. He drained his glass again, his eyes never leaving her face, trying to provoke, but she refused to acknowledge him. 'Simone Parr here, Mrs Quinlan.' John lurched towards the bottle and picked it up. It was empty.

Since Chef was obviously not going to bring influence to bear on the Archers, Danny decided to go there himself. He walked up the hotel drive and spotted the lads – Albie, Joey and Tharmy – scrubbing down the car park with a high-pressure hose and big brushes. Perhaps to compensate for his sexual shortcomings, Albie was in charge of the hose. Tactless as ever he shouted across to Danny, 'Is it true what she's saying?'

'Lucy? Be'ave.' He carried on towards reception, leaving the others arguing among themselves. Tharmy was making a bid for the hose. 'You'll get a go.' Albie kept a tight hold. Tharmy tried to say something. 'When?' interpreted Albie, aggressively.

'Yeah,' Tharmy managed.

'As soon as. Right? Carry on crying and I'll shove it up your rectum.'

Some things never change, thought Danny. He felt more and more separate from the old gang now, as if he'd gone on into a different dimension and left them behind. It added to his feeling of isolation, of being one against the world. He pushed open the heavy swing door. Archer saw Danny coming and tried to waylay him. 'I don't want you in my hotel. You're not –'

'Can I see Lucy please?'

'– welcome here, so just go, please.' He stood in Danny's path.

'Can I see Lucy please?' Danny repeated, determined to get to her.

'No,' he said loudly. Several of the residents, who were reading newspapers in the mock-gentleman's-club leather armchairs, turned to see what was going on.

'Is she in there?' Danny started moving towards the office at the back of reception. Again, Archer tried to stop him. 'Do you mind?' he yelled indignantly.

Danny shoved past him. 'Your daughter's tellin' a pack of lies about me. Right?' He stuck his head into the office and looked around. Lucy wasn't there.

'If you don't go right now, I'm phoning the police.' But Danny was off again, heading for the lounge. 'You're in enough trouble, so please, just go.' Archer pursued him. The heads behind the papers swivelled, relishing the entertainment. Danny spotted Lucy standing in the doorway to the small conservatory on the opposite side of the lounge. She draped herself against the door frame and watched him coming, then, when he had almost reached her, stepped inside and slammed the door, turning the key in the lock. He battered on the door, screaming, 'Open it. Open it,' but she sat down with her back to him among the ferns and trailing hot-house plants and refused to move. Archer hurried back across the lobby, picked up the phone and dialled. 'Police.' He paused. 'Archer, Ullswater Hotel.' Danny shot past him and into the car park. There was another entrance to the conservatory from outside – it was usually reserved for weddings, when a tired old piece of red carpet was rolled out and a couple of bay trees in pots were placed either side of the door. Skidding on a gravelled area and knocking over a garden chair in his haste, he raced past the lounge and round the corner to the exterior door. He rattled it furiously. That, too, was locked. Danny pressed his face against the window and saw Lucy, her legs drawn up in front of her, stare at him provocatively. Then she slid her hand right under her skirt, leant back in her chair and began to arch her body suggestively, watching him all the while from under half-closed eyelids while she moved her arm. Danny turned away, sickened. Her message was self-explanatory.

Once, he thought, he would have shagged her just like that, no problem, wham, bam, thank you mam. That was all she had wanted. She didn't want a boyfriend, nothing that complicated. Lucy was a trophy hunter: she collected scalps. The old Danny wouldn't have found it that oner-ous. But the new Danny, the through-the-looking-glass Danny, had more bloody morals. He'd found his true love and he'd found self-respect. Look where it had got him. If he'd given her one when she came round, Lucy wouldn't be spreading lies about him now. The girls would still have drowned, of course, and if he'd been with Lucy he wouldn't even have seen the boat go down, so by the time they did discover a boat was missing . . . he would still have got the blame. It was a no-win situation. He dug his hands in his pockets and began to walk back up the drive.

Just then, Slater's police car came nosing through the gateway and over the cattlegrid. He pulled up alongside Danny, switched off the engine and wound down the window. 'Stay away from Lucy,' he ordered.

'She's telling a pack of lies about me,' Danny protested.

'Stay away from her.' Danny nodded reluctantly and scuffed his feet. Slater paused, then said, 'You've got a hundred and twenty quid waiting for you at the bookie's. We searched the boathouse – I had a warrant; Juliet knew – and found your account. Next question: how can you afford it, Danny? How can you afford to leave that kind of money just lying there?'

'Pass.'

'Are you on the fiddle?'

'No.'

'It's all cash, isn't it? Must be tempting to let people on and just slot the money. Let a few kids on, even, and just slot it.'

'I'm not on the fiddle. I didn't let the kids go out on that boat.'

'Right.' Slater started the car up again. He looked hard at Danny. 'Stay away –' As if to emphasize the point, another low-flying jet blotted out the rest of his sentence. Slater raised his hand in acknowledgement to Archer, who had been watching them from the hotel lounge window, and drove off.

Archer had his own doubts about his daughter's truthfulness. He knew she was a little minx – sixteen going on twenty and forever flaunting herself; he had a hell of a time keeping her away from the hotel workers – and while he appreciated her obvious charms (in a fatherly way, naturally, he told himself), he was not blind to Lucy's manipulative nature. He'd been on the receiving end of it often enough. She wasn't above flirting with him if she thought she could get her way and she'd swear black was white if it helped her cause. He looked into the conservatory and rapped sharply on the window. She seemed preoccupied. He knocked again and she looked round at him, stretching her bare legs out in front languorously, like a cat. He unclipped the bunch of keys from his belt and opened the door. The air was very close, heavy, a jungly sort of scent. 'You need to keep this door open, it gets too hot otherwise,' he said. She smiled, a secret, infuriating smile. He wanted to shake her. 'He says you're a liar,' Archer snapped, referring to Danny.

Lucy licked her fingers. 'He's the liar.'

'*Is* he?'

She didn't answer. Instead, she closed her eyes dreamily and said, 'Will I have to give evidence?'

'Yes, you'll be the key witness, I should think. So you'd better be right.' Lucy's smile grew broader and broader, until she was one big Cheshire Cat grin.

Bats dipped and swooped around the school house in the evening air. The sky was shot with ominous streaks of yellow and a dark, inky blue, foretelling rain, as the sun went down behind the fells. A September chill was beginning to steal across from the lake. Inside the cottage, John Parr was sprawled in an armchair, a fresh whisky bottle by his side, talking on the phone. 'She's upstairs now. Getting ready. She's shaved her legs. She's tried to hide the fact, cleaned out the bath, but I checked and found tiny bits of stubble. So her legs'll be all smooth. For him. She's putting on her underwear. She's got those knickers. I don't know what they're called but they just hang loosely on her hips. And they look so sexy. And you know why they look so sexy? You know that the slightest little tug and they'll be down. And he'll tug them. And they'll fall. They'll fall all the way down to her ankles because her legs are so smooth. And she'll step out of them. And they'll do it.' He broke down and couldn't go on. A voice at the other end spoke to him gently, sympathetically. There was another silence. Choked and trembling, he put the receiver down and poured yet another unsteady measure. Some of it ran down his chin as he drank. He got up, half fell against a side table, banged his shin and swore foully. The obscenity was out of character, but so was the drinking. So, indeed, was his plan. It was time to assert himself.

The bedroom door was a low, white-painted one made of wooden slats (everything was low in the cottage, it looked idyllic but he was always hitting his head on the

168

beams). It was also on a chain. John pushed it open as far as it would go and saw Simone, wearing a short, tight, black dress, sitting at her dressing-table and pulling that face she always made when she applied mascara. 'Let me in,' he shouted.

'In a minute.' She carried on doing her make-up, completely unperturbed.

'Now.' He beat against the door with his fists in frustration, then tried slamming his shoulder into it. 'I'd like to come in right now.' He slammed his shoulder against the door again, like they did in cop films. 'This is my house and I'd like to come in *right now*.' He gave it all he'd got and, amazingly, the fastening on the door frame broke away and he fell into the room. Simone looked round, playing it cool. He noticed she was wearing the pearl necklace he'd given her as an anniversary present. 'The assertiveness course is working then?' she said airily, looking back in the mirror to brush her hair. He ignored her taunt, got hold of her handbag and yanked out her wallet. Coins fell out and scattered on the bed as he pulled out her credit cards and threw them on the floor. 'I've been too soft with you,' he said, panting, trying to rip a card up. It bent but did not tear. 'Modern Man. Caring, sensitive. But you don't want Modern Man. You want Neanderthal Man. Well, OK, you can have him.' Simone had got up and was edging away but he caught hold of her arm and pushed her back on the bed, pinning her down. She struggled as he ripped at her clothes and the necklace broke, sending pearls bouncing across the carpet.

'Get off me,' she screamed, genuinely alarmed. He was out of control.

'This is my house,' he said through gritted teeth, his face inches from hers, seeing, with some satisfaction, the panic in her eyes. 'We live here because of the job I do. The money we spend comes from the job I do. You contribute absolutely bloody nothing.'

'Get off me. Get off. Stop it. Stop it.' She sobbed, kicking and writhing as John, charged by something he did not know he possessed, forced her dress up round her midriff. The sight of her stocking tops – she never bothered for him – sent him into a fury and he unzipped himself, excited by her naked terror, the sheer primitive emotion. This was what he'd seen through the window that day when she was with Chef: Simone on that other shore, the well-mannered, middle-class woman stripped of everything, *everything*; a slave to that one, all-consuming, burning need. It felt good, this: punishing her and giving her what she really wanted at the same time. He was elated. 'Without me you'd be walking the streets. The car you drive, the clothes you wear, the food you eat. *I own you.*' He thrust hard, his own breath coming in frantic sobs. 'Everything about you, every bloody orifice in your body –'

'Stop it, you filthy bastard. Stop it.' She clawed at his face.

'I own you, you stupid, empty-headed bloody bitch, I own you.'

'*Stop it!*' Suddenly he felt himself go limp and all the strength seemed to go from his body. Simone wrenched free from his grasp and rolled out from under him. They sat on opposite sides of the bed, both of them shaking and crying.

FIFTEEN

Chef and Ruth had married young: she was sixteen, he was eighteen. He had always been considered the pick of the bunch when they were at school – he was good-looking, athletic, cocky, the one you noticed in a crowd – and Ruth had never quite shaken off the idea that she was lucky to have him. That's what the mothers all said at the time, and she believed them. What they also said, and she believed this too, was that mousy little Ruth Tyson would never have caught him if she hadn't been pregnant. The fact that she miscarried two days after the wedding did not earn her any sympathy either. Ruth was undeserving.

The first eight years of their married life were an uphill struggle. Chef – of course, he wasn't known as Chef back then, he was Patrick – did various jobs: quarrying, up on the pass, a laborious, dangerous, ill-paid job; then, when that closed down, forestry work, sawing and hauling lumber. He fell out with the foreman and took a farm job instead, but that was no more successful. It ended in fisticuffs with the farmer's son, who had tried to order him about. After that there was a long period of unemployment, during which Ruth kept them both on her wages from her job in the village post office, until finally, after long years of trying, she conceived again and gave up work to look after baby Thomas. They decided that Patrick needed to train properly at something and, as luck would have it, a position in the hotel became vacant.

Over the next eight years he worked his way up from kitchen porter to head chef – with a spell away at another hotel after he clashed with a previous proprietor – but they took him back at the Ullswater because he was good. Patrick – Chef – had found his niche. There was nothing he liked better than exerting power over others and the heat, sweat and pace of a busy kitchen was an environment in which he flourished. It absorbed his aggression but also stoked it: he was master of his kitchen but only on the indulgence of the tourists and trippers who used the Lakes as their playground. He was *their* servant.

Chef and Ruth still made love – she was useful, submissive, uncomplaining – but it didn't satisfy him any more. So he started philandering, channelling his pent-up sexual energy into affairs, using his bitterness towards the offcomers, initially as a justification, then, increasingly, as a warped, one-man sexual crusade. Ruth got to know about it, naturally – Hawksmere was too small a place for word not to get around – and he became less and less careful, until it got to the stage when he didn't bother to hide it from her at all, and she stopped asking.

He assumed she got some kind of kick out of it, too: perhaps the fact that, whatever he did, he still went back to her bed, was all she wanted. So he began to toy with her, one of those psychological mindgames that couples play, piling on the humiliation by telling her about his women, what he did to them, and still she didn't react. It had become almost an obsession with him to want to break her down, have her explode at him, but the more he flaunted his affairs the less she seemed to care. Until recently.

She'd started making acid remarks and keeping up this vigil by the window. Nothing very impressive but the cracks were beginning to show. Didn't stop her doing what he wanted, though, he thought, sitting in the bath and scooping water over his chest while Ruth soaped his back. It was his night off, but he was going to the hotel anyway. He had some business to attend to. Business he should have seen to a while ago. Ruth knew what kind of business he had in mind so the broadside she delivered as she rinsed him off was unexpected.

'You see old men – well, one or two old men – and you know, just by looking at them, they've "had a good life", slept with lots of women. And you like them for it, respect them for it. You don't think of the pain they've caused. That's safely in the past. No, they had a zest for life, they valued life, they lived it to the full. But you're not old yet. And what you do, and why you do it, it's not life-affirmative at all; it's bitter, *mean*. And you don't value life, of course, because what you did, indirectly I know but, what you did, led to three children dying and I've seen no guilt at all. No remorse. So, all in all, I think I'm beginning to despise you. Ever so slightly, of course.'

The threatened rain had begun to fall, heavily, as Simone Parr left the house. John had hidden the car keys and she had no option but to walk to the hotel. She arrived, soaked, dishevelled, her wet hair dripping down her neck and her make-up all streaked, carrying a small suitcase. Doreen Archer looked up and raised a thinly plucked eyebrow as Simone padded through reception, leaving a trail of wet footprints. She went to the lounge and looked through the open door. Piped piano music was playing softly, the overhead lights had been switched off and the table lamps switched on, casting warm pools of light and throwing other parts of the room into seductive shadows. Arthur Thwaite, in his barman's uniform, served a tray of drinks to a couple in the window seat where she and Chef usually sat. He moved away and she saw their faces: Chef and Lucy Archer. Simone couldn't believe her eyes. She put down her case and took a step into the room, creating a murmur that rippled through the room as people noticed her drowned-rat appearance. Chef looked across at her. Lucy did too. She leaned close and whispered something, her lips brushing his earlobe, and they both glanced at Simone again and laughed. She fled, totally humiliated.

A meeting with Emma was worth the risk of getting chucked out of the hotel again, thought Danny. Besides, Archer didn't usually check out the Ramblers Bar in the evening – he would be too busy flitting between the restaurant and lounge acting important – so it was probably safe. Tharmy (who had custody of the hose at last, Albie having got bored) had caught up with Danny as he walked back up the drive after his run-in with Slater and stammered, 'Emma said to tell you she'd b-b-b-b-be here tonight about t-t-t-t-t-ten,' and Danny's heart had leapt. He showered, shaved and dressed as carefully as he would have for a first date and got there early. Emma was late. By the time she arrived, Danny was in a state. He had convinced himself she wasn't going to show. 'Where's the baby?' he asked, stupid with nerves.

'My mam's minding her. I said I'd only be five minutes.'

His face fell. 'Does she know you're with me?'

'No.'

'We're married, for God's sake. We've got a child. And you've got to sneak out to see me,' he said, piqued.

'Whose fault's that?' Emma wasn't going to give him an easy ride. She missed him like crazy but she'd had a lot of time to think things through. He couldn't answer. She turned her frank, open face up and fixed Danny with her cat's eyes. 'You're a scally from Liverpool. You've got –'

'Thanks.'

' – their daughter – I'm telling you how *they* see it. Not how I see it. You got their daughter pregnant. You took her away to Liverpool. You were too bone idle to get a job. When you *did* get a job you gambled away your wages. You went thieving, got thrown in jail. She came back home. End of a sorry chapter in their daughter's life.

But it's not the end. You turn up again and drown their niece.'

Having it summed up so brutally – and accurately – was devastating. Danny played with the foam in the bottom of his beer glass, tipping it backwards and forwards, unable to look at her. Finally he muttered, 'Nobody's perfect,' but it didn't sound funny, even to him. She stood up abruptly and left.

At the same time in another corner of the bar the kitchen staff were discussing sexual politics. Julie had had a few strong ciders and was getting worked up. 'You always say it. I've been there when you've said it.' She glared accusingly at Albie.

'You're talkin' a load of crap,' he said, swigging from a bottle.

'As soon as you've been with anyone she's "a slag".'

'Bollocks.'

'You said it about me.'

'That's different. You *are* a slag.'

'What?' She took a threatening step towards him. Tharmy, who was refereeing, caught the barmaid's eye – she was new, pretty but shy – and smiled. Albie noticed and said in an aside, 'You've got no chance.' But the barmaid smiled back. Julie and Albie continued to slug it out while Joey, as always, hovered on the edge of the group. Observing Tharmy's tentative flirtation, Joey commented, 'He tried to summon up the courage.' Which was exactly what Tharmy did. He crossed to the bar and smiled at the girl again. She smiled back, waiting for him to speak. It was a long wait. Eventually she said, 'Yes?' Tharmy's mouth puckered as he tried, desperately, to say 'Two pints of bitter.' He couldn't make it past the first 't'. The barmaid's smile had been replaced by a look of horror as Tharmy's battle with the elusive consonant went on and on. He stopped and smiled. She forced a smile back. Tharmy tried again.

The swing doors banged and Danny, who was sitting dejectedly over his ale, looked up, hoping it might be Emma returning. Instead, he saw the bedraggled figure of Simone Parr, carrying a little case, her face a mess of blotches and mascara. She wiped a hand across her cheeks and, spotting someone she recognized, went over to Danny. 'Will you help me?' She was a pathetic sight. Who was he to judge her for what she'd done after Emma's stinging verdict on him? Danny didn't ask any questions, he merely nodded. From across the room there was a crash as Tharmy, who had blown it with the new girl, drove his fist into the bar in frustration and sent a beer glass tumbling to the floor.

Simone looked wiped out. She was chilled and trembling and had a bruise forming on the side of her face. She said she needed somewhere to stay the night but didn't volunteer any information. Danny reckoned he could guess the rest, although he wouldn't have put her husband down as the violent type. They went back to the boathouse, two outcasts together, talking little, each nursing their own, ultimately self-inflicted, wounds. As there was only one rather narrow bunk, he let her have it, saying he'd kip in the chair. Simone did not protest. She lay down and was soon asleep, leaving Danny alone with his thoughts. He sat listening to the patter of the rain on the corrugated-iron roof and Simone's regular breathing and felt himself drifting off into the no-man's-land between dreaming and waking, so that when the words of a poem he'd once heard and liked in Liverpool came into his head he did not know quite how they got there. What they meant, though, was clearer to him than ever before:

'An old experienced singer
Is sitting by the bar,
Brushing ashes from his sleeve
Like one who's travelled far.

Outside it's started raining,
The moon begins her song,
Getting out his Tarot cards
He says, "This won't take long."
He tells me to stop fighting
My mind's demented twin,
He says, "My friend we're all afraid
Beneath these masks of skin".'

Danny woke up stiff and aching with pins and needles in one arm and a new sense of resolution. Simone had gone.

It was the ultimate degradation. She had to ring her own doorbell – her house keys were on the same ring as the confiscated car keys – and hope that her husband would have her back. Simone felt like something the cat had dragged in and worse, and she knew she looked it. What had looked drop-dead sexy when she was getting ready to go out the night before made her look like a tired old tart in the unforgiving morning light. She felt drained, emotionally and physically, by the double blow of her husband's rape and her lover's casual rejection, while overhanging it all was the nagging knowledge that, but for her affair, three children would not have drowned. Simone detested herself, she loathed John, but most of all she hated Chef for using her so callously – using her up; there was nothing left of cool, collected Simone Parr, the headmaster's wife – and then discarding her like a disgusting old rag. Chef had exposed a sexual side of her she hadn't known existed; he had also, she was beginning to discover, put her in touch with a rage she had never experienced before either. It gave her something to hang on to.

After knocking loudly several times – was he rubbing it in or so hungover he couldn't hear her? – John opened the door. He looked equally dreadful, as if he'd slept in his clothes, and his eyes were bloodshot. 'Have you been with him all night?' he demanded, holding on to the door. His breath still stank of whisky. Simone was past caring what he thought. 'What d'you want to hear, John? Yes, I've been with him all night. Yes, he's shagged me silly all night. Yes, he's better than you. Yes, it's twice as long as yours, twice as hard as yours. Is that what you want to hear?' He looked at her with distaste and walked back into the hall, leaving the door open. Simone picked up her case and went inside.

Paula's little coffin was in the Thwaites' living room, the ends resting on a couple of upright chairs. Mourners had been arriving at the wake for the past hour and the house was packed. Children were sitting on the stairs, staring bug-eyed through the banisters at the white box with the brass handles glimpsed through the doorway, wondering if their school friend was really in it. Wondering, too, what she looked like now. The atmosphere was sombre, people sipping sherry and whisky and talking quietly, until Granddad nudged Peter and said, 'We can't let the little lass go without a song. Keep the old Irish tradition going, eh? What was that one you sang at Kathleen's do?'

Peter looked into his father-in-law's rheumy eyes and said, 'I'm not sure if that would be appropriate, Dad.' He cast a questioning glance at Sheila, who was sitting nearby. She nodded. Peter stood up and, resting one hand on the coffin, began to sing. Everyone fell silent. He sang from the heart, with his eyes closed, delivering the old Irving Berlin song in a strong and surprisingly tuneful voice:

> 'I know a millionaire
> Who's burdened down with care,
> A load is on his mind.
> He's thinking of the day
> When he must pass away
> And leave this wealth behind.
> I haven't any gold

To leave when I grow old
Somehow it passed me by.
I'm very poor but still
I'll leave a precious will
When I must say goodbye.
I'll leave the sunshine to the flowers
I'll leave the springtime to the trees
And to the old folks
I'll leave the mem'ries
Of a baby upon their knees
I'll leave the nighttime to the dreamers
I'll leave the songbirds to the blind
I'll leave the moon above
To those in love
When I leave the world behind.
When I leave the world behind.'

Father Matthew, who led the funeral procession from the house to St Michael and Latter Day Saints, was more moved by Peter's singing than he would have thought possible. It seemed to release a wave of emotion: real, powerful, human emotion, expressed in a direct and passionate way, unlike the impersonal dry-as-dust rituals of the Church. They seemed meaningless on the occasion of this small child's burial. So did a lot of other things. Ever since that terrible day when he had knelt and seen the little girl's lifeless body in the police launch, he had been asking questions that God would not – or could not – answer. The event had triggered a deep soul-searching, forcing him to want to be honest about his own crisis of faith with the congregation. If he could not believe in the redeeming power of the Holy Spirit, how could he ask them to? And what could he offer them instead?

Father Matthew had faced dilemmas many times before, but they had always been over what course of action to take or not to take, such as going on a political rally or putting up passive resistance at a demonstration. He had never, until now, had cause to question the bedrock of faith on which his existence as a person and as a priest was founded. Long nights of prayer and meditation had provided no respite: they simply threw his predicament into sharper relief, provoking yet more questions. How had he come to be so complacent? Walking high on the fells he had even considered abandoning the priesthood, especially when he thought of Bernie Quinlan, which he did, often. He had not spent time with her since the drowning, apart from once, when she came to confession and admitted, guiltily, her 'deal' with God at the boat-landing. Even that admission had not shocked him like it might have previously: he was beginning to understand about the ruthlessness of human love.

Father Matthew watched as the pall-bearers, Peter and Arthur at their head, walked with measured pace up the aisle and set down the coffin. He asked the congregation to be seated and looked around at the many familiar, trusting faces before him. He knew what they expected to hear, what they wanted to hear. He took a deep breath. 'I'm not going to insult Arthur and Sheila by mouthing platitudes about the love of God, about Paula being safe in the arms of God, because God seemed to take precious little care of her the day she died. The love of God was strangely absent that day. But it's here now. It's the love of your neighbour. And your friend. That's the love of God.'

He could not depart from the party line at the graveside but the words stuck in his throat and condemned him all the same. 'I am the resurrection and the life. He who believes in me, even if he dies, shall live. And whoever lives and believes in me shall never die.' He heard weeping as the coffin was lowered into the ground and the gulping sobs of little Annie Quinlan, who was clinging to her mother's hand, were the most pitiful of all. Mourners stepped forward one by one and threw flowers into the grave. Paula's friends, tremulous, added little keepsakes and cards they'd made at school. Sheila drew out of her handbag an old teddy bear that had one eye missing and stuffing leaking from his lining – Paula's first toy – and cuddled it to her breast before throwing it in on top of the flowers. Neither she nor Arthur cried: tears were the easy part, the shock reaction. Living with grief every day, seeing Paula's coat hung up, her photograph on the sideboard, her shoes in the cupboard – even the child benefit cheques, which she hadn't got round to cancelling – was much, much harder.

Gradually, people dispersed, leaving the open grave and strolling round the yew-tree-dotted churchyard to other graves of friends and loved ones – most had family buried there. Sheep's wool drifted in the uncut grass. The head-stones went back two centuries: some were carved and polished but many were upstanding irregular-shaped slabs of local slate, reflecting the towering brown peaks that enfolded the little church and its community. The Quin-lans made their way to the grave of Kathleen Toolan, born Kilkenny 1932, died Hawksmere 1980. Peter rested a hand on Granddad's shoulder. Once more he struck up in his rich tenor, this time the strains of 'Abide With Me'. Granddad joined in shakily, then Bernie, then the rest of the family, then others at nearby graves, until the whole churchyard resounded with the hymn.

Danny caught the singing, even though he wasn't there. Knowing the emotions his presence would arouse he had stayed away and was watching the proceedings, saying his own goodbye to the girls, from some distance up a hill. His vantage point was a rocky outcrop – the moorland began the other side of the dry-stone wall enclosing the churchyard, rising fairly steeply to the terrace on which he was hidden – from which he had a good view of the neat, slate-built church with its stumpy tower and gold weathervane. He had been listening to the rooks cawing from a row of tall trees below when he saw the crocodile of mourners leave the church porch and follow the flower-bedecked white coffin to the graveside. He couldn't make out individuals, apart from Father Matthew in his distinctive robes, but he could visualize them. Many of the faces he would have seen, under happier circumstances, at his and Emma's wedding and Samantha's christening. Remembering those occasions made Danny realize that he, too, had his own ties of blood to the small church. When he heard 'Abide With Me' he found himself joining in, even though he knew only half the words.

SIXTEEN

The day after the funeral, Sheila threw herself into an orgy of clearing out. With her daughter in the ground she could not bear to be taunted by physical reminders of her: the pale strands of hair in a comb, the scent of her skin on the sheets, Paula's small pink toothbrush in the glass next to hers and Arthur's. Each separate item was impregnated with memories and meaning, stopping Sheila at every turn. She spoke to Arthur and they made a decision: neither of them wanted to turn her room into a shrine.

When Bernie came round to check on her sister, she found her going through Paula's cupboards and drawers, clothes sorted into piles on the bed and more bags of clothes and toys heaped on the floor. Sheila worked relentlessly with a single-minded focus, allotting articles to a category – keep, chuck, Oxfam – not allowing herself to pick things up and linger over them. She was flushed and breathing hard, strands of hair escaping and falling into her eyes. 'Shall I do it?' asked Bernie, concerned. Sheila did not answer. Instead, she opened a wardrobe and took out a coat on a hanger. 'Would Annie like it? It's hardly worn.'

Bernie didn't know what to say. She could guess what Annie's reaction was likely to be. 'Would you like her to wear it?' she ventured.

'Yes,' said Sheila, decisively.

Annie, predictably, freaked out at the suggestion and locked herself in her room for most of the day. That evening, unable to bear the tensions in the family – Emma was withdrawn, Pete moody and Granddad was driving

Peter mad by reminiscing about the old days in Ireland – Bernie went to confession. She had to get the business about the coat off her chest.

'You couldn't tell Sheila the truth?' suggested Matthew gently.

'"Sorry, Sheila, my daughter won't wear your daughter's coat 'cause your daughter's dead."'

'You wouldn't have to put it quite so bluntly.' He sensed she was pretty strung up. 'How are things at home?'

'No one's killed anyone yet.'

'How's Peter?'

'Peter's a good man,' she said defensively. 'I love him. I've loved him for twenty years. I know I've told you things but I don't want you to use those things. I think it's –'

'I'm not using anything,' he interrupted, protesting.

'– wrong for you to use anything I've told you.'

'I'm not using anything.'

There was a short silence. Bernie said, 'I shouldn't've come.'

Both of them thought the church was empty – they hadn't heard Danny Kavanagh enter and take a seat outside the confessional. He shifted uneasily in his seat, catching snatches of their conversation and wondering if he should make himself scarce. Father Matthew was asking, 'So why did you come?' and his voice was not the dispassionate tone of a confessor.

Bernie replied, 'We were friends. Special friends. I valued that. It was part of my life. Like coming to this church is part of my life. Coming to Mass. Now all of a sudden there's danger in our friendship and I'm the one who has to suffer, I'm the one who has to make sacrifices: keep away from you, from church, from Mass. Well, I'm not prepared to do that. It's your problem as well, Matthew.'

There was a click as she undid the door. Bernie came

out looking upset and was clearly surprised to see Danny. 'All right?' he said self-consciously, but she hurried past him and did not answer. No one else was waiting so he popped his head into the vacated confessional to see if Father Matthew was still open for business. Through the grille he could see the priest, sitting with his head in his hands, apparently lost in thought. 'All right?' Danny said again. Father Matthew looked up, bewildered. For a moment he seemed lost for words, and then, unexpectedly, he asked, 'D'you fancy a drink?'

Danny was relieved: he hadn't been in a confessional since he was ten when his mother used to make him put on his best clothes and go with her. He remembered the oppressive musty smell, counting the knot-holes in the wooden panelling to distract himself from his claustro-phobia, and being afraid of wetting himself and leaving a pool on the seat. There seemed an enormous pressure to feed the faceless presence the other side of the grille with a diet of wrong-doings to earn forgiveness. At that age he would make up sins, coming up with increasingly far-fetched exploits, reasoning that if he racked up the bonus points for things he hadn't done it would put him in credit with God. It seemed unlikely, given the sins the mature Danny had committed, that he was still in the black, but that wasn't what had brought him back to the Church. These days a priest was the only person who would sit down and listen to him.

Matthew said he had a few beers in the fridge at home, which suited Danny fine. He had no wish to go back to the boathouse just at the moment. They sat at the kitchen table, moths banging into the bare light-bulb above them, and snapped the ring-pulls off a couple of cans of lager. 'So,' said Matthew, after a few good swallows of cold beer. Danny wiped his mouth with the back of his hand. 'I want to talk to you about something.'

'Fire away.'

'I wouldn't lie to a priest.'

'No?'

'Out in the street, in the ale-house, fair enough. But not in this situation, y'know what I mean?'

'Yes.' Matthew swatted at a moth.

Danny took a deep breath. 'I didn't let those kids out on the lake. The first time I saw them they were already out there. D'you believe me?' He looked at Matthew anxiously. Matthew fielded the question. 'Why are you telling me this?'

' 'Cause I want you to say you believe me. No one else does.'

'Apart from Emma.'

'Yeah.'

Matthew was silent. Eventually he said, 'Is it drugs?'

'What?'

'Emma was always short of money in Liverpool. Even when you were working. Were you spending your money on drugs?'

Danny was outraged. 'No.'

'On what then?' Matthew persisted, retrieving two more cans from the fridge door.

'I wasn't spending me money on anything,' he muttered, swilling back the remains of the first can and reaching for his second.

'You said you wouldn't lie to a priest,' Matthew said carefully. 'You've just done it. How can I believe anything you tell me?'

Danny was quiet for several minutes. Matthew did not push him, sensing that he was struggling with a difficult dilemma. Finally, Danny admitted, 'I was gambling.'

'Heavily?'

'Yeah.'

'Are you still gambling?'

'Not since the boat went down. I was on the phone to the bookie. That's why the kids were able to sneak into the boat. But I can't tell anyone that and you can't either 'cause I promised Emma I'd never gamble again.' He paused. It was a relief to admit to it at last. 'Do you believe me?' he asked again.

'Did it win?' said Matthew, thinking fast.

'The bet? Yeah. Hundred and twenty quid.'

'What did you spend it on?'

'Nothing. I never picked it up.'

'So, if I phone the bookie's there'll be £120 waiting for Danny Kavanagh?'

Danny put his beer down and stood up. 'Yeah, but you think I'm lying, so forget it.'

'I believe you,' Matthew reassured him.

'Yeah?'

'Yes.'

Danny sat down again and ran his hands through his hair. Suddenly he announced, 'I am guilty, yeah, but not in the way they think.' He was haunted by a picture that would not leave his mind. That morning, he had been rolling a cigarette and waiting for the sun to rise over the lake, as was his wont – he was sleeping little lately and often saw the dawn come up; it still amazed him how different the lake could look every day – when something out on the water caught his eye. Irrationally, his heart started racing – in the dim light, he thought at first it was another body, the bloated corpse of a little girl he had somehow missed when he saw the three of them in the boat. Maybe there had been four after all. But Annie was safe and no one else was missing. Somebody else then? His hand shook as he pulled hard on the roll-up, which crackled and glowed at the tip, scorching his throat as he inhaled. He strained his eyes, staring at the dark mass, until gradually the first rays of light spread down from the opposite fell and skated across the lake, illuminating the scene and changing it from one of blackness and horror to azure harmony. Floating on the tranquil surface was a bouquet of flowers. Inexplicably, Danny found he was crying. 'I promised her I wouldn't gamble,' he continued, trying to explain something to Matthew. 'I was gonna swear on a life, any bleeding life. My granddad lived to ninety-two so I know it's a pile of crap. You know what I mean.' Matthew shook his head, bemused. 'I swore on me granddad's life about a thousand times and every time I was lying through me teeth and nothin' happened to him, so I know it's a pile of crap, but I promised not to gamble and as soon as I pick up the phone to have a little bet a bleedin' boat goes down and three kids –' He rammed his fists into his eyes, unable to go on. 'Shite.'

That Sunday the church was packed, the congregation – many of whom were family and relatives of the deceased – needing to draw succour after the tragedy. The small community was united in grief: a mass of floral tributes had appeared outside the school and a memorial fund had already been set up. It was also united in its strength of feeling about Danny Kavanagh. Father Matthew was aware of this when he prepared his sermon. It meant striking a delicate balance.

Facing the congregation he said: 'We remember poor little Susan Charles and Lisa Graham and Paula Thwaite. And we think of the pain and grief their parents are going through. Lord, hear us.'

'Lord, graciously hear us.'

'And we remember all those involved in that terrible accident. Sarah Kilbride, our doctor; Sergeant Slater and the other police officers; the ambulancemen. And we remember especially a young man who's being blamed for that accident, Danny Kavanagh. Lord, hear us.'

The priest's words came like a kick in the guts for Sheila. She sat, tight-lipped, refusing to join in the response. Confused glances were exchanged as the congregation mumbled, with considerably less enthusiasm, 'Lord, graciously hear us.' Emma Quinlan, her eyes shining, was the only person who spoke the words clearly. Bernie, like Sheila, found it impossible to understand Father Matthew's motives, but her confusion had a different source.

'Lamb of God who takes away the sins of the world,' Matthew intoned.

'Grant us peace.'

'Let us offer each other the sign of peace.' People stood and embraced their neighbours or shook hands with those behind them. Bernie watched as Matthew, making his way down the aisle, hugged several women, saying, 'Peace be with you.' She was on the end of their pew; contact was inevitable. Matthew reached Bernie, looked at her and held out his arms – to the woman standing behind. Bernie was upset, the more so when later he hesitated before giving her the communion wafer. There was an interminable pause as his troubled eyes held hers, until the man behind her coughed, breaking the spell, and Matthew reached out his hand and said shakily, 'Body of Christ.' Sheila Thwaite did not go up to receive communion at all. Instead, she walked out.

She was waiting, a set expression on her face, when the Quinlans left the church. 'Are you OK?' Bernie asked, going over to her.

'Yes,' said Sheila, not taking her eyes off Father Matthew, who was in the porch bidding goodbye to people. When the last person had left, she went over to him and launched a bitter salvo. 'You're a disgrace to the priesthood, Matthew. It's easy to be trendy, easy to pray for killers when it's not your child that's been killed, when it's not you thirsting for justice. You've no idea what it's like to have a child, never mind lose one. You can't possibly know the pain I'm going through, so how dare you come out with phony, trendy shite when I'm sitting in your pew, grieving.' She took a shaky breath and carried on, 'And Paula's funeral – I'm telling you this while I'm in the mood, Matthew. A few home truths. My child's funeral and you're spouting about being angry with God and "community" and "neighbours" and not once did you tell me I'd see Paula again. Nobody, not one single soul, has told me I'll see Paula again.' She started to sob, but brushed the tears away angrily and pulled herself together enough to say, 'And I think I had a right to hear it from my priest. You're a disgrace,' before breaking down completely and stumbling away. Father Matthew, who had not attempted to interrupt or contradict her, turned and walked back inside. Emma chased after her aunt and put an arm around her heaving shoulders. Bernie was left standing at the open door, alone.

Having unburdened himself to Father Matthew, Danny – who was unaware of how publicly the priest had stuck his neck out for him – was determined to talk to Emma, properly. He was ashamed of his flippant response to her the other night; having his record itemized like that had hurt, mostly because, deep down inside, he recognized it as the truth. Long sojourns in the boathouse had given him plenty of time to think things over and after owning up to his gambling problem his perspective had changed. Danny wanted to tell Emma that, which meant bearding Peter Quinlan in his den. He did not expect it to be a pleasant encounter.

Bernie opened the door. A cloud passed across her face when she saw him. 'Is Emma in?' Danny said it assertively; this time he wasn't going to be fobbed off.

'I don't want you coming –' Bernie began.

'*Is Emma in?*' he insisted, loudly.

'– round here, Danny. *No she isn't.*' Bernie raised her own voice to match Danny's.

'You're lying.'

There was a commotion in the hall and Peter Quinlan

appeared behind Bernie. 'You've got a bloody cheek, son,' he said angrily, attempting to get past her, 'coming round here.'

Bernie blocked his way, physically holding Peter back. 'Go in.' She tried to shove him back. Peter was like a ferocious dog straining at the leash. 'You've got some bloody cheek. If I catch –'

'Go,' Bernie screamed at Danny.

'I want to see my wife.'

'– you round here again – if I ever get my hands on you I'm gonna –' Peter was puce. He shook Bernie off and grabbed Danny's collar, half-throttling him.

'I want to see my wife. Right?' choked Danny.

Bernie, agitated, shouted into the house for help. 'Pete, *Pete!*'

'– rip your bloody head off. The fucking grief you've –' Peter was spitting in Danny's face.

Still Danny refused to back down. 'I want to see my wife and bloody kid.'

'– caused around here. The fucking grief you've given everyone. Have you got –' Footsteps as Pete ran down the hall. He took hold of his father's arm, trying to drag him off Danny.

'He's not worth it, Dad. Right?'

'For God's sake, *go*,' Bernie yelled, as Pete separated them.

'No,' Danny said stubbornly. He stood his ground.

'– a bloody conscience, you toe-rag?' Peter continued to bellow at him over his son's shoulder. Pete pushed him back down the hall.

'He's just a scumbag. He's not worth it. He's just a bloody scumbag so leave him.' They disappeared into the living room, from where Peter continued to rant audibly.

Danny and Bernie regarded each other in silence, Bernie wondering how much Danny had overheard outside the confessional. His look said: some. It was a bargaining chip but she wasn't prepared to negotiate. Danny tried anyway. 'I suppose a cup of tea's out the question then?' The door slammed in his face before he had even finished the sentence. He did not see Emma watching from the front bedroom window as he trailed back up the path, although he couldn't fail to miss Sheila Thwaite's drawn features as he passed by their house further down the hill. A low-flying jet shattered the peace once again, its blast like a manifestation of the emotional turbulence that seethed below.

Bernie felt as if her head would explode and the sensation had nothing to do with the window-shaking noise of the jet. She couldn't bear the tension in the room – Peter was pacing like a caged tiger and Pete was still trying to calm him by repeating, 'He's just a scumbag. Don't let him get to y'.' Granddad had made tea and Bernie was waiting, just waiting, for him to sniff the milk. He did, of course. It was one time too many. She got up and left the room. 'Where are you going?' shouted Pete.

'Out.'

Bernie hadn't planned to go to Matthew's, but somehow she ended up at his door. 'You want to talk?' she asked, as casually as she dared.

'Desperately,' he said.

She followed him into the kitchen. Out of habit, he filled the kettle. Despite her own pain, Bernie had been acutely aware that Matthew was undergoing some kind of crisis. The telepathic bond between them had never been broken, merely stretched, and when Sheila had ripped into him, it was, surprisingly, Matthew Bernie had felt for, more than her sister. 'She didn't mean it,' Bernie said, perching on the edge of the table.

Matthew poured boiling water on the tea. 'She meant it,' he replied grimly. He put the tea things on a tray and turned to her. 'You know why I couldn't say it? Because I don't believe it. They're all up there on a cloud, are they?

All the billions who've died, who've been slaughtered, gassed, blown to bits, they're all up there on a cloud, playing their harps. It's a fairy tale. Reality's a little girl, nose and mouth caked in mud, dead. And I couldn't respond to that with a fairy tale. But I should've done. To hell with my integrity, I should've lied through my teeth.' He glanced at the teapot disdainfully. 'You want a drink?'

'No.'

'Glass of wine?'

'No.'

'Have a glass of wine.'

'Do you want one?'

'Yes.'

'Then have one,' she said calmly.

He fetched a bottle of cheap red from a cupboard and got out a corkscrew. 'I don't belong here.' Matthew struggled with the cork. It slid out with a pop and he splashed some into a glass.

'You're the best priest we've ever had.' Bernie meant it.

'I'm a city priest. Derelict flats, abandoned factories, racism, dole queues: I love it. Something to get my teeth into, something to keep me busy, something to stop me thinking, "What the bloody hell am I doing with my life?"' He took a large swig and winced. It was rough stuff.

'She didn't mean it. It was grief talking. She's told me many a time what a wonderful priest you are.' Suddenly, Bernie was panicking. She could hear what he was really saying and she didn't want him to go.

'She's said that?' Matthew looked disbelieving.

'Yes,' Bernie insisted, her eyes on his face. He looked so miserable and vulnerable, standing there in his squalid kitchen with his shoulders all hunched. They fell silent, sensing a moment that had passed before. She wanted to hug him. He wanted to hug her. Both of them knew it would be hard, if not impossible, to stop there: the memory of their kiss by the lake was too strong. Matthew put down his glass and walked round the table towards the door. 'I've got to make a few calls,' he said, going to the phone, which was on a shelf next to the fridge. 'Right,' Bernie replied, watching him dial and hold the receiver to his ear. She raised her hand and slipped out. Matthew waited until she had gone and then replaced the receiver. After that he drank the rest of the bottle of wine.

SEVENTEEN

Ruth wondered who it was this time. Chef came home late smelling different these days. It wasn't Simone Parr's classy perfume, expensive stuff. He reeked of some brazen, in-your-face modern scent. And he had that tanked-up energy he always had at the start of a new affair – it usually spilled over into their bed; Ruth got a bit too, if she was lucky. Or unlucky. Depended on how you looked at it. She eyed Chef, who was spraying anti-perspirant under his arms preparatory to going out. 'I passed my test today,' she announced. It was a big thing for her, striking a blow for independence.

'Yeah?' he said, disinterested, putting on a shirt.

'No need to make a song and dance about it,' she retorted dryly, thinking, why bother?

'What?' He was miles away, thinking of Her already, no doubt.

'Nothing. I thought you might like to take me out. To celebrate.'

'Can't.'

'Why not?' Make him say it.

'Thomas.' Pathetic excuse.

'There's no evidence that he's possessed,' she said hotly. 'I'd manage to find a babysitter somewhere.' Chef didn't bother to reply. 'There's a rumour going round that you've murdered me, buried me under the patio,' Ruth baited him. 'It would be nice for people to see me, just to disprove it.'

Chef slapped on aftershave, bared his teeth in the mirror and, satisfied with his appearance, headed for the door. 'Don't wait up.'

*

Matthew was trembling on a knife edge. One little puff and he'd blow over, into the chasm, falling down and down into the pits of hell. Only he wasn't sure if he believed in the pits of hell and a devil with burning eyes and horns any more than he currently believed in the accepted version of heaven. His overwhelming attraction to Bernie was temptation all right, and he was sorely tempted, but it wasn't Satan whispering in his ear. He had heard enough confessions to know how fallible the human male was. It was him. *He* wanted her.

Yet at the same time as the doubts crowded his brain, his intellect wanted to play dumb. He had invested his entire adult life, almost thirty years, studying for his vocation and giving himself to the priesthood, without questioning whether his belief was founded on shifting sands. It was too much to throw it all away. Emotionally he needed confirmation that this was an aberration, that he was valued for what he did, that it meant something to others. Did it matter what he thought in his heart of hearts? People, people like Sheila Thwaite, needed him: to withhold reassurance from her was to cut her off from her faith. *Her* faith. Not just his. He decided to try to mend fences. Bernie he pushed to the back of his mind.

At the following Sunday service, Sheila made her protest silently, resolutely remaining seated when Matthew said, 'Let us offer each other the sign of peace.' While others hugged and shook hands, she stayed put in her pew, staring glassily ahead. He walked towards her and said, 'Sheila?' but she ignored him. The Quinlans, two rows behind, noticed the snub. This time Bernie stepped out into the aisle, practically waylaying Matthew, demanding that he take notice of her. How strange, she thought, that the only place she was sanctioned to hold him was in church, when it was the Church that was denying them from embracing. But still he avoided her, swerving away to a woman on the other side of the aisle, leaving her feeling more miserable, more rejected and more hopeless than she could ever remember feeling before.

The depression lasted all day. She went about her domestic routine in a haze, hardly noticing what she was doing, operating on autopilot. That evening, as they finished their tea, Peter said suddenly, 'Have you fallen out with him?'

'Who?' Bernie asked, not thinking.

'Father Matthew.'

It was a shock to hear her husband mention Matthew's name, to make any kind of connection between them. She played for time, listening to Annie, who was vying for Pete's attention. 'He says, "D'you want to buy this watch?"'

'Is this one of your stupid jokes?' Pete was scornful.

'It's brill. He says, "This watch'll never lose a second. It's the best watch in the world."'

Bernie looked up at Peter. 'No.'

'So he buys it,' Annie continued. 'That night the gongs go for *News at Ten*. He looks at his watch: half-past five. So he says to his wife, "'Ey, have you been messing around with this telly?"' Her brother pulled an unimpressed face.

'It looked like you've fallen out with him,' Peter remarked.

Emma was feeding the baby, who was sitting in a high chair. 'Come on, just another spoonful. That's a good girl.' Granddad brought in the tea tray.

'We had a few words,' Bernie admitted.

'What about?'

'Sheila.'

'That's not like you.'

'No?' she said, watching Granddad pour.

'No. Put a monkey in a dog collar, you'd worship the ground it walked on.' It was a direct hit, belittling both her faith and her feelings for Matthew. She shot him a poisonous look. Granddad lifted the carton of milk to his nose. Bernie exploded. 'For God's sake, I am sick and tired of you sniffing the bloody milk. Do you think I'd give you sour milk? Have I ever given you sour bloody milk? No. So for Christ's sake, stop sniffing the bloody thing.' The baby squealed. Annie and Pete stopped arguing. Granddad's hand froze where it was, still holding the pint up. Everyone stared at Bernie.

The lads weren't judging Danny: they all knew what a little cow Lucy Archer was. Besides, as Albie pointed out when he rang Danny at the boathouse, the off-comers had to stick together. What he actually said was, 'You don't wanna take any notice of them inbred locals, mate. They're all peculiar in the 'ead. Anyway, we'll see you right – come down the pub with us tomorrow and we'll show 'em.' But it amounted to the same thing.

Danny met up with them in the village store – there was safety in numbers and the old dears behind the counter were too busy tut-tutting over Tharmy's stutter – he was trying to buy a lighter – to go for Danny when he nipped in to buy tobacco. 'Right,' said Albie, cracking his knuckles and grinning broadly, 'Let's go to work.' They lit up outside the shop, donned their shades – it was a blazing hot late-summer day, producing a crop of scarlet-faced walkers – and strolled off up the street four abreast, with attitude. As they rolled up the hill towards the pub, Albie picked up on the thread of an argument he'd obviously been having with Tharmy. 'Look, I know it was you. Right?' Tharmy shook his head, trying to get something out. Albie ploughed on regardless. 'I know it and don't try and say "wasn't" 'cause –'

'Wasn't,' Tharmy managed at last, triumphantly.

'It was. It was –'.

'What's he done?' Danny interrupted.

'– you. Right?' Albie persisted.

'Wasn't.' Now he'd mastered it, Tharmy delighted in the word.

'You're a liar.'

'What's he done?' Danny repeated.

Albie looked embarrassed. 'They're calling me Julie behind my back, aren't they?'

'Wasn't me who started it. Right?' Hostility had made Tharmy unusually eloquent.

Joey, true to form, had been silent so far. He loved the walk, being part of the gang. Looking along the line he announced, '*Reservoir Dogs* comes to mind.'

'Why Julie?' asked Danny.

'You know why,' Albie said, obstreperously.

'I don't.'

'Julie Andrews. "Do, a deer." And it's down to him. Right? That gobshite.' Danny felt an involuntary smile crease his face. It was good to be back on familiar ground.

'I never said nothin'. Right? I never –' Tharmy protested.

'You did, you lying get.'

'– started nothing.'

The conversation continued in the same vein but Danny's attention wandered as he caught sight of Arthur Thwaite walking towards them. It was a meeting he had been dreading and he was glad to have back-up. Arthur eyeballed him, his expression murderous. As he drew level, he spat in Danny's face. The message was clear: you are the lowest form of life to crawl this earth. Stunned, Danny wiped his mouth on his sleeve. None of the others had even noticed.

In many ways, Emma was as isolated as Danny. She was tainted by association with him, which meant it was impossible to stand up for him in public, or in front of her family, without getting flack. Especially because of Paula. All things considered, it was easier to keep a low profile, which was why she hadn't come down when he called round a few days ago. Home life was tense enough as it was. Privately, she found it hard to believe what people were saying, but a nagging worm of doubt remained at the back of her mind. He had lied to her enough times in the past, hadn't he? So he wanted to see her. Why? To feed her more stories? Better to get on with her own life, concentrate on bringing up Samantha. She rejoiced in her baby, playing with her, holding her, watching her change, grow, develop. But even that didn't come guilt-free. Her aunt Sheila, keeping up a vigil at her window as if she was waiting for Paula to return from school, followed Emma with her eyes when she walked past the house with the pram. It was beginning to get to her, so much so that she went round to see Father Matthew, somebody else whose name had apparently become *persona non grata* in the family.

'I never thought I'd get pregnant. I never thought I'd have a baby. That was for other women,' she began. 'I didn't think I was capable of it. But I was and, to tell you the truth, I was quite proud. Not right away. That was all panic and what-do-I-tell-me-mam, but after a bit I was quite proud. I'd achieved something. And I liked showing her off, showing my baby off. But then Sheila goes and loses her child, so I can't show my child off to Sheila any more because, well I can't, I can't even walk past her house without thinking: is she in there, watching me with my baby?'

'It'll get easier with time,' Matthew said.

Emma shook her head. 'No. Because who's the father of my child? Danny. Who's to blame for the death of her child? Danny. What does that do to her?'

'Danny's not to blame,' he said quietly.

'That's how she sees it.'

'She's wrong.'

Emma studied him carefully. 'You know that?'

'Yes. He might *feel* guilty but he isn't.'

'Feel guilty?' she pressed.

'Yes.'

'Why?'

'They did get into the boat.'

'When his back was turned.'

'Yes.'

'He hasn't got eyes in the back of his head.'

'I know.'

'So why feel guilty?'

'You should talk to Danny,' Matthew replied, realizing he had overstepped the mark.

'Have you talked to him?'

'Yes.'

'What are you hiding from me?' she demanded.

'Talk to Danny,' he said again.

Gambling was something you just did. It was as if it was in your blood, as if you were born to it. Thinking back, Danny couldn't recall what age he'd started betting, but he was very young, still a child. The bus stopped at some traffic lights on the outskirts of Penrith and he looked out of the window and saw a gang of young boys sitting on a wall, pushing each other, smoking, jeering at people in their cars. Then he remembered. It was the same time that he stopped going to church. Instead of spinning the priest a web of fictional sins, he'd had real ones that he didn't want to own up to.

There was a bloke who used to stand on the street corner on a Saturday who took illegal bets. Danny had done it for a dare, the first time, but when he ended up with four times his pocket money, he was hooked. It became a regular thing, he looked forward to Saturdays impatiently, and long before he was old enough to go into a betting shop he would loiter outside and ask someone to put a bet on – for his dad, he told them. Race days at Aintree were a family treat – everyone in Liverpool went to the Grand National – and once he'd experienced the thrill of being in the crowd as the field thundered past, he sometimes sloped off to meetings at nearby Chester and Haydock, where the bookies on the course would take bets from youngsters, so long as there wasn't a bobby around. He asked his dad to take him to the stadium for a night out at the dogs, and quickly became addicted to that, too. Not that he ever used the word addicted. It was just a bit of fun.

Danny had never examined why he gambled, or tried to explain it, to himself or anyone else. Admitting to Father Matthew that he was gambling had been a breakthrough. Accepting all the consequences of his gambling was much, much harder. Not even being sent to prison or losing his wife and child had stopped him. It had taken the deaths of three small girls to bring him to his senses. If he hadn't been placing a bet, they would never have gone out on the lake and drowned. So they paid the price. His price. One hundred and twenty quid. Divide that by three: £40 a head. He could throw that away tomorrow on one race. Life was cheap indeed.

He found the meeting room, which was bare and functional with a circle of hard chairs set out on the dusty floor and lots of ashtrays and a coffee machine on a table on the side. About a dozen other people were standing round, wearing shuttered expressions and smoking furiously. Danny was greeted by a middle-aged woman with short grey hair and a friendly face, who asked, 'Are you new?' When he nodded, dumbly, she got him a coffee, told him not to worry and introduced him to the group. They looked surprisingly normal.

When Danny's turn came to speak he didn't know what he was going to say. He stood up, glancing at the faces around him. This was what came out: 'It's the old woman who swallows a fly. Then a spider to catch the fly. And then a bird and a cat and God knows what. That's me when I'm doing me brains in. Lose a tenner. Lose twenty chasin' that tenner. Lose forty chasin' that twenty. And I'd blame her for it. I can't go home to her with half me wages; I'll get one of those looks, won't I? So I lose the other half chasin' that first half and go home absolutely bleedin' skint and I'm blamin' her or some jockey or some bleedin' trainer. I'd be blaming anyone but meself.'

Emma couldn't get Father Matthew's words out of her head. What had Danny told him? Why should he feel guilty if he had no reason to? Mulling it over as she walked back home, she reached a decision. She would have to go round there and talk to him.

Granddad was snoring in his favourite armchair when Emma got in, a newspaper rising and falling on his chest. Bernie was sitting on the sofa, her eyes closed. At first Emma thought her mother was asleep too, until she saw the rosary beads in her lap and noticed her lips moving silently. Her dad and Pete were nowhere to be seen – down the pub, boozing, she surmised. Emma went upstairs to look in on Samantha, feeling the back of her neck to check her temperature and tucking in the covers. She crept back downstairs, opened the living-room door and whispered, 'Mam.' Bernie opened her eyes. 'Can you listen out for Sammie? I'm going round to Delilah's for a bit.' Bernie nodded, shut her eyes again and continued her prayers.

It was dark when Emma reached the boathouse and she was glad to see Danny's light on. She was a little spooked by the walk: she had forgotten to take a torch and the final stretch along the footpath by the lake had been pretty creepy. There were lots of rustlings in the bushes; foxes, probably, but you never knew what weirdos were about. She tapped and called, 'It's me.' He opened the door, surprised.

'I've not long got in meself,' Danny said.

'Where?' Emma stepped inside.

'Oh, just out.' He did not elaborate. They looked at each other, both remembering the last time she had come round, the thunderstorm, their passionate kiss. This time Emma kept her distance. 'D'you want a cuppa?' Danny put the kettle on the Baby Belling. She glanced around the dimly lit boathouse, noticing how few things he had. Apart from the small cooker there was a toaster and a big, old-fashioned sink, but that was about it for mod cons. It was a pretty basic set-up. He was still reading poetry – Gerard Manley Hopkins had obviously survived the bailiffs' visit to their high-rise flat – and it looked as if he had been writing something, too, as she could see his scribble on an A4 pad by the bed. Emma wondered if Danny was lonely. She watched as he poured scalding water on to a teabag in a mug.

'What?' he asked, aware that she was observing him and feeling a little uneasy. Emma did not respond. 'What?' he said again. He never could read her mind. There was a slight scuffling noise outside. Hedgehogs trawling through the rubbish again, he thought. It was amazing the racket they made. Badgers came too, sometimes, if he left food out for them. Danny had sat out on a few balmy nights and watched the cubs rootling around with their mother.

'What did you tell Matthew?' Emma said suddenly.

'What?' he repeated, thrown.

'You heard.'

'Nothing.' What exactly had Matthew been saying?

'What do you feel guilty about?' Emma said fiercely, her cat's eyes glinting in the half-light.

So he'd talked. Some priest. 'He's got no right to be spouting to you about –'

'What do you feel guilty about?' She wasn't going to let it drop.

'– anything I've said. Nothing. I feel guilty about nothing.'

She moved closer to him, a full-scale row brewing.

'You've told him things that you haven't told me and I want –'

'I've told him nothing.'

' – to know what they are. I've got a right to –'

'I've told him nothing.'

' – know what they are 'cause I'm your wife and I'm going through it just as –'

'I don't know what you're talking about. Right?' he said furiously.

' – much as you are –'

A sharp knock on the door stopped them in mid-flow. One visitor a night was fairly unusual; two was unprecedented. 'Yeah?' Danny shouted, assuming it was Albie or Tharmy. No reply. Another knock. Must be Tharmy then. He went to the door, turned the key in the lock and opened it a crack to peer out. Immediately, men wearing dark clothes and balaclavas like terrorists stormed in and swarmed all over him shouting the place down. One of them got him in a headlock, screaming 'You fucker! You little bastard! You're gonna pay for what you did,' in his ear, forcing Danny's arm up behind his back so that he yelled in agony. 'Who are you, for fuck's sake?' he panted through gritted teeth, struggling. 'Get off me. Right? Get off me and get the fuck out of here. Get off – aargh.' He doubled up as another man punched him in the stomach, then kicked his legs from under him so that he crashed to the floor. Blood streamed from his nose. He felt a boot grinding into his back and screamed. Emma, backed into a corner, screamed too, as one of the gang grabbed her by the upper arms and shouted hoarsely, 'You keep out of this. We don't want to hurt you. It's him we want.'

'What for? You get your hands off me.' She tried to lash out but he held on to her tight. 'Let – me – go.' She let her body go limp suddenly so that his hold on her loosened, then dropped down and wrenched her shoulders free. He did not attempt to tackle her again; he went over to the others who were sticking the boot into Danny on the floor. Danny was curled in a foetal position, groaning and crying out with each kick. Emma was horrified. 'Stop it! Stop it! Leave him alone. What are you doing? Where are you going? *Let him go*,' she sobbed, as they half dragged, half carried Danny out of the door.

Danny was carted towards the lake, held horizontally, one man to each arm and leg. 'We know what you did, you scumbag. Let's see how you like it, shall we? Let's see how you like it under the water. Do you know what it's like to drown, Danny?' one of them ranted as they ran with him.

'I didn't do nothing. Right? I didn't do nothing for Christ's sake. She's telling a pack of lies about me. I didn't do nothing,' he repeated, over and over again. The four continued to shout abuse as they ran along the jetty with him and flung him down on the duckboards, his upper body hanging over the side. Then, the shock of freezing water filling his eyes, his ears and his nose as his head was plunged under and held down. They brought him up, gasping and screaming his innocence, while the ranting man yanked hold of him by the hair and said, 'You tell the fucking truth. Have you got that, you Scouse bastard? You tell the fucking truth at that inquest or we'll come back and drown you for real.' He forced his head back and under again. This time Danny wasn't quick enough and he swallowed a load of water and felt some trickle into his chest and came up coughing and retching. 'Ready to tell the truth, yet?' another roared. They ducked him again and again, and each time they let him up for air he croaked, 'I didn't do nothing. She's telling a pack of lies,' before the lake closed over his head. Just as he knew he had no resistance left, they let go and ran off, leaving Danny floundering and choking on the jetty.

Emma, who had been watching, terrified, from a distance, was in time to witness a car's headlights sweep up the track as the men got away. She ran down to the shore, her heart in her mouth, fearful of what she might find. Danny was on his hands and knees, vomiting up water and trembling violently, his lungs working like bellows. She knelt down beside him and rocked him against her. 'It's OK, Danny, I'm here. You're safe now. I've got you. I'm here.'

Danny couldn't face another night by himself in the boat-house after what happened. He'd hardly slept – every rustling leaf and fox's bark had made his heart race – and, when a mallard skidded on to the lake with a clatter of wings, he was halfway out of bed before he realized what it was. By then it was dawn and he went outside and saw evidence of his attackers – a jumble of footprints in the mud by the shore, tyre marks on the grass – but nothing that he could identify them by. All the same, Danny had a shrewd idea who the ringleader was and he wouldn't have lacked for volunteers.

That evening, desperate for company, he met up with the kitchen staff at the Ramblers Bar and told them all about it. 'Did you recognize any of them?' asked Julie, frowning at the cards in her hand. They were sitting round a table, playing pontoon for small stakes. Danny was watching. 'Twist,' she added. Albie turned over a nine of hearts.

'They wore masks,' Danny said.

'Their *voices*.'

'They all sound alike, don't they. Sheep-shaggers.' It was no use saying who he suspected; they'd only come back and give him a worse hiding if word got out that he was mouthing off.

'Well?' interrupted Albie, the dealer, impatiently.

'I'm thinking,' Julie insisted. She turned to Danny again. 'Did you tell the police?'

'Be'ave.' He pulled a finger across his throat. Julie didn't catch on.

'You should've done.' Albie sighed loudly. 'Twist

again,' she decided. He gave her a another card. Julie looked pleased. 'Stick.'

Albie turned to Joey. 'Yeah?'

Joey, hesitating, explained, 'He was caught in two minds.'

'What happens at an inquest?' Julie ploughed on.

'They decide the cause of death, don't they?' Danny kept his eyes on the cards.

'They drowned.'

'They *know* that,' he replied, nettled.

'So why have an inquest?'

'They're trying to blame someone, aren't they? They're trying to blame me.'

Albie tapped the table. 'Well?'

'He decided to twist,' said Joey. Albie turned over the ten of clubs. 'And instantly regretted it.' Joey had bust.

Julie, seeing Danny was upset, laid her hand on his arm. 'Why don't you just do one?'

'A runner? Where to?'

'Back to Liverpool.'

'You're jokin', aren't y'?' He snatched his arm away.

It was Tharmy's turn but he was having trouble saying 'twist'. Albie, looking around, noticed Ruth standing at the bar. She held his gaze. 'Who's that?' he asked, whistling softly.

Julie glanced up. 'Don't know.' The identity of Chef's wife had remained a mystery to the kitchen staff. 'Anywhere then,' she continued, speaking to Danny.

'She's giving me the eye.' Albie was excited. She was an older woman, yes, but they tended to be more appreciative. And they had more patience.

'My wife and kid are here,' Danny said.

'You hardly ever see them.'

'I see them.'

Albie returned his attention to the table. 'What do you want to do?' he bullied Tharmy, who was still trying, and failing, to say 'twist'. Albie turned over a card – a king – for him, making Tharmy go bust. He swept up Tharmy's money. 'What are you doing?' demanded Tharmy, suddenly eloquent.

'You wanted to twist.'

'I didn't.'

'You were trying to say "twist".'

'I was trying to say "stick",' he protested.

'You lying bastard.'

'I was trying to say "stick".'

'You've just said "stick". You've just said it twice. So how come you couldn't say it before?' Albie had him there.

'Give us me fucking money.'

'Fuck off. Say "twist".'

'Give us it.' Tharmy reached for the pile.

Albie put his hand over it. 'Say "twist". Say "twist" and I'll believe you.' Tharmy made a goldfish face but couldn't get the word out.

'Sussed. Right? That's how you were before. Right?' Tharmy's mouth puckered. 'That's how your mouth was before,' Albie said. 'If you were tryin' to say "stick" you'd go like that, wouldn't y'? St-st-st-' He pushed his lips out. Tharmy was still making a fish face.

'He thought: Thank God it's not snap,' observed Joey.

John Parr was pouring out his heart again on the phone – a modern cordless model – a glass of scotch by his side. He was not drunk, merely talkative, but then it was still early in the evening. 'The first time was nine months ago apparently. Boxing night. They did it in room 34 of the hotel.' He got up and began pacing the living room. 'I asked her if she still loves him. She said no. I asked her if she hates him. She said yes. But why does she hate him? She hates him because he hurt her so much. And he could only hurt her so much because she loved him.'

Hearing a car pull up outside, John peered through the window and saw Simone get out. Arthur Thwaite, who was walking up the drive towards the house, hailed her. She stopped unloading the supermarket shopping from the boot to talk to him. Judging by their demeanour they were having a bit of a row, but John was too caught up in his own tortured world to register much. He switched his attention back to the phone.

'Sex. Everything's sex. She was his little Christmas present. Like a new hat, pair of socks, pair of gloves. He's used them for a bit but now he's cast them off and I'm supposed to pick them up and wear them again, but they're stretched now, out of shape, distorted, and stained, and they smell of him –'

'Who is it?' asked Simone, coming through the door laden with bags. John put his hand over the mouthpiece. 'A parent.' She went out again to retrieve the rest of the shopping. He replaced the receiver. At the other end of the line, Ruth heard a dead tone.

It took Arthur twenty minutes to walk to the hotel; twenty minutes during which the rage that had been burning in him as bright as a memorial flame flared into white-hot fury. Tharmy had witnessed the John-Simone-Chef dust-up on the day of the drowning and word had got around quickly. It didn't take a genius to work out why the headmaster wasn't in school and looking after the kids and Danny Kavanagh had apparently confirmed it to the kitchen staff. Now that Arthur had told Simone exactly what he thought of her he was going to sort out Chef. Properly.

He barged into the kitchen, which was at the height of madness with dinner, and collided with a waitress carrying a pile of dishes. Arthur pushed her out of the way, sending the crockery flying. Pieces of fine porcelain scattered across the tiles, causing everyone to stop their frantic preparation duties and look up. Chef marched round to remonstrate and saw the barman advancing. 'You're dead,' Arthur spat.

'Stay that side, Arthur,' warned Chef, reaching for a weapon. His fingers curled around the handle of a heavy frying pan. Arthur, making his way along the serving counter, took no notice. 'Our Paula drowned 'cause of you.'

'Stay that side.' Chef stood like a boxer, waiting.

Arthur kept on coming, stepping into Chef's hallowed territory. 'Our Paula drowned 'cause you couldn't keep your hands to your bloody self.' Chef swiped at him with the frying pan, catching him a glancing blow on the side of his head. 'Stay away, Arthur.' Arthur launched a flying tackle that unbalanced Chef and dislodged a bubbling cauldron of soup from the cooker, narrowly missing scalding a porter. Both men went sprawling.

Archer, detecting sounds of a fracas, came hurrying across the dining room. A few curious glances were being cast towards the kitchen, but most diners seemed not to have noticed anything amiss. A red-faced Cumbrian man was placing an order, instructing the waitress minutely on his steak: 'Very rare. In fact, pull its horns out, wipe its arse and stick it on me plate.' There was another tremendous crash of breaking crockery. This time, people did look. Archer burst into the kitchen just in time to see his barman and his head chef stagger into a tall trolley loaded with pans, locked in combat. Sizing up the situation, he backed out and returned to the restaurant. 'I'm sorry, ladies and gentlemen, but there will be a slight delay to dinner,' he announced.

As understatements go, this was a beauty. None of the kitchen staff was pretending to do any cooking: they were too busy cheering and yelling for the two protagonists. Arthur and Chef had fallen out of the back door into a small yard, which was piled high with cardboard boxes and catering-sized cans of cooking oil. They landed in a heap but Chef was quicker on his feet and ready for Arthur when he got up. They circled each other warily. Chef feinted a punch, Arthur went for him, and Chef side-stepped it, thumping Arthur on the jaw. Arthur tottered a few steps but stayed upright and got stuck in again, charging into Chef and knocking his legs from under him. Chef was felled like a great tree, toppling over backwards, unable to stop himself. Arthur jumped on top of him and smashed him in the face.

Danny, who was in the Ramblers Bar having a drink and waiting for the others to come off work, also heard the noise and came round the back to investigate. He saw a large crowd of people gathered round Chef and Arthur, who were rolling on the ground swapping blow for blow. Danny pushed through to the front and shouted at the top of his voice for Arthur. Bloodied but unbowed, he was giving Chef the biggest pasting of his life and for a time it looked as if they were evenly matched. Finally, however, Chef's superior muscle power won out and he fetched Arthur such a crack that he could not get up. Chef went for the kill, raining punches on him until Arthur stopped moving completely. He gave him a last, vicious kick in the ribs and walked off, shooting a look of hatred at Danny as he shoved past him.

The next day Danny had a visitor. He was clearing the picnic tables outside the boathouse, sweeping the crumbs on to the grass for the chaffinches, when Father Matthew's car came bouncing up the track. Matthew was on a mission to try and heal the torn community, which, so far, hadn't proved very successful. After hearing about the fight at the hotel he had gone round to visit the Thwaites, only to be told to stay away from the house by a grim-faced Sheila. She had not forgiven him for Paula's funeral and he was beginning to doubt whether she ever would. He was hoping to tackle the situation from a different angle by reasoning with Danny.

'I want you to go to Sergeant Slater and tell him the truth. You –'

Danny saw where he was coming from and said, flatly, 'No'.

'– were on the phone. There'll be an itemized list of phone calls –'

'No.'

'– to prove it.'

'No.'

'Then let me tell Sheila Thwaite,' Matthew begged. 'She's lost her –'

'No.'

'– child. She's got a right to know the truth about her child's death; who's to blame, who's –'

'Look, what I told you I told you in strictest confidence.'

'– not to blame. She's got a right to know the truth.'

'In strictest bloody confidence and you've got no right to go blabbing to anyone,' Danny snapped.

'I've gone out on a limb for you. I've asked for prayers for you and it's driven a wedge between me and Sheila Thwaite and that's got to stop because she needs me. She needs her priest,' said Matthew.

Danny was adamant. 'I'll lose Emma. If she finds out I was on the phone to the bookie, that's it.' A group of people were waiting on the boat-landing. He called across to them, 'I'll be right with you.' To Father Matthew he said, 'See Lucy Archer.'

'Mum and Dad are working,' Lucy said, when she opened the door and saw Father Matthew.

'That's OK. It's you I've come to see, Lucy,' he replied, stepping inside uninvited.

'Why?' she pouted, tossing her long hair over her shoulders.

'I want to have a little chat.'

'Oh.' She turned and walked back up the hall, swinging her hips in a pair of cut-off denims. It might be fun, she thought idly, to get the stuffy old priest in a lather. She threw herself down on the leather sofa in the lounge, reclining along its length as if he was a shrink and she was the patient on the couch.

Matthew wasn't playing games. 'Look at me, Lucy,' he said, sternly, pulling up a chair. She opened her eyes. 'Sit up.' Lucy propped herself up on her elbows. 'Properly, please. This is serious.' Lucy sat, slightly chastened, her legs tucked under.

'You want to get married one day, Lucy?' She nodded. 'Have children?'

'Yes.'

'How many?'

'Three.'

'Arthur and Sheila Thwaite can't have any more children.' Matthew watched her face. She had the grace to colour ever so slightly but recovered quickly. 'You can imagine how important it is for them to know the truth. The truth about how Paula died,' he continued, speaking quietly.

'Yes,' she agreed, almost whispering.

'Without the truth, they can't even begin to grieve. Can you see that?' Matthew explained.

'Yes.' She wouldn't meet his eyes.

He paused for a few seconds, letting his words sink in. Then he asked, 'When's the inquest?'

'Next week.'

'Will you tell the truth at the inquest, Lucy? Please,' he pleaded. She nodded again dumbly. At last, Matthew thought. Finally we're getting somewhere. He couldn't imagine why she would want to lie in the first place. Attention-seeking, probably; that's what came of being an only child. She'd always come across as rather spoiled.

Looking at her now – Lucy was sucking her thumb in a childish but oddly explicit manner – she was the picture of contrition. Lucy coiled a long curl around her finger and appeared to stare at his crotch as if fascinated by it. Matthew realized he had lost his thread. He cleared his throat. 'What will you say?' he pressed.

She looked up at him with wide blue eyes and said, sweetly, 'Danny Kavanagh took money off those kids and pushed them out on to the lake.'

Matthew was appalled. 'Lucy, I know that's –'

'Danny Kavanagh took money off them and pushed them out on to the lake,' Lucy repeated, as if she had learned it by heart. She tilted her chin at him and smiled.

A train of young children processed up the aisle bearing gifts of food, singing:

> 'All that I am,
> All that I do,
> All that I ever have
> I offer it to you.'

The idea of the special offertory was to compile food parcels to be sent out to the homeless, but Father Matthew was also hoping that focusing on the children would have a beneficial effect on everyone. He studied the congregation and saw faces relax and soften as the children placed their gifts – cans of condensed milk, packets of pasta and rice, soup, cereal, tinned meat and fish – on the altar. Sheila Thwaite was looking at the children, too, but it was impossible to read her expression.

As usual, Matthew went down amongst the churchgoers to bid them peace, hugging people and shaking hands. He did not attempt to approach Sheila but when he saw Bernie's face he knew he could not evade her a third time. He had no wish to; the reason for avoiding physical contact had always been to protect her, not to hurt her –

although he knew how much it had – and he was too weakened by self-doubt to keep up the resistance any longer. The urge to hold her was overwhelming. Especially when her frank eyes held out such an invitation. She stepped up to him and said, 'Peace be with you,' and her look said, 'I'm not afraid if you aren't.' Matthew put his arms around her and buried his face in her hair. It was so natural, so right. So inevitable. He felt her breath escape in a long, quivering sigh on his neck, while in his head the children's voices echoed the paean of devotion:

'All that I am,
All that I do,
All that I ever have,
I offer it to you.'

Afterwards, Bernie came back with him to help sort the food into parcels. They unloaded it on to the kitchen table and made a pretence at getting started, both of them in a state of heightened awareness. Having fought the attraction for so long, their brief embrace was loaded with a significance neither of them could ignore. It seemed to Matthew he was on a journey to a destination he knew not where, with no means of controlling it or getting off. If it was a one-way ticket to damnation, then so be it, he thought. Surprisingly, he did not seem to care any more.

He tried to play it cool. Picking up a tin of low-calorie baked beans, he read, ' "Thirty-five per cent less sodium and twenty-five per cent less calories".'

'Hmm?' said Bernie, stuffing spaghetti into a box. Her hands trembled slightly.

'It should be, "Thirty-five per cent less sodium and twenty-five per cent fewer calories.'

'Really?' She walked round the table, as if coming to peer at the label, standing close to him so that their shoulders were almost touching. He held the baked beans up for her to examine. Bernie took the tin from him, her fingers caressing his.

'Very common error,' Matthew said huskily. 'I've often thought of forming a pressure group. The RSPLF. The Royal Society for the Protection of Less and Fewer.'

'Really?' She put the tin on the table. He could smell her perfume. He wanted, desperately, to taste her skin. She peeped up at him from under her dark eyelashes and he saw a smile playing on her lips.

'Yes,' he replied, turning to face her, encouraged. He put a finger under her chin, drawing her mouth towards his. She returned his gaze steadily, acquiescing. Then, someone pressed the doorbell. Neither of them wanted to break the spell but the person with their finger on the buzzer was persistent. The next round would have to wait. 'Will you come back tonight?' Matthew asked gently, stroking Bernie's cheek.

'Yes,' she whispered, her eyes glowing.

Once she had made the decision, Bernie assumed the rest would be simple. She wasn't sure exactly when she had made up her mind to commit adultery – the drowning had something to do with it; seeing how life could be snatched away, just like that, without getting a chance to tie up loose ends or say goodbyes or do the things you'd always planned to do. It had made her see how little her life was. If she was asked to summarize her existence on a piece of paper, it wouldn't make very exciting reading: a couple of innocent teenage flirtations, lost her virginity on her wedding night, three kids, no career. No flings, either; she'd always been faithful. And where was she now? A forty-five-year-old waitress with a body that was slowly falling apart and a husband who had sex with her out of habit rather than desire. Not much of a reward for sticking to the rules.

It wasn't that she didn't love Peter. She did. But that

didn't stop her loving Matthew, too. Love. The word tripped her up. *Did* she love Matthew, or was it something less noble, more basic? Standing next to him in the kitchen she had been intensely aware of the current between them. It was as if all the little downy hairs on her body were bristling like a cat's whiskers, picking up every nuance of his presence. And there had been another sensation; one she had never experienced before. An ache, a wanton, physical ache, Down There. Bernie's face was flushed as she made her way home. She was sure everyone could see what she was thinking. Her skin felt totally transparent, like a newly hatched insect. Vulnerable to everything.

She was so preoccupied that she didn't notice Danny Kavanagh standing on the pavement outside their gate and nearly blundered into him. 'Oh, sorry.' Too late, Bernie saw the jean-clad legs, crossed at the ankle, and looked up to find him glaring at her, his arms folded defiantly. 'I'm staying here. Right? Till my wife and child come out that house and see me. Not on the sly. We can do that. But with your knowledge. Right?' Flustered, Bernie scuttled past him and shot inside. Danny had overheard her talking to Matthew in the confessional. She prayed he couldn't read the infidelity that must be written all over her face.

NINETEEN

Bernie had anticipated feeling guilty, but afterwards, not beforehand. She did not know how she was going to get through the next seven hours, living with the deception that lay ahead. There were practical arrangements to consider – she still had to come up with a plausible excuse for going out – but the emotional complications proved more difficult. Bernie was sure – well, pretty sure – that Peter had never been unfaithful to her, which made it all the more difficult to justify. It could not be justified, she thought, rubbing in fat and flour and letting the breadcrumb-like mixture trickle through her fingers. This was something selfish and indulgent that she was going to do for her. All the same, she had to make it up to Peter somehow. So she was cooking him his favourite meal.

She added cold water to the bowl and formed the pastry into a ball, kneading it for a minute or two before covering it and putting it in the fridge to rest. Next she peeled a pile of Bramleys, coring and slicing them and putting them to one side sprinkled with lemon juice. A joint of gammon, tied with string, was already simmering on the cooker in a stock of onions, carrots, parsley stalks, bay-leaves and black peppercorns. Bernie turned her attention to the bucket of potatoes on the draining-board and began peeling them methodically. Peter loved his mash, preferably with a pool of melting butter on top. She also had a large, fresh, green cabbage, which Annie and Pete would probably moan about but Peter, who relished traditional dishes, also consumed with great gusto, usually mixed in with his mashed potatoes.

What next? Bernie wiped her hands on her apron,

glancing up at the kitchen clock. Better to keep busy, and not think about the evening. Ah, yes, the pie. She floured a board and got out the pastry, cutting the ball in half and rolling it out thinly to cover the base and sides of a huge dish. The apples went in, layered with plenty of sugar, a handful of raisins, some cloves and a good pinch of cinnamon. Draping it over the rolling pin, she placed the rest of the pastry carefully on top to make a lid, brushing the edges with beaten egg and pinching them together to seal them. Then she trimmed them with a knife, knocking up the edges to give them a fluted effect, and rolled out the trimmings to make leaf shapes to decorate the pie with. A final glazing of the beaten egg and it was ready for the oven: a real labour of love.

When Peter got home the over-sensitive smoke alarm was belting out its manic shriek and the comforting smell of home cooking filled the house. He took off his coat and went into the kitchen, to find Bernie, besmirched with flour, poring over the stove. 'Is that what I think it is?' he asked, sniffing appreciatively.

'Boiled bacon and cabbage,' she replied, prodding the joint with a fork.

'Yesss!' Peter punched the air in delight.

'Apple pie and custard for afters,' Bernie added, stirring away busily and keeping her back to him. Peter walked up behind her, grabbed her bum and gave her a slobbery kiss on her neck. 'You little beaut,' he said, ruffling her hair, and went off to the living room to sit down with the paper. Bernie bit her lip.

The food was wolfed down by everybody without comment. Conversation was limited – a sure sign of success – although little Annie insisted that Granddad test her on her multiplication tables. 'Six eights,' he said, munching rapidly.

'Forty-eight.'

'Six nines.'

There was a pause as Annie recited the nine times table to herself. 'Fifty-four.'

'The water hot?' young Pete asked, glancing up at Bernie.

'I'm first for a bath,' she said firmly.

'Nine eights.'

'You're going out?' Peter looked surprised.

'Whist drive,' she explained.

'Got yeeeeeeeeer!' Granddad squealed. Bernie jumped, guiltily.

'Seventy-four?' Annie faltered.

'Wrong.'

'Seventeeeeee-two,' she whooped triumphantly.

Bernie couldn't stomach any pie.

She took her time in the bath, adding some posh foaming stuff that Emma had given her for Christmas. Relaxing in the scented steam she raised an arm and soaped it languorously, watching the suds slide down her skin, then soaped her breasts with her hands, slowly, lovingly, watching the brown nipples stiffen and stand out, glistening. She leaned her head back and tried to imagine how Matthew would feel, grazing on her body, but there was something fundamentally wrong with the fantasy. However hard she tried, Bernie could not envisage him without his dog collar. Her erotic day-dreams were interrupted by a sharp rap on the door. 'Are you making your will out in there?' Pete shouted. She stopped massaging her breasts and sat up suddenly, creating a tidal wave that splashed over the side of the bath and soaked the carpet.

Bernie dressed extra carefully, styling her hair, applying make-up – including a soft, pink lipstick – and dabbing perfume behind her ears, on her wrists and, after a moment's hesitation, in her cleavage. 'You look lovely,' Emma said when she came downstairs.

'Thanks,' Bernie replied, a trifle breathlessly. Just then Pete shot past, bare-chested, and announced crossly, 'No shirt.' Bernie shrugged. Pete looked taken aback and began rooting under the stairs, hurling old trainers and football socks out behind him like a terrier digging a hole. The two women looked at each other and laughed. Putting on her coat, Bernie said, 'Will you do the dishes?'

Emma stopped smiling. 'Is he' – indicating her brother – 'allergic to hot water?'

'*Please*,' Bernie pleaded.

'All right.'

She stepped out into the evening air and started walking. 'Bernie,' Peter's voice shouted. Bernie froze in her tracks, utter dread flooding through her. How had he guessed? She turned and saw her husband gesticulate from the garden, then open the gate and come down the street towards her in his carpet slippers. 'What's wrong?' he asked, seeing her expression.

'Nothing.'

He drew closer. 'You didn't say goodbye.'

She breathed a sigh of relief. 'I'm late,' she said impatiently.

'*Is* there something wrong?' Peter was studying her face. Her knew her too well.

'No, I'm late, that's all.' She glanced at her watch.

He leant forward and kissed her lightly on the lips. 'Bye,' he said softly.

Bernie's brown eyes were clouded. 'Bye,' she replied automatically, still standing there.

'Well, go on, then.' Peter gave her a little push and a wave as she trotted off, stumbling a little on her best high heels. Watching her progress – she'll break an ankle in those, he thought; don't know why she feels she has to compete with Doreen Archer – he noticed Danny Kavanagh loitering further down the street. He had half a mind to go and see him off, but thought better of it: what he really wanted to do after that nice tea was flop in front of the telly.

Bernie saw Danny, too, and was certain Peter would come haring down the road to yell at him. Her plan, it seemed, was doomed, especially if Danny started talking. She checked behind her, but Peter was retreating into the house. Bernie walked past Danny as casually as she could, feeling like some painted strumpet. Danny's eyes bored into her but he said nothing.

She completed the half-mile or so to Matthew's house without further incident, but just as she was about to turn into the driveway, two more familiar figures approached from the direction of the woods beyond the church. It was Lucy Archer – with Chef. He had his arm around her waist and she was leaning against him and giggling madly. Unable to decide on the best course of action, Bernie stopped and took off a shoe, tapping it on the pavement as if there was a stone in it. 'Evening,' Chef grunted. Lucy made big eyes at her. 'Hello, Mrs Quinlan. You look smart.' Bernie assumed she was being facetious. Lucy must have guessed what she was up to. 'Thanks,' she smiled weakly. They strolled on, Lucy glancing back over her shoulder and staring keenly for a moment. Bernie put the shoe back on, hitched her handbag strap up and waited until they had disappeared round the corner. Her heart was pounding and her mouth was so dry that her tongue stuck to the roof of her mouth. She took a deep breath and walked up to the front door. There was a light on inside. Bernie rang the bell, stepped back and waited, looking around her to make sure no one else had spotted her. A black-clad figure was visible through the frosted glass. The door opened. Bernie goggled. It was a priest. But it wasn't Matthew.

They regarded each other in silence for a few seconds. At last he inquired, 'Can I help you?' She closed her mouth, swallowed, and tried to talk. No words came out. 'Can I help you?' he asked again, looking concerned.

Bernie did not know what sense to make of this. Matthew had been so certain. Hadn't he said, 'Come back tonight'? He had been going to kiss her earlier, without a doubt. This man must be an unannounced visitor. That was it: some cleric popping round for a sherry that he hadn't been able to get rid of. She managed to say, 'Is Matthew in?' in a reasonably normal voice.

'He's gone away for a few days.' The words ripped into her like shards of flying glass. She might have known she was clutching at straws. Matthew had bottled out. He would say he had done it for her but she didn't want that, she didn't want protecting. She wanted him. Bernie nodded, forcing a social smile to her lips.

'I'm Steve. Can I help?' he asked in a kindly manner.

'No, er, it was nothing. Thanks.' She turned away before he caught sight of the tears that were threatening to come.

Bernie made the whist drive with five minutes to spare and was glad, for once, of Doreen Archer's mind-numbing commentary. Doreen didn't expect audience participation, which was just as well as Bernie was locked in a world of her own.

'Lord Lichfield. I honestly couldn't believe it,' clucked Doreen, laying a card. 'I'm the highest lady. Omar Shariff's the highest man. The two of us –' she broke off suddenly, looking at Bernie severely. 'Third player always plays high.'

'Sorry?' Bernie didn't even know what she'd just put down.

'Third player always plays high,' Doreen repeated, momentarily exasperated.

'Sorry,' mumbled Bernie.

'Anyway, the two of us are shaking hands. There's a

flash of a camera. I look. It's Lord Lichfield.' The other couple at their table tried to appear impressed. It was getting harder as the evening drew on. Bernie was quiet. 'Wonderful man. Lovely teeth,' Doreen gushed.

By the time Bernie got home, her feet were killing her and she felt stupid; stupid and gullible and ridiculous and pathetic. She flagellated herself with adjectives, hating herself for ever having entertained the idea that she and Matthew . . . she couldn't even say it to herself now, it sounded so coarse, so unrealistic.

Peter was in the kitchen when she came in, making tea. He stuck his head round the door and saw Bernie bearing a potted plant. 'You won?'

'Booby prize.'

'Want a cup?'

'Please.'

She was positioning the plant on the hall table when she heard him pad up behind her. He put his arms around her middle, buried his head in her hair and held her tight. 'You smell lovely,' he said.

Danny's vigil eventually paid off. The following day he was waiting down the street from the Quinlans' house when he saw Emma coming down the hill with the pram. 'How are you?' she asked, concerned – it was the first time she had seen him since the attack – touching a bruise that stood out, livid, on his forehead. 'I've been really worried.'

He winced. 'OK, so long as you don't squeeze me too hard,' he said, hoping she would. Emma smiled but did not embrace him; their meeting was too public for that. 'I'm off this morning – Juliet's working,' he added. 'I was goin' to take some flowers down the graveyard. Wanna come?' Immediately, he wished he hadn't told her – it sounded like an admission of guilt – but Emma seemed pleased. 'All right,' she said, looking at him with her head on one side, her eyes bright. It was as if she was trying to detect a subtext; Danny had seen blackbirds stand like that when they were listening for worms underground. 'Can I push?' he said, looking at Samantha, who was flexing her chubby fingers and working up to a wail. Emma laughed. 'Come on, then. It'll calm her down a bit.' The Kavanaghs descended into the village, garnering several disapproving glances on the way.

This time, Emma didn't quiz Danny about what Father Matthew had said, and Danny decided not to let things get heavy. He wanted to regain her trust and he was prepared, now, to play it slowly. They bought flowers at the village store and strolled on to the church, talking little. It was not an uncomfortable silence. At the wooden latch-gate they paused. In the churchyard, Arthur and Sheila Thwaite were standing by Paula's grave as Sonny Clarke, the stonemason, erected her marble headstone. It stood out as white and proud as a new tooth amongst the moss-covered slabs and granite crosses.

A car going past on the road backfired, awakening Samantha with a start. She turned puce and began to yell, causing Sheila to glance up. Emma rocked the baby in her arms, shushing her, then handed her to Danny. 'Here, you hold her – no, upright, against your chest, like this.' He felt the child's wet cheek on his and was filled with an indescribable tenderness. The baby took a snuffly breath and settled her face into the crook of his neck, quietening as Danny gently rubbed her back. Emma picked up the bouquet. 'Stay there. I'll take these in.' She opened the gate and marched down the gravel path alongside the dry-stone wall that encircled the churchyard. Sheila and Arthur watched her, casting occasional black looks at Danny. Emma realized her timing was bad, but she wanted to prove that Danny cared, even though, judging by the expressions on her aunt and uncle's faces, he was clearly not welcome. Emma wasn't even sure that she was. 'It's lovely,' she said falteringly, indicating the headstone. They did not respond. Sheila's eyes were hollow; Arthur's, furious. Awkwardly, she bent down and placed the flowers on the grave, then turned and walked back towards Danny and Samantha. She did not see Arthur kick the bouquet high into the air in a shower of petals and fall anonymously into a patch of long grass. Danny did, but he did not say anything.

Doreen and Cecil Archer were working late in the hotel office, yawning as they ploughed their way through a pile of suppliers' invoices. Doreen, who was not flying in hostess mode that evening, wore a cardigan and a severe pair of glasses, which she kept on a chain around her neck. Archer was sucking absent-mindedly on a mint humbug. Just as they were debating whether to try out a cheaper butcher, one of the lights on the control panel began to flash and the sound of two people having apparently athletic sexual intercourse was broadcast quite clearly. 'They've knocked the phone off the hook,' Doreen said, amused. This kind of thing happened from time to time. Archer peered at the throbbing red light. 'Room 34.' The rhythmic sound of a headboard knocking against a wall and springs creaking violently continued to reverberate around the office. Doreen had a smile playing around her lips but Archer was not amused. It was rather too sustained a performance for his liking. No bloke could keep up that kind of pace for so long. 'Go up and tell them,' he said, twitchily.

'*What?*' She was aghast at the suggestion.

'Go and tell them,' he insisted.

'They'd die.'

'They'd sooner that than *this*.' He couldn't take much more of the woman's gasping breaths and the bloke's vigorous thrusting.

Doreen took off her glasses, wondering why he was

getting so het-up. 'They obviously don't know we can hear them. What they don't know won't hurt.'

Archer returned, huffily, to his book-keeping, but he couldn't concentrate. Surely it should be over by now? Finally, he flung down his pen in exasperation. Doreen gave him a look. 'What?' he demanded.

'Nothing,' she said, airily.

The woman upstairs let out a piercing scream. Doreen couldn't imagine what he was doing to her but whatever it was, it sounded fun. Sort of how you expected Imran Khan to be . . . Archer, unable to bear it a second longer, jumped up and scanned the hotel reservation plan. 'Thirty-four's empty,' he said in surprise.

'*She* seems occupied,' Doreen joked.

'Yes, yes, yes, do it to me, do it to me, oh yesss!' the woman shouted, climaxing.

Archer did a double-take at the voice. 'It's Lucy,' he said, wonderingly. Doreen's smile faded fast as she realized her husband was right. He got the master key and strode out of the office, Doreen hot on his heels.

The couple were so preoccupied they didn't hear the door being unlocked. Archer was treated to the sight of his little girl enjoying uninhibited coitus with his head chef in a manner that suggested she was no virgin. Doreen whipped her glasses back on her nose and gaped. Lucy, who was on her back, legs wrapped round Chef's waist, saw them before he did. For a grisly second, Archer thought she was going to carry on the performance, showing herself to him – her father – in that awful, exposed way, but then she stopped moving and Chef looked at her questioningly and she said, 'We've got company.' He looked round and rolled off. Lucy, naked, eventually covered herself with a sheet.

'Get dressed,' snapped Doreen at them both. Her eyes followed Chef as he walked brazenly past her to put on his clothes.

'Will you wait outside?' Lucy said sulkily to her father.

Archer looked glazed. 'Yes,' he replied, and propelled his wife from the room. Alone again, Lucy and Chef smirked at each other unrepentantly. Each had found the perfect match. For now, anyway.

Out in the corridor, Doreen was hissing, 'You *can't* sack him.'

'I've got to sack him.' Archer was recovering.

'Wait till we find another chef, then sack him,' said Doreen, ever the pragmatist, lowering her tone as a nun in wimple and habit approached them. 'Evening,' they chorused politely.

'Good evening.' She inclined her head and took out a key.

'I've got to do *something*,' Archer asserted.

There was a sharp intake of breath behind them as the nun, who had obviously been given number 34 without it being crossed off on the reservation plan, unlocked the door and discovered Lucy, standing completely naked, in the middle of her room. Chef, who was dressed, leered at the quivering, middle-aged woman, causing her to clutch at her crucifix as if he were the Antichrist.

''Scuse me,' said Archer, hastily, grasping, too late, what had occurred and taking the nun firmly by the elbow. 'I think there's been some mistake.' His profuse apologies could be heard all the way down the corridor as he led her away.

Chef winked at Lucy and swung jauntily out of the room, only to run into Doreen. 'You'll pay for the room of course. I'll stop it out of your wages,' she said icily. He ignored her and swaggered past. What Lucy did now was her own business; she was sixteen, it was legal and she loved it. Doreen knew she was fighting a losing battle, too. 'Try to leave the nun alone,' she sighed, as he disappeared from view.

Back in the room, Lucy was now partially dressed.

Doreen regarded her, hands on hips, her lips compressed. 'That wasn't your first time.'

'It was.'

'Lucy, I heard it. You didn't sound particularly –' she searched for the right word, '*apprehensive.*'

'With him. My first time with him,' Lucy explained, spelling it out as if her mother was particularly dense.

'There have been others?' Doreen said faintly.

'Yes.' Lucy zipped up her skirt and sat on the bed to put on her shoes, as cool as a cucumber.

'How many?' She hardly dared ask. Lucy looked up at her, raising an eyebrow. 'Approximately.' Doreen didn't want half the hotel staff enumerated.

'One.'

'You're lying,' Doreen said, disgusted. Downstairs in the office, Archer caught the tail end of the exchange – the phone, forgotten, was still off the hook. 'You're a slut,' he heard his wife shout, her dreams of appearing in *Hello!* magazine at Lucy's wedding to a wealthy aristocrat evaporating fast. 'My daughter's a slut.'

Arthur Thwaite had been suspended from duties for a week since his fight with Chef and there was a new, rather officious barman in charge of the Ramblers Bar. He was a stickler for timekeeping and chucked the last few drinkers out on the dot at 11.00 p.m. Chef, who had sunk a few, weaved his way up the hotel driveway, whistling, his hands in his pockets. Danny, who had also been drinking in the Ramblers and had just come out of the gents toilet, was some distance behind him, staying in the shadows. He remembered the unpleasant look Chef had given him the last time they met. A car jolted over the cattlegrid and came down the drive towards them. Chef stepped over to the edge of the grass, out of the way. Suddenly, the headlights came on full beam and the car swerved directly at Chef. It struck him with a sickening, bone-crunching thud, sending his body flying into the middle of the road. Danny stared, horrified, as the car screeched to a halt, revved up and reversed rapidly over Chef's prone form, tyres squealing. Chef let out a hideous scream. But twice wasn't enough for the driver. Whoever it was wanted to make sure Chef was good and dead. They stopped again, slammed the car into first gear, put their foot down and drove at him a third time, ramming the body and dragging it for several yards under the wheels, before screeching off down the semi-circular drive and out through the other gateway. Danny ran over to the inert heap spreadeagled on the tarmac, which had been mangled in a thick, dark pool of blood, just like the sauce in one of Chef's signature dishes.

TWENTY

An ambulance arrived to shovel Chef up and take him to hospital. For a few hours it was touch and go but, with characteristic pig-headedness, he refused to die. The alcohol he had drunk probably saved him, the surgeon pointed out to Ruth, when she eventually turned up several hours later: the fact that his muscles were relaxed had helped to – he was about to say 'minimize his injuries', but glancing at Chef, who had his skull and jaw held together with an elaborate arrangement of wires and his body encased in plaster and bandages from head to toe, he changed his mind. The man's injuries would leave him permanently disabled, but to what extent couldn't be known at this stage. Even if he did manage to walk again it would be a long, slow process and the poor chap would have to be on painkillers for the rest of his life. 'Well, he probably wouldn't have survived,' the surgeon concluded, lamely.

'Oh,' Ruth said. Her expression was unreadable.

Later in the morning, Sergeant Eddie Slater arrived. He looked at Chef, who was still unconscious, and winced. 'How are you?' he asked Ruth, taking a seat by the bed. It was hard to find a space that wasn't occupied by tubes and monitors. 'Fine,' she replied, looking remarkably calm. Still in shock, Slater surmised. He flicked open his notebook and coughed gently. 'We think it was intentional,' he announced. There was no easy way to break this sort of news.

'Really?' Ruth did not seem particularly surprised.

'Can you think of anyone who'd want to do this to him?' Slater inquired.

'Hmm.' Ruth leaned back in her chair. 'Stephanie and Norman Peploe. He screwed her a few years ago, dumped her. Teresa and Graham Harris, screwed and dumped. Barbara and David Samuelson, screwed and dumped,' she enumerated, ticking them off on her fingers. 'Liam and Julie Howard. Lisa and Jamie Pope. Frankie and Jean Thistlethwaite, now divorced. Nicola and James O'Reilly. Wendy and Tommy Brown. Simone and John Parr –'

'Hang on,' said Slater, scribbling furiously. 'I can't keep up with you.'

The list of suspects turned out to be so extensive that Slater had to set up an incident room at the small police station and enlist the help of a WPC to co-ordinate the investigation. He decided to tackle the locals first. Half of Hawksmere, it seemed, had been requested to come in for interview. By the end of the day he was more confused than ever. They all had strong motives and, what was more, they made no attempt to hide their delight at the news. Slater, who prided himself on his close links with the community, was dismayed that he was so out of touch with the depth of feeling about Chef. He flipped back through his notes and highlighted the following statements:

Arthur Thwaite: 'It wasn't me. I'd've used a bloody steam-roller. I'd've made sure.'
Cecil Archer: 'Yes, we caught that man having sex with Lucy. And so, yes, I'm delighted he's been hurt. I'm disappointed he's not paralysed from the waist down, actually, but it wasn't me driving that car.'
John Parr: 'Nothing trivial, I hope. Fractured skull at least. Crushed testicles.'
Simone Parr: 'If you find out who it was behind that wheel, let me know, won't you? I owe them a drink.'
Danny Kavanagh: 'Right. I tried to kill him. I killed the

kids on the lake; I tried to kill the chef; if there's any foot-and-mouth this year, you can put that down to me and all. A bit of mad cow disease, I'll cough for that as well. Is there anything else I can do for you?'

Ruth, Chef's wife, remained stoical throughout. When Slater went round to see her and deliver a progress report – and to check if there were any more names she had remembered – she merely smiled philosophically. 'So many people hated him, didn't they? I doubt you'll ever find the real culprit.' She sipped her tea. Slater paused, his cup to his lips, as he noticed the car parked outside. It looked very clean, as if it had been newly washed. An uncomfortable thought suddenly occurred to him. 'You passed your test recently.'

Ruth smiled again and stretched her legs out in front of her sensuously, like a cat. 'Yes,' she purred contentedly and yawned, showing a little pink tongue and white, sharp teeth.

It was Bernie's turn on the flower rota. She approached the church of St Michael and Latter Day Saints with a feeling of dread. Which would be worse, she asked herself: seeing this Father Steve in there – who must suspect something, the way she had behaved on the doorstep – or bumping into Matthew? But then it crossed her mind that Matthew might never come back, that she, Bernie Quinlan, *wicked* Bernie Quinlan, had driven him away for ever, and the thought that she might not see him again was unbearable.

Her crisis of conscience was solved for her by the chugging diesel-engine noise of a taxi, which swept past her and stopped outside the church. Father Matthew got out and waited while the driver extracted a small case from the boot. Bernie drew level. 'Hello,' she said, hesitantly. For a moment, she thought he was not going to acknowledge her. When he did look at her, his face was different. The Matthew she knew, and loved, had been replaced by a distant, unsmiling man with cold eyes. 'Hello,' he replied stiffly. Then he turned back to the driver, pressing a note into his hand, and said, 'Keep the change.' He picked up his case and walked to the priest's house, which was next to the church down an overgrown driveway, and went inside, shutting the door.

Bernie walked into the cool interior of the church and breathed in the familiar heavy scent of flowers and incense as if it were a drug that would calm her. It usually did – normally she enjoyed the solitude, tending the vases, trimming and rearranging the displays, adding fresh water; it made her feel at peace – but today the routine did not offer any reassurance. She looked up at the nave ceiling, which was painted turquoise with little gold stars. It had always seemed to suggest innocence, something sublime. Not any more. Naïvety, yes; the naïvety of a child's vision of the world, but something else, too: a wilful ignorance on the part of adults, a conspiracy that pretended the sky was always blue and God was in his heaven and everything would be all right if you did what he commanded. She hacked haphazardly at an arrangement of rust-and-yellow chrysanthemums, tears blurring her sight. From behind her, footsteps echoed on the stone-flagged floor.

'Where did you go?' Bernie said, not looking round. She knew it was Matthew. She knew the way he walked – strode – she knew what shoes he was wearing, she knew when he would stop and genuflect. She knew him inside out. But not inside her. He obviously didn't want that kind of knowledge after all.

'On a retreat. I spoke to the bishop. His advice was go away and think about it.'

'You told the bishop about us?' Bernie was even more wounded.

'Yes. He told me the best thing was to get away. Second best was take you away for a weekend, give you a good rogering, get it all out of my system. I chose the former.' Matthew spoke harshly, as if he intended to hurt her. 'Apparently, it's all down to arrested adolescence. A build-up of wild oats. One long dirty weekend should do the trick, the bishop says.'

Bernie, who still had her back to him, began to weep, silently. He saw her shoulders shake and carried on: 'In seminary there was this textbook. I looked up women in the index. It said, "Women, see under Danger".' Bernie's weeping was no longer noiseless. She fell on her knees, knocking over the vase, so that water flooded the crimson carpet by the altar and spread out into an ever-widening dark patch. Matthew, having taken the bishop's advice, retreated back up the aisle, stumbling a little as he went.

Peter Quinlan couldn't believe Danny Kavanagh had the sheer brass neck to carry on hanging about in the street, waiting for Emma. She must be giving him some encouragement, he reasoned, because he was turning up every day like a bad penny. The very sight of Danny got Peter in a bate: he had spotted him while he was out digging the front garden and had come storming into the house to have it out with his daughter.

'That Scouser's outside again, up to no good,' he ranted.

'Oh, is he?' Emma continued to feed Samantha spoonfuls of gloopy puree, most of which was sliding down the baby's chin. 'Come on, open,' she coaxed, remaining nonchalant.

'Are you still seeing him?' Peter demanded, disbelievingly.

'Yes.'

'Why?'

'Why?' She looked at her father as if this was a ridiculous question. Peter didn't see it that way.

'Yeah. Why?' he repeated, ignoring the sarcasm.

'He's my husband. He's her father,' Emma said, pointing with the messy spoon. Samantha grabbed it, spattering mashed swede and carrot across the room. Just then, the smoke alarm went off again, filling the house with its high-pitched, insistent shriek. Peter went to switch the damn thing off before he burst a blood vessel.

'What set that off?' he asked, popping his head round the kitchen door, the smoke alarm silenced. Bernie was chopping vegetables with her back to him while saucepans bubbled on the stove. The chops under the grill – there was still a freezer-load of mutton to get through – had obviously been responsible. Bernie did not answer. Peter could tell from the tension in her neck that something was up. 'Hey.' He went up to her and turned her round, tilting her face up towards him. She was weeping; big fat tears coursing down her cheeks. 'What's wrong?' he asked, gentle now, concerned.

Bernie sniffed loudly. 'Onions.' There were indeed onions on the chopping block, but they didn't normally make her cry like that. He tried to rub the tears away with his thumbs but they kept on coming, splashing on to her upper lip and dampening her blouse. 'It's the onions,' she insisted defiantly, mopping herself up with a paper towel and glaring at him red-eyed. She shook his hands off and returned to her cooking. Peter remained unconvinced.

That evening he went to see Father Matthew. Peter wasn't a regular at confession – not like Bernie – it made him feel too uncomfortable, but he knew there was something going on with his wife. If anyone should be able to read between the lines it ought to be the priest.

'It can't be easy for her. Running a home's difficult at the best of times. But now she's got Emma and the baby,' Matthew pointed out, cautiously. They were sitting in a pew – the church was otherwise deserted – in deference to Peter's request. He had said he wanted an informal chat, not the whole shebang.

'You think it's that?'

He hesitated. 'Do you?'

The implication hidden in the question ruffled Peter's feathers. 'I do my bit.' he said, jutting out his jaw.

'I know.'

'I'm old-fashioned, I know, but there are ways of doing things, Matthew. This isn't London. There's ways of doing things round here and they've stood the test of time.'

'She's never criticized you. She thinks you're a wonderful husband.'

That made Peter even more suspicious. What exactly had Bernie been saying about their marriage, he wondered. That sort of stuff, between man and wife, was private. He didn't like the thought of her and Matthew having cosy little chats about him. Peter studied the priest through narrowed eyes. 'But?'

'Sorry?' Matthew was looking increasingly discomfited by their talk.

'A woman says a thing like that, there's always a but. "He's a wonderful husband, but . . ."'

Matthew paused, then bowled it back at him again. 'Do you think there's a but?'

Peter grimaced. Obviously there was, or they wouldn't be having this peculiar conversation. But what was it?

Finally, Bernie was lying in Matthew's arms. After all the angst and pain and longing and rejection they had given in to their feelings and let it happen. They were as warm and snug as two bugs in a rug, wrapped up in a cocoon of cotton wool, protected from the world and all its condemnations, safe from guilt and recriminations. To be with him, naked, feeling his weight on her and the rasp of his belly as he rocked in and out of her, was all she asked. To touch the pulse beating wildly in his neck and taste his sweat and feel his lips seeking urgently for her breast was all she wanted. 'All that I am/All that I do/All that I ever have/I offer it to you.' She did not open her eyes. If she kept them closed she could shut out reality and keep them both suspended in this glorious, everlasting present.

'There's nothing to forgive. Nothing whatsoever,' he said to Bernie the following evening at confession.

'There is.'

'Nothing ever happened.'

'No? I woke up the other day, early hours of the morning, somebody making love to me. I thought it was you. I was still half asleep, half conscious, and I began to realize it probably wasn't you, it was Peter. And I wanted to stay like that, half asleep, half conscious, because that way it could still be you, it could still possibly be you. That's a man I've loved for over twenty years and you tell me there's nothing to forgive.'

Matthew gazed at Bernie and his heart ached. He still wanted, desperately, to kiss her. A few days' religious brainwashing hadn't really flushed her out of his system. He'd been given the theological equivalent of a few cold showers but the effect had been very temporary. She was too deeply ingrained. He wished it had been him, making love to her, giving her pleasure instead of all this suffering. Bernie, looking into his eyes, saw the mask he had been wearing since his return slip so that, for a few, brief seconds, they were back in the kitchen and trembling on the verge of discovery again. Then he replaced it with a frown, stood up and said a curt, 'Goodnight,' leaving her alone in the quiet church with the guttering shadows of candles dancing like flames on the white walls.

In between doorstepping Emma and dealing with the steady trickle of customers who still wanted to take boats out – the season was stretching on as tourists made the most of the Indian summer – Danny was keeping an eye out for Lucy Archer. She was the only person who could clear his name. He couldn't – wouldn't – save himself by giving evidence about his win at the bookie's for fear of ruining his precarious relationship with Emma. They met up for walks with the baby whenever they could, now; a sedate courtship compared to the heady rush of last summer and their alfresco sexual adventures, but Danny didn't mind. He enjoyed being with them both, playing with little Sammie and talking to Emma. They were developing a new emotional intimacy. He told her about his visits to Gamblers Anonymous – he had continued to go to the meetings in Penrith – and was honest about his history of gambling. Emma listened, saying little, but she did not condemn him. Danny was beginning to feel as if they were on the right road at last, although the fast-approaching inquest hung over it like a great black cloud.

If he couldn't get Lucy to tell the truth, he would have no future in Hawksmere. Even if he wasn't drowned in the dead of night by the gang of masked men, he and Emma would never be able to settle down and live as a family in the community. Emma would be ostracized too – she was getting a hard enough time of it as it was – and as for going back to Liverpool with him, he knew the answer to that. He was too big a risk. There were too many bad memories. These days Emma held a part of herself in reserve. Danny sensed this: it was a safety precaution, insurance against him letting her down again.

He knew what Lucy's game was. The saying, 'Hell hath no fury like a woman scorned' had not, until recently, held much meaning for him. Presumably she wanted to hear him beg. She got off on sexual power: her exhibition in the conservatory was demonstration enough of that. Keeping Danny in thrall was obviously giving her an enormous buzz. And since Chef was out of action –

permanently, by all accounts – she'd need to get her kicks elsewhere. Well, she wasn't having his balls for her collection. She needed to be told this was serious. Lives had been lost already and more were at stake.

The following Saturday, Danny spotted Lucy waiting at the bus stop in the village, all dolled up for an afternoon in town. She saw him at the same time and looked nervously about. The bus was approaching. Danny hurtled down the road towards her. Lucy got on and paid for her ticket. The bus was pulling away by the time Danny reached it. He ran alongside, hammering on the doors and shouting, forcing the driver to stop and open the doors. Danny bounded on board the platform. 'I just want to talk to her,' he said, indicating Lucy, who was cowering in a seat halfway back.

'Where are you going?' The driver wasn't interested in his motives, only his destination.

'I'm going nowhere. I've got no money.' Never had he spoken a truer word.

'Then you're gonna have to get off, son,' said the driver in an I'm-being-reasonable-here voice.

Danny ignored him and advanced towards Lucy. 'They nearly drowned me the other night, you stupid bitch,' he yelled. 'They think it's down to me. There's three kids dead and they think it's down to me so you'd better start telling –'

The driver stood up, getting less reasonable. 'Will you get off my bus please, son?'

' – the truth. It's not a fucking game, you know what I mean? I'm sorry I knocked you back. Right? If that's why you're doing this, I'm sorry.'

'Will you get off this bus right now?'

Danny kept going tenaciously, his eyes fixed on Lucy's face. 'Right? I'm really sorry. And I can understand you having a go but blaming me for the death of three kids is a bit over the fucking top. Right?'

The driver had him by the arm. 'Look, I'll phone the police.' He started to haul him back up the aisle.

'So tell the truth. No one's gonna blame you. Everyone's gonna understand. Right?' he pleaded, clinging on to the luggage rack while the driver continued to tug at his sleeve. The other passengers were hanging on to every word. Lucy was pale. Danny shook the driver's hand away angrily. 'I'm getting off.'

The driver was equally fed up. 'I'm late, son.'

Danny clambered down from the platform, still shouting, 'So tell the truth. Right? Tell the truth.' The doors sighed shut in his face. He watched as the driver got back behind the wheel. Once more, the bus started to move off. Danny ran alongside again, jumping up and banging on the window where Lucy was sitting. 'Tell the truth. Tell the truth, Lucy, please. Tell the fucking truth. Tell the truth. Right? Tell the truth.'

Matthew was having trouble with his U-bend. No amount of plunging would unblock it and the plug hole had regurgitated a load of tea leaves which were floating in the grimy kitchen sink. With some reservations he had called out Peter Quinlan, whose handyman business covered most things, to tackle the job for him. Peter peered into the sink and said, 'Too much tea and sympathy, Matthew, that's your problem,' and undid the cupboard doors underneath. He dispatched Matthew to switch the water off and got to work with an adjustable spanner. It was an easy job, but he wouldn't have expected Matthew to dirty his hands: priests were supposed to operate on a higher plane than other men, after all. He'd probably just pray for a miracle. Peter snorted quietly at his joke.

'Turn it on,' he shouted.

'What?' Matthew's voice came back faintly. Peter sighed and wriggled out from under the sink just as the phone started to ring. 'Turn it on,' he called again to Matthew, who was upstairs. 'Shall I get your phone?' he added.

'Please.'

Peter picked up the receiver. 'Hello?'

'Hello.' It sounded like – why on earth would it be? – but it sounded like his wife. Before he had time to say anything there was a sudden torrent of water from beneath the sink. 'Turn it off,' he bellowed hastily upstairs.

'What?'

'Turn it off.' The flood ceased abruptly. 'Hello?' he said again. Whoever it was had rung off. He was sure it was Bernie. She must have been going to pass on a message to him about another call-out. So why put the phone down? Unless it wasn't him she was after. He remembered Matthew saying, 'Do you think there's a but?' and went cold. There was a way to check. Peter dialled 1471 and heard his own telephone number recited back to him. He, Peter Quinlan, was the butt. The joke was on him.

'No luck?' asked Matthew, entering the kitchen to find Peter packing up his tools.

'You'll need a plumber,' he replied, and left without bidding him goodbye.

TWENTY-ONE

The thought that there might be something going on between Bernie and Matthew continued to burrow, maggot-like, deeper and deeper into Peter's brain as the day went on. He could not concentrate on his other jobs with such an idea festering away, and by the time he got home he was in a black mood. It was not improved by Danny Kavanagh phoning to speak to Emma. 'She's not in,' Peter said roughly, and when Danny protested he slammed the phone down. Emma and Bernie looked up questioningly as he came back into the living room. 'Danny,' he grunted, throwing himself into an armchair. Emma continued to play with Samantha, ignoring her father's slight. She sang to the baby, taking the child's chubby hands in hers and reciting over and over again:

> 'Clap hands, Daddy come home,
> Bring little Jo-Jo a cake and a bun.
> Jam in the middle, cherry on the top,
> Hurry up Daddy and don't you stop.'

The rest of the family were in, too: Granddad was falling asleep in front of the television and Pete and Annie were on the floor having a game – amicably for once – of topple bricks. Pete extracted a block carefully from the middle of the edifice, keeping up a running commentary as he did so. 'There's a hush throughout the auditorium. "Surely not, surely not –" but *yes*, he does it!' Now it was Annie's turn. 'And you can't help but feel sorry for his young opponent,' Pete continued, making his fist into a microphone. 'To meet a man like this at the top of his form.'

Peter's gaze wandered from his two youngest to Bernie, who appeared to be miles away, staring into the middle distance with unfocused eyes. Where was she? He thought he knew her backwards, but now he wasn't so sure. Eventually she became aware that he was studying her and asked, 'What?' Peter did not reply. Instead, he got up and went out. They heard the van start and drive off down the road.

It was time for confession, Peter decided. And not necessarily his. He parked outside the church and walked in. There was no one else waiting so he opened the confessional door and sat down. Matthew, who had also, apparently, been deep in thought, jumped when he saw his face. 'Hello, Peter.'

'Bless me, Father, for I have sinned,' Peter said rapidly.

'May the Lord help you to confess your sins with true sorrow,' Matthew responded.

Peter didn't beat about the bush. 'There's something wrong with Bernie.'

Matthew hesitated. 'Something physical?'

Peter gave him a you-know-what-I-mean look through the grille. 'Emotional. She's been crying a bit. In a world of her own.'

'Have you spoken to her?' Matthew did not meet his eyes.

'I've tried. You know when I was fixing the pipe; trying to fix the pipe?'

'Yes.'

'She phoned. I answered. She put the phone down. Why would she do that?'

'I don't know.'

'Are you screwing my wife?' Peter demanded brusquely.

'I beg your pardon?' Matthew was stunned, both at the accusation and the insight.

'*Are you screwing my wife?*'

'No.'

'This is the sacrament of penance, Matthew. If you lie during this, you might as well walk out there and piss on the altar.'

'I'm not lying. I'm not screwing your wife,' Matthew said defensively.

'Have you tried to screw my wife?'

'No.'

'Have you contemplated screwing my wife?'

There was a pause. Peter, almost sobbing with rage, banged his fist on the side of the confessional. '*Have you contemplated screwing my wife?*'

Matthew sighed. 'I'm only human, Peter.'

What kind of answer was that? It was a yes, that's what it was. Had Bernie wanted it, too? To commit adultery with a priest? 'Did she give you any encouragement?' he shouted.

'You'll have to ask her that.'

'Did she give you any fucking encouragement?' He was desperate to know.

Matthew remained resolute. 'I'm not prepared to answer that. I'm sorry.'

Peter stared at him, his colour high, breathing hard. Matthew was glad that there was a wall, however thin, between them. Peter stormed, 'You spout about sacrifice, Matthew. But the only sacrifice you're asked to make is to keep your hands to yourself. You can't manage it. Christ went to the cross; all you're asked to do is keep your hands to yourself and you can't. You're a disgrace.'

'Yes,' Matthew agreed, ashamed.

'And this isn't just any old woman, Matthew. This is my wife. I'm your parishioner. You're supposed to give me a bit of support. A bit of emotional and spiritual support. You mess about with my wife, you're not just failing to support me, you're breaking my fucking heart.'

'Nothing ever happened, I promise you.'

'And it won't, Matthew. You see, you mess about with

women and you're just like any other man. And I'll treat you like any other man. And if I caught any other man messing about with my wife, I'd rip his dick off. OK?'

Peter was very quiet when he got home. He said nothing to Bernie, and she didn't ask where he'd been.

It was the final scene, at the airport. The bit where Rick gives Ilsa the letters of transit and tells her that if she doesn't go with Lazlo she'll always regret it and she says, 'What about us?' and he replies 'We'll always have Paris.' Bernie was there on the tarmac in Ingrid Bergman's shoes, torn between two lovers: the man who needed her and the man who was her grand passion. When Bogie said, 'It doesn't take much to see that the problems of three little people don't amount to a hill o' beans in this crazy world,' she found tears pricking at the back of her eyes; not because that was the effect *Casablanca* always had but because it really meant something to her now. What was she doing, jeopardizing her marriage, her children, everything she had, for a selfish impulse, an impossible fling? It could never have gone anywhere with Matthew. One night of passion – and it might not have been that good, she consoled herself, remembering his clumsy schoolboy kiss – and she could have lost everything. Bernie remembered Matthew and their ridiculous conversation over the tin of baked beans and smiled, in spite of herself. A hill of low-calorie beans at that . . .

Peter, who was sitting next to Bernie on the sofa, looked at her profile in the reflected light of the flickering black-and-white movie and smiled too. As Bogart said, 'Here's looking at you, kid,' Peter touched Bernie's cheek and whispered, 'I love you.' It was something he hadn't said to her for a long time, he realized. She turned to him, her face lit up with delight. 'How much?' she whispered back, mischievously.

'This much,' he said, extending his arms as if he'd caught the biggest fish in the world.

'Prove it,' she laughed, as the credits rolled.

'How?'

She pointed upstairs. Peter took her hand. They climbed the stairs together and at the top of the landing she stopped, put a finger to her lips and indicated a door. Peter understood. He removed the smoke alarm, handing it to her like a trophy. 'Thank you,' Bernie said, from the bottom of her heart.

Chef had been sent home early – his hospital bed was needed – gathering quite a crowd as he was lowered into his wheelchair by two hefty ambulancemen. ' 'E don't look too hot,' a neighbour tut-tutted. 'Can't see *him* getting up to his tricks again in a hurry.' Chef, who in his plaster casts, bandages and head brace looked like a horror-flick hybrid of *The Mummy* and *Hellraiser*, was trundled into the house. His eyes, burning with fury, were all that moved.

During his sojourn in hospital Ruth had reinvented herself. The long-suffering, passive, dowdy wife had been replaced by a confident, attractive, sexually voracious woman. After years of being humiliated and taunted by Chef, revenge was sweet. Dumb and immobile, he could only watch, helpless, as she got herself ready for a night out with her new lover, putting on a floorshow that sent his blood pressure rocketing.

'Simone Parr used to shave her legs for you, I believe. Why's it so sexy, do you think?' she mused as, wrapped in the scantiest of towels, she shaved her own, still-good legs. 'I think it's to do with anticipation. You shave them, therefore you anticipate somebody fondling them. No fondling, no need to shave.' Ruth smiled at Chef brightly. She put on a pair of silky high-cut knickers – new ones; she'd splashed out on lingerie – and fastened a lacy black bra. 'You'll notice it's a front-fastening bra. He's a bit clumsy, you see. All thumbs.' Next she picked up a suspender belt, dancing in front of Chef and whirling it around on one finger like a stripper before doing it up and fastening her stockings. 'Turn him wild, black suspenders. "Sussies" he calls them,' she said, confidentially. 'It's funny, isn't it: nakedness isn't sexy at all. But the slight concealment of nakedness, *well*. And it's not the things you expect, is it?' Ruth looked at Chef as if expecting an answer, then shrugged her shoulders. 'This suspender belt, for instance, it's to hold my stockings up, that's all, to make my legs look good. So it's strange that it should be thought so sexy; sexier than the stockings, sexier than my legs even. Hmm?' Chef, his jaw firmly wired up, could only roll his eyes.

Ruth sat down at her dressing-table in her underwear and began applying make-up. 'He's young, excitable. Gets there far too soon, if you know what I mean. But six or seven quickies make up for one long slowie, don't you think?' She outlined her lips and filled them in with glossy red lipstick. 'And I've got to admit I find it flattering, the fact that I can get him going six or seven times without massaging his ego, so to speak.' She winked at Chef in the mirror, then dabbed perfume between her breasts and on her wrists and neck. Finally, she stepped into a short, clingy, low-cut dress – also new – which made the most of her trim figure, and slipped on a pair of high heels. 'There.' She posed for him, hands on hips, one leg slightly in front, like a model. 'What do you think?' Ruth looked stunning and she knew it.

'We do it in room 34 of the Ullswater Hotel. It's the last one they let, so it's usually empty. Unless the hotel's heaving, of course,' she said, patting her recently-cut hair as she delivered the *coup de grâce*. 'Obviously, it's not the best room they've got, but it serves its purpose. Double bed and what-have-you. He works there, you see. A bit of urban rough.' And with that Ruth bent and kissed Chef lightly on the forehead, leaving a vivid lipstick imprint. 'Be good,' she said merrily. 'Don't wait up.'

The evening before the inquest, Sheila Thwaite went down to the churchyard and stood at Paula's grave. Arthur, having drunk half a bottle of whisky, had passed out in the chair at home and she felt utterly alone. The flowers on the grave had wilted in the late summer sunshine, giving it a forlorn look. She gathered the dead blooms up, noticing the wilted petals scattered like confetti where Arthur had kicked Danny Kavanagh's bouquet. Sheila stared at the little mound of raised earth. She couldn't believe that her daughter was decaying beneath her feet, that that was the end of Paula and she would never see her again. Every afternoon when the school children went past in noisy gangs she half expected her home, running down the path with her copper-coloured hair streaming behind her. It was still a surprise, somehow, when she didn't eventually turn up in time for tea. On several occasions Sheila had laid three places or prepared three portions without even realizing.

In the dim light she saw someone move out of the corner of her eye. It was Father Matthew, locking up the church for the night. He felt her eyes on him and looked up. 'Sheila,' he called, but she turned her back resolutely. She had not spoken to him since her outburst; did not attend confession, and sat at the back at Mass, refusing to take the sacrament or to wish him or others peace. Her grief was fierce and internal and that was how she wanted to keep it, enfolded in her womb. That space inside her, the space that had once nurtured Paula as an unborn child, was the only physical protection she could offer. It was good to feel her anger and sorrow churning in her belly like the movements of a restless foetus. By nursing it, she could keep Paula alive.

Matthew would not be put off. She heard his footsteps swishing through the dewy grass as he came over and stood beside her. Neither of them spoke. Finally, he said, 'I know how difficult tomorrow's going to be for you and Arthur, going back over everything that happened. But I hope it brings some kind of resolution for you.'

'Like what? It won't bring our Paula back, will it? The coroner's not going to wave a magic wand and say, "Here's your little girl, she's OK after all",' Sheila spat.

'No. But knowing the truth about how she died will help.'

'I know the truth, for God's sake. We all do. And I hope Danny Kavanagh gets his comeuppance for it.'

'Let's not prejudge things.'

'Drowning's too good for him. Once you're dead, the pain stops. I want him to know how it feels to lose someone that's a part of you and to go on hurting and hurting for the rest of your life.'

'We've only got Lucy's word about Danny's involvement.'

'Do you know' – Sheila looked at Matthew with crazed eyes, her voice catching – 'sometimes I see Emma, my own niece, walk by with that baby and I want to run out and snatch it from her and hurl it into the lake and say, "There, *now* we're quits. His child's life for mine." That's the resolution I dream about.' She broke into wild sobs and buckled at the knees, tipping forward on to the grave and screaming hysterically, 'Paula, Paula, Paula,' her fingers scrabbling at the newly laid turves. Matthew, wretched at the profundity of her anguish and his inability to comfort her, knelt down beside Sheila. A great outpouring of grief seemed to spurt from her jerking body as if from a main artery, pumping out like it would never stop. He looked around for help, fearing she was having some sort of fit, but there was nobody around and he didn't like to leave her. Gradually, however, the madness subsided and she lay, curled into a ball, her cheeks caked with dirt, huge shuddering gasps racking her body.

'Sheila,' he said softly, 'come on now. Let's get you home.' Slowly she raised herself up, looking dazed. There were petals and twigs in her hair and her clothes were grass-stained and crumpled.

'Oh Matthew,' she gulped. Still on his knees, he rocked her in his arms until her violent trembling ceased. 'May God forgive me for what I said.'

The boathouse was closed for the day – both Danny and Juliet were attending the inquest – so there was little for Danny to do when he got up but smoke and fret. He felt like a condemned man awaiting execution. Watching the dawn spread fingers of gold across the fells and tint the surface of the water, he drank in every detail, every subtle shift in shade and colour, every bird noise and plop and ripple of the lake as if for the very last time. His future in Hawksmere depended entirely on the outcome of the inquest.

Emma arrived, as arranged, at 8.30 a.m., with a zipped-up suit bag in the shopping tray of the pram. She looked on critically as Danny buttoned the freshly ironed shirt and pulled on the trousers, and when his nervous fingers fumbled with the tie she said, 'Here, let me do it.' Frowning slightly in concentration, she untied and retied the knot while Danny gazed into her face as if he were trying to imprint it on his mind. 'There.' She gave it a final tweak and smiled at him. The domesticity of the moment was not lost on either of them. It was almost like old times, except that the last time he had worn a tie was for his court appearance. He slipped on the jacket – it was a little long in the arms but fitted well across the shoulders – and said, 'How's that?'

'Nice.' She glanced at her watch. 'I've got to get back.' They were both tense. Danny had no idea what she was thinking. There were so many things he wanted to say to her but it seemed too late for any of them now. 'Right.' He pushed his hair out of his eyes. Emma remained looking at him, as if trying to decide something. 'The truth'll come out,' she said softly, giving him a sudden hug. He clutched hold of her hard.

'Yeah,' he whispered, although he very much doubted it.

He doubted it even more when he saw Lucy Archer approach the coroner's court with her parents an hour and a half later. Danny was standing outside, smoking, when he spotted them. Lucy noticed Danny at the same time and gave him her butter-wouldn't-melt pout. She had come done up for her command performance, dressed demurely in a designer suit that somehow managed to suggest she was wearing nothing underneath. Her hair was pulled back with a Madonna-ish centre parting, two long curls hanging down either side of her face. Around her neck she wore a crucifix on a chain. It was an image calculated to present a picture of guileless innocence.

Danny's heart sank. 'Tell the truth, Lucy,' he said, stepping in front of them. Cecil Archer was furious. 'I'm no expert but I'm pretty sure you're –'

'Tell the truth in there Lucy, please.' He put his hands on her shoulders and tried to make her meet his eyes. She flashed him a mulish expression from under heavily mascaraed lids and did not reply.

Doreen twittered and Archer grabbed his daughter and steered her away, '– not supposed to talk to a key witness.'

Danny danced after them, pleading, 'Please, Lucy. Please, tell the truth.'

Archer ushered his wife and daughter through the doors, turning round to snap, 'So do you *mind* –' He remained blocking the doorway until Doreen and Lucy were well inside.

Danny glared at him furiously. 'She's telling a pack of

lies and you know it. You know what a conniving little bitch she is. You've seen her in action, chasing the staff. You know about her and Chef. She's doing this to get back at me.'

'Cecil,' Doreen's voice called. 'Are you coming?'

Archer put his face so close to Danny's he could see the blackheads in his pores. 'Unlike you, you Scouse piece of shit, my daughter has been brought up properly. And that doesn't include tearing apart a community like you've done. Lucy is a bright, well-educated girl who knows the difference between right and wrong. So, if she says she's telling the truth, I believe her.'

'Cecil, you're holding up the lift.'

'All right,' he yelled back furiously and stamped inside the building. Danny pounded the wall in despair.

More cars drew up and the Quinlans and the Thwaites got out. Sheila looked white and exhausted and Bernie had an arm around her shoulders. The two women walked past Danny without acknowledging him but the men, following behind, glowered contemptuously. Arthur stopped in front of him and his eyes were like flints. Danny stared back, unflinching. They disappeared inside. Emma, who had been trailing along at the back, pressed his hand briefly and mouthed, 'Good luck.'

'Come on, sis,' Pete, who was waiting in reception, grumbled. He stuck his head out of the door to haul her in and did a double-take at Danny's outfit. 'That's my suit.'

TWENTY-TWO

The coroner's court was an old-fashioned, high-ceilinged room with plain white walls and a row of windows set, rather oddly, along the top of the wall behind the bench, so that the slanting light streamed in from one direction only, as if through a window in a prison cell. Danny supposed the effect was intentional. The public gallery was packed; everybody in Hawksmere seemed to have turned out, including some he wouldn't have expected – Albie, for example, who was accompanied by Ruth.

The coroner himself was an elegant, silver-haired man with winged eyebrows and a piercing expression. 'As coroner, my task is quite straightforward: I have to determine the cause of death,' he announced, eyes sweeping the courtroom. 'In an ideal world I could do that without apportioning blame or implying guilt. But this isn't an ideal world. The law allows for people who feel they might be incriminated by these proceedings to be present throughout and, when appropriate, to ask their own questions of any witnesses I call. And that is why Mr Daniel Kavanagh and Mrs Juliet Bray will be present throughout this hearing.'

Simone Parr was the first to be called to the witness box. She looked delicate and wan but her apparent fragility was misleading. When questioned about the affair that led to her husband's absence from the school, the speech she so coolly delivered was as pitiless as a public castration. 'We came from the city. Noise. Panic. A village school in the Lake District – it was a dream come true. And the house they were giving us – ivy up the wall, apple trees in the back, a river at the bottom of the garden. We couldn't believe our luck.' She glanced across at John, who was sitting, white-faced, on the front bench in the public gallery. 'But the novelty soon wears off. You realize you're not living in the Lake District, you're living in a little village in the Lake District: petty, parochial, claustro-phobic. And you're getting older. And your husband's getting older, sucked dry by that school, chalk dust in his veins, utterly devoid of conversation.' John's eyes were shut, as if trying to block out her words. 'You try to escape the boredom,' Simone continued, twisting the knife she had plunged into him. 'But there are only two things you can do in a little village in the Lake District. One's drink. The other's sex.'

John Parr put his head in his hands. He was so distressed by his wife's betrayal that it was several minutes before he was able to collect himself enough to give evidence. He clung on to the edge of the box, fighting back tears as he spoke. 'I suspected my wife was having an affair. Suspected isn't the word. I *knew*. As good as knew,' he said shakily. He drew a large white handkerchief from the pocket of his sports jacket and blew his nose. 'If she'd tried to hide it, I'd've taken some comfort from that. "At least she cared enough about me to try to hide it." But she didn't.' He bit his lip and dropped his head for a moment. Then he looked up, red-eyed and turned to the coroner. 'I followed her,' he admitted, lifting his chin. 'I left the children unattended to follow my wife.' Susan Charles's father cried 'Shame' and a murmur rippled through the onlookers. Simone Parr sat bolt upright, staring straight ahead. At least, she thought, we won't have to live here any longer. It was obvious John would get the sack. With any luck he could still get a job in some inner-city school – if he managed to stay on top of his drinking – allowing them to be painlessly reabsorbed into the anonymity of urban life. And if he couldn't hack it, she'd leave him and get herself a job and a decent man. Snivelling on the stand there he looked totally pathetic.

'Daniel Kavanagh was talking to you?' the coroner quizzed Lucy Archer.

'Yes.'

'What was he saying?'

'He wanted me to go in the boathouse with him.'

'What for?'

Lucy raised her eyebrows. 'Sex,' she replied, in a tone that suggested, 'What else?', as if being waylaid by men was a cross she had to bear. Emma glared at her furiously.

'And where were the children at this stage?' the coroner continued in his kindly uncle vein.

'In the boat,' she said, tossing her head. 'He was talking to me and pushing them out.'

Danny jumped up and shouted, 'She's lying!', causing heads to swivel round and stare. He slumped back down in despair. The coroner ignored his outburst and carried on with his cross-examination. 'Did the children pay Mr Kavanagh?'

'Yes.'

'How much?'

'Three pounds.'

'A pound each?'

'Yes,' she said firmly.

'How did they pay it?'

Lucy was temporarily flummoxed. 'I'm sorry?'

He leaned forward, examining her hawkishly. 'Did they each pay a pound coin? Did one child pay for all three? Did he have to give them change?'

She considered. 'They each paid a pound.'

'Wasn't that awkward for them?'

'No.' Lucy looked surprised.

'They were on the lake, being pushed out. How did they reach him?'

She missed a beat, then decided, 'They paid before. Before they were pushed out.'

'I see.' The coroner leant back and folded his hands. 'Was there anybody else around?'

'No.'

'Mrs Bray?'

'No.'

'Do you like Daniel Kavanagh?' the coroner asked unexpectedly.

Lucy looked across at Danny, enjoying herself immensely. 'No.'

'Did you like him? Did you "fancy" him? Do you still use "fancy"?' he inquired gravely, as if hampered by antediluvian tendencies.

'Yes. I mean, we use it. I didn't fancy him, no.'

'Not at all?' It was his turn to raise his impressive eyebrows.

'No.'

'So why go to the boat-landing?'

Lucy was thrown off course. 'I just did,' she stumbled, blinking.

'You'd be alone. With a man you didn't like,' he reasoned.

'The children were there.'

'But you stayed. After he pushed the children out. You were alone with him.'

'Yes.' She was a little less buoyant now.

'With a man you didn't like. A man suggesting sex.' A touch of steel was creeping into his voice. Cecil and Doreen Archer exchanged glances.

'Yes,' Lucy said, subdued.

'Why didn't you walk away?'

'I don't know,' she replied sullenly, enmeshed in her own story.

He paused. He tried the uncle approach again. 'I was young once, Lucy.' An understanding twinkle. 'Somebody hurts you; you tell a spiteful lie about them. You think you can retract that lie but everything gets so serious and it goes on so long that you can't. To retract it would make you look foolish, childish. But that's not true. To stick to the lie is childish. The brave thing, the adult thing, is to tell the truth. Yes?'

'Yes.'

It was clear to everyone what the coroner thought. Archer cringed. An expensive education wasted, he thought. We've stuck up for that little madam and now she's going to drag us through the mire. In his heart of hearts he had suspected all along that she was lying. Blood was thicker than water, so they'd given her the benefit of the doubt. But this was real blood they were talking about and the stretch of water the children had drowned in provided his hotel's livelihood. He couldn't defend her any more. He didn't want to: he wanted to disown her. He also wanted her to tell the truth.

Danny could hardly bear to listen as the coroner asked Lucy patiently, 'Did you lie about Daniel Kavanagh?'

Silence. Everyone in the courtroom seemed to be holding their breath. 'No,' said Lucy.

The coroner tried again. 'You remember shortly after the boat went down, Sergeant Slater asked you a question?'

'Yes.' She looked at him suspiciously.

'He asked you how many children were in the boat.'

'Yes.'

'You said you couldn't be sure.'

'Yes.'

'But you remember quite clearly now.'

'Yes.'

'Why couldn't you be sure at the time?'

'I was upset,' she said defiantly.

'Hmm.' He gave her another chance. 'Can I ask you again, Lucy? Did you lie about Daniel Kavanagh?'

'No.'

'Could you be *mistaken* about Daniel Kavanagh?'

'No.'

'Would you like some time to think it over? Would you like to talk to your parents about it?' Archer tried to attract her attention, but Lucy steadfastly ignored him.

'No.'

Having given her every opportunity to come clean, the coroner dropped his uncle act and got heavy. 'When did you arrive at the boat-landing?' he said tersely.

'I'm not sure.'

'How long were you there before the boat went down?' She considered. 'About ten minutes.'

'We know the boat sank at 12.40, because that's when you dialled 999. Yes?'

'Ye-es.'

'So you must have got to the boat-landing about 12.30.' It sounded reasonable. 'Yes,' she replied, more positively.

'So from 12.30 to 12.40 you were with Daniel Kavanagh on the boat-landing.'

'Yes.'

'He was never in the boathouse, as he claims?'

'No.'

'Would you?' The coroner turned to a clerk, who produced a phone bill from his papers and took it over to Lucy. 'That's an itemized list of phone calls from the boathouse. At 12.37, Lucy, when you say he was with you, Daniel Kavanagh was on the phone in the boathouse. How do you explain that?'

Lucy was still trying to keep up. She barely glanced at the sheet of paper. All she knew was that she had been caught and, this time, there was no way out. People were nudging each other, whispering. The Archers looked grim. Danny sat, stunned, wondering how on earth they had come by the information. Only one other person knew, and he was bound not to reveal privileged information by his word as a priest. Danny stared at Father Matthew, who shifted in his seat and looked away.

'How do you explain it?' insisted the coroner once again.

Lucy hung her head. 'I can't.'

After an adjournment for lunch it was Danny's turn in the witness box. The clerk presented him with papers, too. 'Is that the statement you made to Sergeant Slater?' the coroner asked.

He scanned the documents. 'Yes.'

'Is it true?'

Matthew had told Slater about the call, so he would also have told him who he was on the phone to. The clerk would probably produce the proof – a receipt for his unclaimed winnings – if he denied it. Danny felt trapped. 'Most of it,' he answered reluctantly.

'Which bits aren't true?'

'The bit where I say I can't remember what I was doing in the boathouse. I can remember.'

'You were on the phone,' the coroner prompted.

'Yeah. Look, I know where you got this from. I told someone in total confidence and he had no right –'

'People have a right to know –' Matthew boomed from the public gallery, interrupting him.

'– to go mouthing off about it. No right whatsoever.'

'– how their children died, the truth about how their children died,' Matthew persisted.

There was a shocked silence. 'Why did you lie?' asked the coroner, more gently.

Danny swallowed. 'I was on the phone to the bookie.' He looked across at Emma, pleading mutely for clemency. She looked stunned. At last he said hoarsely, 'I didn't want my wife to find out because I'd promised her I'd never gamble again.'

*

The coroner delivered his verdict soon afterwards. Having denounced Lucy Archer for her spiteful vendetta against Danny, he turned his attention to the others implicated in the hearing. 'As for John Parr, an experienced head teacher, his behaviour was a disgrace. No matter what personal trauma he was going through, leaving primary-school-age children unattended is unforgivable.' Simone glanced at John, who sat rigid in his seat, and she felt a tiny pang of remorse.

'That leaves us with Mr Daniel Kavanagh,' the coroner continued solemnly. 'He's got nothing to reproach himself for. On the contrary, he acted immediately and risked his own life to try and save those poor children. Lies have been told about his young man, but in my opinion he is a hero. May I offer –' He paused as Danny, exonerated, broke down and began to sob helplessly, overwhelmed at having his name cleared but, equally, at the price he'd paid to do it. 'May I offer my deepest sympathy to the families of these children. Blame can be apportioned, but not guilt. This was a tragic accident.'

Arthur and Sheila Thwaite and Bernie and Peter Quinlan comforted each other while Emma sat, tight-lipped and inconsolable. Danny's sobs continued to echo in the still, high-walled chamber. He knew by her face that Emma, who had supported him and believed in him when everyone else had condemned him, would never forgive him this time. Afterwards, he waited for her in the corridor. The Quinlans and the Thwaites filed past, subdued. They seemed faintly embarrassed: none of them would meet his eyes. Emma, following behind, stopped and gave him a look of total disgust. It was a look he had seen her wear only once before, when she came to collect him from the police station in Liverpool. 'I'm sorry,' he said hopelessly, but she turned on her heel and ran to catch up with her family. Danny leaned his head back against the wall and tried to shut out the tears that were once again threatening to squeeze from under his eyelids. He had lost Emma for good. There didn't seem to be any point in carrying on.

No one seemed to want to bring up Danny's name. Her parents and Pete, who could usually be relied on to bad-mouth him at the slightest provocation, were strangely quiet when they got home, pussyfooting around Emma as if they were uncertain of what to say. 'I don't expect we'll see the Parrs here much longer. And Lucy'll probably be packed off to some exclusive boarding school on the other side of the Pennines,' remarked Bernie, who was cutting sandwiches for tea.

'Good riddance,' muttered Peter.

'Pity. I was hopin' I was in with a chance now she's legal,' Pete said.

Emma felt as if she was going to burst. For once, she wanted them to have a go. She wanted her father to say something about 'that shiftless Scouser' so that she could let rip and scream, 'Yes, OK, you were right, all of you. I should never have married him, never have given him a second chance. He's a gambler and a liar and he always will be and now he's a murderer too, not a hero like that man said.' But they didn't.

Finally, she could bear it no longer. Leaving Samantha in Bernie's care, she went round to Father Matthew's house. It was dusk and the pine-scented air flickered with bats, circling and swooping in the fading light. Wild flowers were folding their petals as the dew fell, suddenly reminding Emma of the time when Danny walked her home from the disco and she'd pointed out the red campion to him under the street lamp. That was the night she'd secretly decided that he was the one she wanted. She'd been charmed by him – his good looks, his scally humour, his quick mind, his suggestion of urban glamour. You never quite knew where you were with Danny; he was exciting, different. Dangerous. Just how dangerous it had taken her until now to work out.

She remembered Father Matthew saying, 'He might *feel* guilty but he isn't,' and it puzzled her. To her mind he was more culpable than the Parrs and Chef. It was a view Matthew apparently still held. 'You must be pleased that Danny's been cleared,' he said when he opened the door.

'He shouldn't have been,' she snapped. How could a priest say that?

Matthew extended his arm. 'Come inside, Emma.' She followed him into the kitchen. Without asking, he poured her a glass of wine. 'I thought I might see you,' he said, handing it to her.

Emma did not touch it. 'You don't understand.'

'Correct.'

'He promised he'd never gamble again. But he did. And my cousin drowned because of it. OK, he could've been phoning anyone, but he wasn't; he was phoning the bookie. And that's why our Paula drowned,' she cried desperately.

Matthew sat down heavily and patted the chair next to him. She took it, reluctantly. 'The whole village was blaming him. All he had to do was tell the truth: he was on the phone. Bookie, pie-shop, greengrocer, it wouldn't't've mattered, he was on the phone, the lad couldn't be blamed, they'd've all accepted that.' He took a sip of his wine and winced. 'All bar you. So he took all that blame, all that abuse, because he didn't want to lose you. I call that love.' He stared at her over the top of his glass. Emma didn't know what to say. She had never thought of it that way.

Still wearing Pete's trousers and shirt, Danny clambered into the wooden rowing boat. He untied the rope and pushed off from the jetty. There was no wind – the lake was as flat as a millpond – and the full moon sparkled on the surface, casting an ethereal beam across the black water. He dipped his oars, dissipating the reflected light into a myriad bouncing specks, and began to row out towards the middle. The lake was over seven miles long and more than half a mile wide and he rowed with grim determination, gritting his teeth, the chords of his neck standing out like rods as he hauled on the oars with all his strength.

Further out, the temperature became colder, as if he were entering another, more sinister zone, and the noise from the distant road was deadened by mist smoking off the surface. Danny realized he had lost his bearings but did not let up. All he could see was Emma: her face on the bus that first time; her eyes looking deep into his when they made love on the fellside; her glow of joy when she showed him their baby. Her look of utter condemnation after the inquest. He rowed harder.

Matthew's words kept going round in Emma's mind all the way home. Danny had been spat at, beaten up and half drowned. He had become a hate figure ostracized by the whole community. He would have incriminated himself at the inquest. Just to protect her. But it didn't take away from the fact that he was gambling. His addiction had cost lives. She looked in on the sleeping baby. Her child, hers and Danny's. A quiet voice at the back of her head whispered, 'What if he'd been on the phone to you. What then? Would you be responsible, too?' The list of 'what ifs' grew longer and longer. What if the girls hadn't played truant? What if they hadn't met Granddad? What if the jet hadn't flown over? What if Danny had made the call five minutes earlier? Was it just a series of random events that had lead to a tragic accident? The coroner's words came back to her: 'Blame can be apportioned but not guilt.'

*

He was under the water again, going down, down, down into the dark glacial depths, the netherworld beneath the lake where many had perished over the centuries. His chest was bursting but even the roaring in his ears couldn't mask the siren voices of the drowned, luring him, singing to him, 'Give up. Give up. Join us.' Then his hands touched a body and he tried to take it up and it was so heavy he thought he'd never make it and the chorus in his ears grew louder and louder. 'This is where you belong. Join us.'

It was Emma who had broken the spell. His love for her that had given him the superhuman strength to kick upwards towards the light one more time when it seemed every last molecule of oxygen had gone from his body. He wanted to live so badly that he kept swimming and kicking and fighting until his head erupted into the living world and he sucked sweet air into his lungs again. It was like being reborn.

Danny stared at the misty water, remembering it all again: carrying Susan Charles's slime-covered body out of the lake, seeing Arthur and Sheila Thwaite's grieving faces, watching the train of mourners in the graveyard as the strains of 'Abide With Me' floated up to him on the mountainside. He stopped rowing.

Emma watched the baby's chest rise and fall, rise and fall, living her fragile life breath by breath. Sometimes, in the night, Samantha would appear to stop breathing and Emma would hang over the side, ready to blow new life back into her, and then Samantha would give a little snort and carry on and Emma's world, so perilously balanced, would right itself again. Death would come one day, a day far away, but not that day. Whether she would be able to intervene or prevent it, Emma had no way of knowing. She kissed her finger, planted it gently on the child's cheek, and crept out. She had to see Danny.

The moon was up, making it easy for Emma to pick her way along the footpath leading to the boathouse. She felt a sense of urgency, without knowing why. The door was ajar. She pushed it open and looked inside. No lights on. 'Danny?' she called, listening. There was no reply. A terrible thought suddenly struck her. Emma turned and ran down to the shore.

Danny bent over the oars, exhausted by the strenuous rowing. His heart was beating furiously, the sweat-soaked shirt clinging to his body, and it took him several minutes to recover. He put the oars in the rowlocks and let the boat drift. When, finally, he looked up, the momentum had carried him into the path of moonlight so that he was illuminated, as if on a stage.

He put his hand in his pocket, took out a coin and examined it, turning it over in his fingers. He was a gambler. He knew the odds. The girls hadn't. Emma hadn't. Gambling was in his blood: it had given him a reason for living but it had also destroyed everything dear to him. His addiction was the controlling force of his life. It always had been.

But never again. He had sworn on a life, any life, and look what had happened. The only life he had a right to gamble with was his own. So why not let chance decide, once and for all? A last flip of a coin for the ultimate stake. He tossed the coin upwards, sending it spinning into the moonlight, twisting and turning in the silvery radiance, his one, bright hope.